Gauchos Cannot

Sing Soprano

Robert Scott

BLACK ROSE
writing™

First printing

This is a work of fiction. Names, characters, businesses, places, events and incidents are either the products of the author's imagination or used in a fictitious manner. Any resemblance to actual persons, living or dead, or actual events is purely coincidental.

ISBN: 978-1-61296-501-7

PUBLISHED BY BLACK ROSE WRITING

www.blackrosewriting.com

Printed in the United States of America

Suggested retail price $16.95

Gauchos Cannot Sing Soprano is printed in Calibri

To Steve Tucker: Whose enduring wry wit and sharp eye
are as invaluable as ever.

With much thanks to family and friends for all their support throughout the effort to produce this work, especially Michelle Robinson.

Gauchos Cannot

Sing Soprano

It's gotten worse; much worse in our maddeningly absurd attempt at existing within a surgically-clean society, (purr, goes the kitty...) germ-based epidemics, economic systemic cronyism... furthermore, and much worse, our democracy... even more atrocious... arms' races–much, much worse... Ah, "... lawyers, guns and money!"

Could it be that our immune systems are down–that basically, we are all extremely weak. Let's go... can we, please. I mean, does anyone really think we are here. We've arrived? Nothing more to do? (Ya know, like a child asking while heading to granny's for Christmas–are we there, yet?)

In a nutshell–'No'.

There is more work yet to be done.

Chapter 1

On the night of his birth, a sudden and prodigious storm unleashed a flurry of lightning whose sweet claps of thunder clamored from ballooned hammer-heads of great heights in the skies above this otherwise in-descript mid-sized prairie town. Later, some would claim, a magnificent, super-charged lightning bolt struck a cell-tower's eight-story antennae rising atop the very hospital and at the exact moment that Jaime Gabriel Holbrook exited his mother's semi-glorious birth-canal.

True enough, absent typical steering winds, a lower-atmospheric pressure cell spawned a somehow-surprise monster storm, who cannily proceeded with its torrent in a sinking, swirling fashion in nearly the same median-divided lane for most of three hours. During this prolonged liquid pummeling, Mariella Christi Holbrook heaved, groaned and grunted to summon every ounce of energy she could muster to push forth her only child. Did some of this storm's electrical energy pool play a role? Some would indeed say, yes. Even in Mariella's heavily medicated stupor, she detected a look of obdurate consternation upon the obstetrician's face.

"What?" she mustered. "What is it?"

"No, no, now. Nothing to worry," the doctor replied, rather dryly, as doctors are seemingly prone to employ such tonal duplicity as they patronize. Not being one to accept such at face value, Mariella insisted further explanation to the doctor's curious-stricken mug. But having by now already passed along the pinkish womb-jelly

7

covered, spotted miniature being to attending nurses for cleaning and other customary procedures, he met Mariella's eye momentarily, then simply ignored her request.

Only a short time later, however, a nurse handed a blanket-wrapped Jaime to his mother. Shortly thereafter, Adrian Holbrook, beaming proud father, removed the blanket so as to be able to hold his son to the heavens free and natural, as he himself once had been. At this moment, both immediately believed they understood what had earlier pasted such a quizzical expression upon their doctor's countenance.

In fact, Adrian already had questioned the reported weight of 9 lbs., 6 oz. Not that this amount registered beyond reason, but Jaime did appear less than robust in overall size. Only during that time when Adrian held his arms fully extended with his son did both parents witness the answer. While certainly nothing of Herculean proportions, relative to the newborn's size, however, his pair of baby testes could not be said to be in direct proportion to the rest of his clammy-skinned self. Baby balls? More like...needing extra postage. They resembled that of, say, more a four-year-old lad–maybe six, seven? Who could ever know? Yet, no one of their right mind could question the singular fact–the boy does possess a pair.

"Please, Adrian! That's enough," Mariella implored her husband. "Give him back."

Adrian's smile beamed, unable to control the swelling of pride.

"That's my boy!" he burst. "That's my boy!"

"I said, give him back. Now! I mean it, you," Mariella belted.

Obligingly, Adrian returned the boy to his mother's waiting arms, who quickly re-wrapped the child in blanket and drew him tightly to her bosom. Two afternoons later, before checking out, our young couple openly discussed the situation with the doctor. He confirmed that Mr. Jaime Gabriel Holbrook did possess above average-sized testes for a newborn, but further explanation could not be provided lest they tempt legalities to ripple forth fangs. Besides, he did add, such measurements are meaningless, empirically speaking. Litigiousness has no place in a baby ward, after-all, he threw in. No worries, he continued. These things tend to work themselves out. He is otherwise healthy. Mariella reluctantly accepted. Adrian swelled inside, his fatherly cup he didn't even know he metaphorically held in his smallish-hands, spilling over.

To back up just a tad, dear readers, our new parents fell in love, (lust, if truth be told) their senior year of high school. Evidence to this showed on Mariella's belly soon thereafter. Adrian dutifully took the expecting mother as his wife, although she did make him wait several days before saying 'yes' to his marriage proposal. Yet, here they are today, alas, neither possessing a blimy smidgen of insight as to the cause of our aforementioned young lad's positive condition, if not downright outlook.

But let it be stated here toward the beginning of our journey: The golden leaves of Colombia have been eliminated as a suspect, usual or otherwise. Whom or what can be said to blame? Groucho Marx's ghost, it has been noted by a few, often appears above the intersection of Laurel Canyon and Mulholland Drive during celebrations of All-Hallows. Should we start there? The balls are natural, people. Please.

Speaking of spicier spices, saffron also has been eliminated as our chief consultant as to the culprit of said's, well... you know. Nye. Nye. Nye... And they're off, a voice floated down.

Chapter 2

"Up?" the boy sheepishly spoke, his first word; oddly, phrased as a question.

"Well," mother replied, "if you have to ask...."

"Up?" Jaime repeated.

"You, you, ya-think?" she bemoaned. "Your head is pointed which direction?"

"Up?"

"Helloooo, silly goose. Yes, it is pointed up!" she said, exasperated. "You are correct. Si'."

"Ohhh! His first word! He said it. Adrian..."

Chapter 3

"Crocus sativus," Mariella sometimes pontificated while in the kitchen.

Latin speakers once used it to mean saffron, if they could afford such multiple-syllable words. Mariella employed the Googled knowledge to impress Adrian when explaining its savored richness, its potency despite an overall subtleness. The color most of all she liked–burned-orange with a pinched reddish-brown edge, she would explain to anyone.

"It actually affects the taste as much as anything," she sometimes boasted of its two-tone pedigree.

"Mommy?" Jaime learned to whine when a desire encroached his thoughts.

"Not now, son. Mommy's busy. Please, son. Not now. Please. I'm begging you. Don't you see I'm cooking!

"Damn you, heifer-ass, fat-nutted bastard!"

"Mommy's sorry... I'm just tired."

Later that next afternoon.... more of the same.

Chapter 4

In morning's early light silver streaks
Dice blue-bonnet flakes of star dust,
Upon which fall a rays' firth and girth,
Not a lot, mind you, dearest of all,
But it packs a punch. Which leads any gifted,
Or even a talented mess, to ascertain eternity.
If only everyone could digress.

Adrian adored Jaime, droopy shorts and all. A better time in history it could not have been, what with saggin's trendiness and what-not. But... Do I really need to go forth?

Hint: (URL addresses that end with XXX)
A writer must skip the Lou, here.
He cleaned up. You know he did. Do not kid yourself. Please. Don't. I'm serious.

Top-10 Pairs in Modern Times

1. John & Paul
2. Fred & Ginger
3. Peanut butter & Chocolate
4. Cops & Donuts
5. Gin & Tonic
6. Sonny & Cher
7. Sonny & Crocket
8. Milk & Cookies
9. Peas & Carrots
10. Judy Garland & a Microphone

Chapter 5

Speaking of significant pairs....
But let us pause, first, though. For just a moment.

By third grade, our lad with the bodacious pair required a seat equipped with extra padding and a wide bottom. Special educational sorts perfectly attended to this need, however, and with only minimal detection of outward disregard. The seat worked well. The trick proved to be hiding this arrangement's purpose from other students.

Jaime, or WB as some classmates now called him, sported a savvy personality. Suave and svelte. Of course, one's mind drifts to "Old Spice" and grandpa's aftershaves, but still.... Jaime's reputation by middle school truly exceeded even the roof of those above such things. By middle school Jaime Gabby Holbrook easily, despite some reluctance that could not be masked, and a tenderness in the mid-section that lingered from the onset of puberty, agreed to his mom's strongest suggestion (against dad's weak dissent) and signed away his right to participate in any extra-curricular school activities involving athletics. Not to be concerned in the first place, however, because our mate failed to locate an athletic supporter (matching cup not necessarily included) large enough to protect, fit comfortably, etc. If not for his precious cargo... Mariella could only shake her head in shame, turning to exit the last sports shop she knew to search for something that could handle her baby's abundance of juevos.

"I guess you'll have to learn band," Mariella said blandly.

"I could play tuba," Jaime added ho-humly.

What more could she do? Additional handicap applications are being considered.

Chapter 6

At the least, even! Even a waist-band size small enough to fit my boy, Mariella continued in the car. Any cup that might fit for protection only came available in waist sizes far too large. If only I knew how to sew, she whispered aloud. Jaime's digital ear piece piping hot, hip-hop sounds prevented the voice of his mother from reaching inside his brain. He still rode the rear seat en-route to, well, anywhere. Mariella demanded as such in lieu to whispers behind her back of unspeakable ideas, notions, etc. It would just be better, let's say. Safer.

For time's sake, here, dear readers, let's fast forward. Shall we?

Oh, to hell with it. Let's!

As Jaime reached for his salad-day's chilled fork, academics took a willing back seat to Hollywood-style bedroom antics. With the days of roses and wine, crystal and spice and more, (what, with the proliferation of XXX.coms and all), Jaime began to see a path toward greener pastures. By his senior year of high school, his tuba playing abilities having not taken flight, actual left-coast milk producers convinced Mariella that Jaime's truly best shot at achieving financial freedom lay in the flow of money shots and silicone-sisters that cash of any currency and denomination always chases.

Jaime, nearly convinced by said solipsism, only realized within minutes of lending his signature to a professional pornography contract that it might actually limit his earning capacity in the long run.

And, voila. Off our boy goes.

Yes!

Chapter 7

At this stage of his life's journey, our dearest protagonist learns how difficult and grimy hitch hiking successfully can be. In fact, if such witnesses can be found, and produced, I must add (at the strong urging of multiple attorneys), bounty will be paid (cash only, as to be expected. And well under any table(s)).

Yet, Jaime picked up the craft in no time–relatively speaking of course. Also turns out that using projectile-shaped body parts is better practiced outside city limits. Any city, Jaime correctly inferred; thus, he only twice encountered trouble with 'local' authorities. And only twice because.... well, maybe it's better to save such things for later. Much later, probably. Like right toward the end, perhaps?

"Where ya' headed?" Three words Jaime Gabriel Holbrook grew to love more than, well, certainly many things.

Chapter 8

Guillotines & Automatic Weapons
"Off with their heads."
Now, these four puppies can be taken in any number of various scenarios:
Un–a la, Mr. Maximilian
Dueax–Marie Antoinette
Twa~!–Mr. Mr. (inside joke, dearest of all readers. Explanations to follow within four, eh, maybe twelve chapters).
At last... let's get ready for quatroooooooooooooooooooooo!
Silence.
"What?"
 Uh-ooooooooooooo... oh, to end all...
Four–Many Hermitic heifers!
"Off with their heads."
Gabby loved 'em–those four of most famous, and infamous, words.
"Off with their heads."
It became his nome-deseuer.
"Hey 'off'," friends eventually shortened it to. (But with that 'hey dude', gnarly San Diego drawl and syrupy snicker follow-up)
"Off."
"Yo."
"What up?"
"You know it."

"Know it."

"You knows I know."

"But it, still? Just, it...?"

The look. That 'off' look.

"Naw cutty."

To write that Jaime "Off" Hollywoodbrook figuratively tore down the neon lights of lower Sunset-the-Boulevard before he fled; to say such words...one should digress, really. So I will.

Jaime "Off" Hollywoodbrook had wiped the field, playing like a player as it may be.

"Here's to freeloaders of the world," Jaime raised a crystal champagne glass, just before not signing that contract, during a particularly glitzy dinner celebrating a spectacularly profitable year among Hollywood's adult-film crowd, including but not limited to producers, directors, key grips and pages. But digestion is where the fizzle meets the waiter bringing the check.

"What's that?" a thick, Jersey-accented fella with pizza-face cheeks and cadaver-flavored skin, demanded of Jaime's freeloader toast.

"Pardon?" Jaime politely paused to oblige.

"Who da fuck? Da freeloaders, you stupid fuck!"

A more quizzical diagnosis could not be prevented.

"Mafia one and mafia two," Jaime stated with astute boldness.

"What the...?" The fella's brow insisted.

"Government and the mob."

"Which ones?" the Jersey kid boiled.

"Well, not the good ones," Off proclaimed, now definitely losing his patience; yet, strangely, not his sudden erection. A calling? (Later, dear readers. Later...) "There are no good governments, and only a couple of really bad cosa nostras. No, wait. Both make things cost more than they otherwise would. Unfettered, you know. Unfettered."

"Fuhgedaboutit! Ahh!" Jersey scoffed.

"Anyhow, to freeloaders, including those fuckin' So-Cali producers. Sons of bitches!"

Cue to sounds of glass being thrashed.

That guns were not drawn until much later that same evening can only be accounted to the fact that everything's laid back in Southern California. The rain, the people, and yes, even some of the more traditional mobsters. But when it does rain, it can unleash–m-fer's. And it did rain later, just after midnight.

Jaime soon learned of So-Cal's weight, only narrowly escaping by the skin of his oversized balls. Not literally, of course. I mean, he's alive, and everything. But....

Let's just begin this new era by saying just that.

A new era thus began. And our boy's off and running again. This time, however, in a directly opposite direction as before. Which means little to a compass-illiterate young man looking for the one way toward New York, New York. Specifically, he sought the Tribeca district within Manhattan. Far from Canal, though. More towards the western side of the triangle. Not too close to Wall Street, you know. De Niro could not be found, let's just leave it at that.

Jaime also discovered a new path to follow, or at least make attempt at–acting with his britches buttoned. Quite the concept it turned out for him–financially, spiritually, health-wise. You name it really. It was a nice move. Once he arrived, of course. And once he, you know, cut his teeth, so to speak.

Yes, you've by now most likely deduced a retreat to be en-vogue. It's true. Let's stop here at 1st and 1st and allow the nexus to take a timeout.

Five years earlier. (It took four years for Jaime to make it far enough eastward over the Rockies via Albuquerque, in-between visits to grandma's for chicken soup, more directional mishaps, bla-bla-bla and what-not.) And finally on to where it really all began–the Back Bay–which turned out to be far more down to earth than he could have ever imagined. Fantasy more suited his fancies, as it happens. So shortly he dropped down to ole' New York.

Here it only took a few weeks to top the charts. But I digress. More on La Mella, large, l8r.

The adventure from southern Cali-porn-i-A, turns out to be mighty, mightily interesting on its own merits. So let's...

It began soon after the first driver found the shoulder of Hwy. 1 South. Jaime, for whatever reasons, could not handle his directions well in southern California, or almost anywhere, except home, as it turns out. One could ascertain that a general direction of east could easily be deduced while residing near the pacific coast of the United States. (now there's a paradoxical notion: as if east or west could be anywhere other than due!). However, parts of the coast line found nearest Los Angeles do face southward, but still, most people can find, at least, come close to east or west.

And Guadalajara will do!

Oh, those hard-headed donkeys. (Both figuratively and otherwise).

. . .

Eight hours later, void of even an A.M.-radio station, Jaime's driver proposed the following:

"Clear the county of all bovines... cows," he clarified to thwart Jaime's initial, mystified response.

"I know what a fucking bovine is, man! Shit. Moron," Jaime whispered below his breath.

"Excuse me," said the man behind the steering wheel of the first vehicle to carry our main character more than five miles. They had, indeed, traveled through two western states together.

"Cows...why clear the county? And do you mean every last one?"

After some convincing, and being that Jaime hadn't actually seen any cattle along the road, he naturally assumed there probably could not be more than a hundred, at most. More wrong, as it would be, Jaime should have to search long and hard to experience. Still, he bought into the man's dialectical musings, something about mad cows, obesity epidemic, cancer, Hinduism and his daughter's newly-found love to a vegan icon. (What is that, anyway?) Jaime's vulnerable emotional state of being deserves most of the blame, however, for the ensuing criminality. And as tempting as it may be to note the horrific state of mind cattle endure during any legal massacre in a corporate-operated slaughter house, Jaime's actions

22

here and now are certainly reprehensible.

Never-the-less, our young man now thusly finds his ass on the ever-loving, mother-toting run. And yes, not much longer after the killing outbreak began within said Kettle County, Gabby did attempt to flee the scene, large-bellied female cow in-toe. During his heifer-cleansing spree, guilt at-last prevailed, once he realized, nearly too late as it turns out, he had been flatly used; or so it seemed, anyway. Up to this moment in time, everything had made such perfect sense, (and yes, dear readers, any description of a thousand murdered livestock will not be provided due to the graphic nature of such violence; however, it should be noted, not needlessly either, that most never knew what hit 'em and it didn't actually produce a blood bath, as it were).

Until he deconstructed the logic behind this ride-provider's so-called disgust for red-meat, plus vegan idolatry, the possibility to such a thing actually existing had seemed far from fathomable. (Not that any sacred cow, or more, could know why, but half-way across the sphere called earth, at the exact moment Gabby's light bulb clicked on as to the vagrancies of veganism (in his mind, dear readers, not yours) a small herd of cows in Bombay, India, fainted, almost simultaneously.)

Back out west Gabby fell stock in the middle of a situation in which he attempted to escape a horde of way-pissed-off ranchers, one large female shorthorn with. And this cannot, in this occasion, be characterized as that of being simple to execute. In fact, if such analyses might be had, "quite difficult" comes to mind. And a feat of greater strength, one can scarcely imagine, I suspect.

Yet, Jaime fled swiftly, all things considered.

In the end, it must be stated, he left, well, like this–enlightened.

As to this enlightenment, let's hold off for the chapter. His harried harangue aside, his use of many skills, social and otherwise, to garner the onset of his near-fatal escape, will provide much more entertainment value.

And so, nine-hundred ninety-nine dead cows later, Jaime Gabriel Holbrook, stopped just short of euthanizing (his terminology, not mine) the final Kettle County bovine. And though Jaime could not have a clue as to the sudden fainting spell that spread like Arizona wildfire among a few more Bombay sacred cattle, a brief moment of silence before the storm allowed him to detect a siren's wail. Then he heard what he thought could be only the low rumblings of an angry mob. Angry ranchers. Armed angry ranchers!

"How could anyone admire someone, let alone worship, anyone who eats from that derived from anything resembling a face? Large rocks have faces for Christ sake," he would cry before a swelling crowd.

"Kill him!" the crowd responded in a low grumble.

Ten Most Infamous Pairs of Modern Times

1. Hitler & Mussolini
2. Bonnie & Clyde
3. Tonya Harding & Jeff Gillooly
4. Oil & Water
5. Gin & Tonic
6. Prohibition & Alcohol
7. Mark David Chapman & "Catcher in the Rye"
8. Donny & Marie
9. Truth & World Wide Web
10. Coke & New recipe

Chapter 9

That a rope of any size should be handy, could cause one of any generation surprise enough–at least a wrinkle of the crescent. So the truth that one with a harness intact lay just within Jaime's reach, seemed as close to divine intervention (Christian, Hindu, Seek or otherwise) that he had ever before experienced. Jaime Gabriel adroitly snagged the connection to Kettle County's remaining living cow, and off they went. That also he located commercial wire snips, spotted right in the bed of a stranded Chevy pick-up abandoned near a ragged barbed-wire fence-line, and this oh-so-useful tool being found just as the sounds of mob-mentality and closing-in-on-your-ass-sirens drew nearer, proves providence knows no boundaries. He really could not have been more fortuitous.

Chop, chop and three strands of semi-tout barbed-wire fence gave forth an out, whose option they gladly exercised. As the topographical serendipity would also prove, a gully awaited their scamper; one conveniently enough equipped by a path providing a winding, naturally formed, spring flashflood river bed, sandy and a little rocky at-present. In less than ten minutes, though, our fleeing duo managed to wind past another twist in the gully and completely free themselves of anyone's sight. The mob wrestled with how the obvious pair could have vanished so suddenly, and then quickly attributed this bafflement to a get-away vehicle, one equipped, of-course, with some sort of bovine transportation device.

Funny how rapidly a mob's collective angst can fizzle. But fizzle it did, until a few remaining smaller groups each devised a plan—the best of which consisted in most part to immediately contact the federal Farm B, just after local insurance representatives had been notified. No local authorities, mob leaders decided. They'd only have its hand out, at best.

Meanwhile, Jaime and Fuzzy (his heifer needed a name, right) felt they had put enough distance between themselves and whatever pursuant flocks remained. Tired could not begin to shed light on just how exhausted both were. Fuzzy hadn't moved more than a half-step at a time since that warm, spring afternoon when she had to maneuver her hind quarters in a more southerly direction to avoid hordes of horseflies and unwanted advances. Her rump did itch and the southern gale force felt fine. Oh so nice.

At the moment, however, she wondered why her human would lead them down such a dry creek bed. Grass, man. Doesn't he even know? Cows like grass. Fresh, somewhat green, preferably, and just beyond reach, if possible. Jaime fell into a dream, of sorts, as it portrayed himself using his blessed talent in a freak-show carnival. Only two bits to gaze the wonderful pair, (17+ - admitted, only). The dream ended with a Bible-thumping mob in hot pursuit. Luckily, the sound of scuffling hooves awoke Jaime just before a pack of zealots screamed, nearly in unison it must be noted, those dreaded four words: "Off with his head."

For the next of three, maybe four hours, the two hustled along the meandering sandy-bottomed creek's ever-flattening banks, until it opened unto a nearly lush verdant field. He let the heifer run un-tethered until two minutes later she promptly plopped.

He found an overgrown abandoned shack in the back corner in a shadow cove. Inside remained a good-week's supply of oats. Someone was still using the shack for cover. At worse they could hole up here until the oat supply is spent and hopefully find enough time to plan a final escape. But would time in itself suffice?

The answer, in a nutshell, would be yes. But how to boil the oats? And just like that, our young man-on-the-lamb found his sweet ass faced with Homo Sapien's two most basic obstacles for oh-so many centuries, until more recent times: fire and clean water

On more than one occasion it has been suggested that lightening showed the way to early man's jump to using fire for warmth and chow. In more recent times scientist discovered that strikes of lightening set off a chemical chain reaction creating bountiful amounts of nitrate, which the accompanying rain absorbs and carries to waiting roots of all plant life. Perhaps this fact even played a role in Jaime's unique extremities. Never the less, finding flint certainly aided man's movement forward in progress. But yellow-green dells do not easily reveal hidden flint reserves, perhaps buried just beneath the bountiful terracotta. And clean water? Now there's a whole 'nother beast, (see sub-Saharan Africa, India, ancient Somaliland pirates, etc...)

What kind of animals typically choose not to run in the face of fear? Polar Bears, lions and suddenly Jaime Gabriel Hollywoodbrook. (I mean, after-all, he literally owns a pair, a rather hefty set....well, you get the picture.)

As for anyone else, why wouldn't you run? Its greatest pleasure lies in that excess of adrenalin and endorphins magically created for all, to be released closest to physical exhaustion as one can near. After a sweet, restful sleep, Jaime awoke to remember another favorite Mariella Holbrook maxim: "Don't sweat the small shit."

Mother Holbrook loved to remind him of this during his childhood, often more than a dozen times in a single day. After admiring sheets of silky, gold sunlight, filter through majestic pines, he remembered more....

"But the devil is in the details," he finally began to retort, back when, after many months, maybe years.

"Yes, but we are not afraid. We have Jesus on our side...you see," mother Holbrook often added, for additional support, a warm smile flowing across her clear face. "We have that little man already defeated. So don't bother me with this whiney-ass shit, 'cause we don't care," she would then state, without fail, wagging finger not excluded.

"But...?"

"But nothing," she'd beat him to the punch.

"But...?"

"I said, 'But nothing.' Now, move around, people! Now! Move!"

Sound of spattered-feet stomping about, enter here.

And thus our embattled, perhaps even maligned, friend, one said, Jaime Holbrook of Hollywoodbrook farms, made a U-turn; (technically it measured less than 180 degrees. But who's counting?) having now reached the understanding that running, if not completely fleeing, any scene, no matter how bad, can never fully solve any given problem. It is not a solution–should not be considered as even an option, he went on to conclude.

By the time he returned, however, few signs of life existed. Scarcely the sound of a gossiping pack of teen-agers, packed tightly, four per pick-up cab, whistled past the DQ. Otherwise... crickets. Chirp...

Chirp...

Chirp.

Chapter 10

"Gotta get off that Greyhound express. It's such a hard habit to kick, though–tough cookie," Jaime mumbled to no one in particular.

"Excuse me?" a strange voice broke in.

"Yes?"

"Are you speaking to me?" asked a grayish woman with rosy-rich cheeks painted on silk-chocolate skin.

"No 'mam. No. I'm just.... ah, it's nothin', lady."

"Shuga, you can spill it with me's. That's what we're all here for, sweetie. To help each other pull through. It's a wicked storm out there. Sure is. What's weighing on your mind?"

He hesitated, at first, knowing full well he would quickly open his heart. Nothing beats a nice stranger waiting in a Gallup, New Mexico, Greyhound depot en-route to wherever. Her eyes twinkled. He studied them more closely and she let him; adoring his admiration of her. She seemed as an angel. Perhaps... no? She....

"I have really big balls," he let forth.

Yes, she smiled, nodding in affirmation without so much as a flinch of surprise.

"No, I mean, literally. I have huge testicles. Physically," he continued, starting to spread apart his thighs.

"Oh, I know, honey. I know. What is it, though, that's really bothering you?" the kindly woman implored, somehow knowingly.

"Well, I...I've quit my job," he began, scratching his scalp, pausing to wonder if she meant she knew of his big balls, or just about some being bigger than others? "I'm headed to New York City, to be an actor, you know. And, well...I sorta got side tracked and what-not. I mean, ah fuhgedaboutit," he stopped short, abruptly.

"No, sweetie. I understand. You go ahead," she sparkled.

"Well.." he pondered, sincerely. "Well, I encountered a rather strange, strange, most odd-of-all ducks. He just... well, he just really tripped me out. I mean, this dude *is* a trip. I swear."

"Oh, don't swear, honey," she smiled. "Never swear aloud."

"Ok," he agreed with ease, wondering if it would still be okay to imagine a swear?

"Anyway," he continued to her steady twinkle of the eyes. "I want to be an actor. A real actor, right. Well, I'm going to be, I should say. A real actor," he paused to note her reaction—another simple nod of affirmation.

"Well, so I gave up, because this guy that I rode with for such a long ways... I mean, he was kind enough to give me a lift and all, but then he started in about how cows are the cause of, well their red meat is the culprit, mostly. I mean, it's the root of heart disease and cancer, from the carcinogens people ingest on bar-b-que weekends." (don't get me started on the benefits of medium-rare, let alone tar-tar)

"And obesity, and global warming," he continued. "And rising deficient immune systems. It really just has no end. And he's right. I see that now. And I saw it at first," he studied the ladies eyes more deeply. "But in-between. This is where the trouble lies."

"Well, I do understand," the nice woman responded, becoming anxious, almost agitated, suddenly. "But, that's my bus. Be good. You will survive if you just follow your instincts. You're okay. Bless your little heart," she ended, patting his knee before blending behind a swirling flock of would-be riders.

"I'm okay," Jaime repeated to himself a few times. "Okay."

Now emotionally re-charged, Jaime sprang back behind a mask of confidence and used his ticket to overcome his directionally-challenged senses. Head east, young man. Head east. New York, your mother awaits you. But first, untie that bitch!

How many people never understand, from lack of first-hand

experience or otherwise, just how many stops a Greyhound bus driver takes, even midst crossing a fucking desert, no less? How many, Jaime wondered openly.

"It's ridiculous," most concurred, albeit, a captive audience, no doubt.

"Ehh, what are you gonna do?" another, older man with gaunt cheeks and large, ruddy ears sprouting a field of white hair, interjected.

"But..." Jaime began in an attempt to further the obvious.

"But nothing, smart ass," the old man interceded again to cut ole' 'Off' off at the knees. "If you could afford another form of transportation, you'd be in it, instead. Now shut your ass, before I close it for you."

Jaime quietly acknowledged the supremacy in logic and authority and slept until Amarillo. By next morning, Tulsa, Oklahoma greeted his morning sunshine. Rolling green hills placed a smile on his face. Through the Ozarks and Great Smokies they continued.

"Welcome to the Pine Curtain," he overhead a passenger utter as the bus at-last entered the confines of West Virginia's winding state boundary.

"Pine Curtain?" Jaime gently shook his skull in confusion.

"Starts down 'bout Tyler, Texas ways, and gets real thick, 'fer sure, as soon as Shreveport. Don't change from there 'til that 'Lantic Ocean. Damn skippy," the man reiterated.

"Is that right?" Jaime nodded, now in agreement, despite having not an inkling as to the man's point.

As it turns out, the strange fellow from the Greyhound makes a somewhat known argument–that being that attitudes tend to tighten proportionally to the density of said, 'pine forests'. Thus, a la, pine curtain translates into bigoted politics and religion, let alone education and extra-curricular activities. Look at the sample of evidence; the body of work–lest you detect a sprinkling of a May Queen's skeptical musings in your bosom, dear reader.

Assassinations, for one: Martin Luther King. J.F.K. (Yes, Dallas technically is west of Tyler, but not by much. Besides, anyone truly in the know, knows that the 'West' actually starts at the easternmost border of Fort Worth, Texas. And Dallas is for damn sure east of beautiful Fort Worth. Hello eastern NFL division, anyone? Single blue-gray star....

Politics, for two: Bull Connor, Lyndon LaRouche, David Duke, Strom Thurman, Robert "Sheets" Byrd, etc., etc., etcetera.

Education: The Little Rock Nine and the lovely state of Mississippi. (all apologies Faulkner fans)

The West Memphis Three?

Moonshine?

Religion?

(Need a writer really provide more here? Let's digress...)

Credence to the merits of said 'Pine Curtain' theory, could at least be debated civilly. (Now there's irony)

"Everyone's living in their own unique dream. They just don't know it," Jaime suddenly realized.

"Ah, they ..." but his next thought evaded him.

Then, from out of no-where, a warm voice spiraled downward again.

"Early bird gets the worm," it sounded.

"What the...?" Jaime belted!

"If all you are is a ream of light," the voice continued.

"Yes?" Jaime replied, quizzically.

But just as quickly as it entered our protagonist's field of noise, it disappeared without so much as a sneeze.

Chapter 11

"Mazda or Noah?"

This proposition came forth from Gabby's next potential lift, heading back east, as it turns out. For time's sake, dear readers, Jaime's inattentiveness led to him riding westward through Ohio, Nebraska, and southeastern Colorado, before realizing the error, once again, of his directional ways. Pueblo holds its own summer charms, however.

"Guillotine," Jaime said.

"No," his newest potential driver responded sternly. "Between those two only."

"Oh... Noah?"

"Wrong answer. Get in, anyway," a Hopi Indian travelling upstream complied. "Gets cold here in the desert at night."

"Who's Mazda anyway?"

"Boy... you are lost," the cinnamon-colored man laughed.

"I know. I appreciate it," Jaime said as he bowed his head humbly.

"Do you know of chariot gods, or ancient battles in the sky?" the Hopi explained as his '59-flatbed gained a post-ton of speed.

"Like Star Wars or somethin'?"

"Sorta," Hopi replied, now studying Jaime's chiseled cheeks admiringly. "You have high cheek bones."

"You're not a Hollywood porn producer, are you?"

"A what?"

"You've never heard of ....?"

And thusly, the following six-hour trek ensued quickly, as time travel goes, with flowing conversation of pre-ice-age civilizations and *"Californicationism"* and how a Hopi Indian from southwestern Arizona wound up in Pueblo. This most-beautiful exchange of words and its associative idealism ended with two agreements:

One: For most women, in general, men are just a photograph–interchangeable like so many cheap frames. Isle candy, hopefully loaded and healthy, and with flowing hair. (Ugly, but true, no?)

Two: A photograph can possibly rob a human being of its soul. Or at least put a chink in its armor.

The gist of these ideas can be summarized properly as: mythologies of the ancient world (any part, east or west, north or south, and any other direction there-abouts) possibly may be steeped in more actual history than modern-day tales written by winners of military might. Majestic cities, long since buried by rising sea levels from the melting of ice, suggest for many archeological scholars the evidence of highly advanced societies–far too advanced to fit squarely into the notion of man being highly developed, relatively speaking, mind you, for less than 5,000 years.

Might the gods of old truly have existed? Might these tales explain why monotheism won the day, eventually? That being, one omnipotent supreme-being easier to bow before and acknowledge, as such, than many, varied, often angry gods–ones not necessarily seeking the lowly meek's approval, patronage or following?

To say a thousand stars dance among a long desert's night represents more than understatement. It nears heresy, to a writer's mind, anyway, I suspect. Jaime lie in awe.

"This cluster here," our Hopi gladly explained, drawing a line in the midnight realm.

"That one?" Jaime pointed to the same.

"Yes."

"The Milky Way?"

"No. Many city folk say the same. But they too are wrong. There is the milky way," he aimed farther right and higher, and much deeper.

"Ohhhh," Jaime acknowledged.

"What I'm showing you is simply the belt of Orion."

"Orion?"

"Yes. Well, he died at the stinger of Scorpio."

"Oh?" Jaime uttered.

"You are a scorpion, no?" Hopi asked as he rolled slightly toward Jaime.

"I don't know, to tell you the truth. I was never allowed to know my birthday. It's one of the larger mysteries whose answer I seek."

"The desert is the place for you, for sure," the Hopi stated plainly, though with great confidence.

"You think?"

"I do. You must be a scorpion. Scorpions make the desert home, especially at night," Hopi concluded before returning to other tales of lore—the least of which included the notion that.... the possibility of humans witnessing first-hand the birth of Orion. It represents the most important event to ever be passed down as legend. Which, as legends go, speaks well to its credence. It definitely has passed the smell-test of time, let us agree. (Urban legends (any) eat your hearts out! (You know you cannot endure))

Secondly, a reader of any era should note the deeper meaning of the possibility of humans being present at the birth of a cluster of stars, no matter how many light years earlier it might have actually occurred. A spectacle, at the least.

"If you're not finding what you need, drop something you already hold—figuratively or literally," Hopi spoke after an interlude of who knows how long?

"Figuratively and literally, you say," Jaime repeated with impressed smeared across his face like a one-year-old's birthday cake.

"Do you hunt?" Hopi asked without segue's permission.

"Pussy," Jaime stated with a robust laugh.

Hopi cracked up, too. Two more hours passed in silence at just

36

that thought. Orion's birth my ass.

"Desert life provides few places to hide," Hopi whispered, breaking another long drought of noise. "Everything is exposed and reduced to its most basic element."

"I see that," Jaime said. "Are you hungry, at all?"

"I'll be right back," Hopi said, suddenly standing, knees creaking as he did.

Jaime wondered to where his Indian host had left? His truck, maybe? Did he have some food in there? Maybe water? Hopi returned with a pile of timber, apparently from a stockpile in the rusted-out bed of his pick-up.

"Here... make a fire," Hopi ordered, dropping an armful of dried limbs before Jaime's feet. "I'll get some cactus."

"Is it good?" Jaime asked, feeling foolish immediately for reminding himself of the spoiled attitudes of southern Californians.

"Better than potatoes," Hopi replied. "Sweet, too."

The corners of Japer's mouth moistened, slightly; as much as can be expected in two-percent humidity. He arranged pieces of wood in a tee-pee fashion, pausing momentarily for fear of political incorrectness, but then thought better of it. Why would a shape offend his new friend, particularly one so perfectly conducive to fire? Should he start the blaze? He decided to wait. In his temporary lonely state, he felt a chill overcome him. So he stood to search for any loose scraps of something to burn which he might find despite the intense darkness. He quickly abandoned the idea, however, upon seeing Hopi in stride, dragging two large limbs of cacti.

"Pencil Cholla," Hopi said, smiling. "Very juicy. Oh, you didn't need to wait for the fire."

"I didn't know," Jaime said.

"Are you thirsty?" Hopi asked.

Jaime's face answered without reply.

Hopi extended an arm-shaped piece above his shoulders, eyeing for Jaime to lean beneath. Hopi made cuts in the heart of the cactus until a thin, but steady flow of sweet water dropped from underneath the prickly fruit, splashing onto Jaime's tongue and lips, down his throat.

"Thank you," Jaime offered, softly cleaning his lips with his left forefinger. "What's your name?"

"Chris," the Hopi answered.

"You are left handed?" Chris inquired.

Jaime nodded in agreement, hoping the fact didn't change his status.

"Interesting," Chris offered. "A left-handed scorpion is rare. Maybe you are on the cusp?"

"Cusp?"

"Cusp," Chris conferred.

"Of...?"

"Of being an actual scorpion," he continued.

Jaime could only shake his head in wonderment, as Chris now eyed the unlighted tee-pee of wood.

"Do you have a match?" Jaime asked meekly.

"No," Chris responded. "But this will work.'

Chris laid a rather small, Jaime thought, slate of flint in the palm of his hand. Jaime held it, somewhat bewildered as to the process.

"Strike it against this rock," Chris instructed. "Let the sparks fall to this," he added, placing a nest of dried shavings just outside the tee-pee of wood's perimeter. Where did the shavings come from so quickly, Jaime wondered?

A few attempts later and Jaime gently blew into a single plume of smoke he somehow could see. It lightly, but rapidly flamed, and Chris pushed the pile beneath the timber and aided the effort with his own exhales. In no time, a whiff of white smoke spiraled heavenward. Thirty minutes later Chris held slices of desert fruit on a pike-like stick out to the growing orange glow that captured Jaime's gaze to nearly hypnotic states of euphoria. Occasionally, a hazy blue flame appeared, steady at the base of their roast.

"The hunter's prize," Chris stated.

"How long?" Jaime asked, unable to contain his anticipation at-hand.

"Not much more," Chris said. "Little more, only."

When the first bite of Cholla entered Jaime's mouth, he honestly felt he had never before tasted anything quite as satisfying.

Certainly better than any who-ha he ever placed trembled lips upon, he thought. And this Hopi knew his cactus well, for the Cholla's texture reminded Jaime completely of potato, and indeed its taste contained a slight sweetness. Chris' eyes revealed his own satisfaction at having enlightened yet another to but one of many of the desert's little-known treasures. Another hour passed in silence as each relished in the vastness of eternal skies and its imposing dominance on a single psyche.

"Hard to believe just how far away all that really is, eh?" Jaime offered, weakening spellbound glares.

"It is far. Yes," Chris whispered. "But how far may turn out to be the wrong observation."

"How so?"

"The better question may be, how near, new friend. How near," he reiterated.

"But, it's so far," Jaime said mildly.

"Yes, but how near?"

"Well, it's like this... got about as far east as Texas, once...and, damn bartender tells me that everything domestic is two bucks, you know. So I order a Budweiser, but later, see, I notice they have Shiner Bock. It's domestic, right? German shit from the hill country of Texas, no?"

"I don't know," Jaime admitted, more curious to how this would relate to the distance of stars.

"Trust me, it is."

Chris waited for a reply to his request of immunity, but Jaime's frozen glare told him all was well.

"Anyway, long story short, they don't include Shiner Bock as domestic... something about it being better brewed, but not really... then, maybe it's because of it being a Bock... it doesn't matter. Point is, it's not included... an asterisk, as I like to say."

"It's bait and switch," Jaime agreed, thinking back on his first contract, suddenly.

"Yes, but see, I have a bucket of asterisks I'd like to have my way with," Hopi said softly, but with certainty.

"Do say," Jaime abided.

"Like... oh, there's too fucking many," Chris said, thrashing his arms momentarily. "You're a little nuts, man."

"Did you say, 'You're a little nuts, Meg?'"

"What," Chris asked, bewildered and now standing up to stretch.

"Nothing," Jaime cowered. "What's wrong?"

"I said, 'man' not 'Meg', man," Chris clarified.

"Do you smell that?" Chris segued, seamlessly.

"What?" Jaime questioned. "I didn't..."

"No. Not a gasser... cosmic burnt... orangey..."

Jaime didn't dare to enter this opaque scene. After all, he didn't even complete high school, let alone master the ole' Bard.

"Did you read Ed Doveer?" Jaime asked, out of clear darkness.

"Shakespeare, you mean?" Chris returned volley.

"I guess," Jaime agreed, reluctantly lowering his face to the scorpion inching stealth-like upon his outer shin, protected only by blue jean.

"Scorpions live and hunt in the desert, right?" Jaime quickly asked.

"They do. Why do .... you...; hold very tight," Chris stated as he slightly, ever so gently, slowly lifted his right palm, facing sand-ward. "Hold, it..."

Bam!

"Go!"

Let the ringing of 9mm shells thrashing through dry air reign supreme.

"Hit the floor," Chris shouted but in a hushed fashion.

"Do you think someone could actually shoot a chigger?" Jaime whispered next, oddly.

Chris' nose remained to the earth.

Silence.

"Silence," Hopi breathed aloud, gently.

More silence.

"What is that?"

"Unless it's a genetically altered scorpion with a small, semi-automatic handgun, I don't know," Chris replied. "But... I don't hear sand."

"Sand?" Jaime questioned.

"Feets across the sand," the Hopi named Chris explained, now rising in a push-up style in order to twist onto his plumpish hindquarters. "Did you just ask me if I think someone can shoot a chigger?"

Jaime nodded so.

"With what? A pea shooter?"

"No, silly red man. A bullet. From a gun," Jaime nodded, now adversely.

"Not unless by accident, I would have to say," Chris stated in all seriousness.

Silence.

More of the same.

"I had to hear growing up, how my great-grandmother, she shot three—on three different occasions, at that!"

"How do you know?" Chris asked, besmirched.

"I guess I don't," Jaime acknowledged to both. "There's still a bullet hole in her living-room ceiling. At least there used to be."

Truth be had, dear readers, five bullet holes, from three separate occurrences, did in fact exist for many years, until the razed bulldozers made its appearance upon that squalid scene. Such a successful experiment that white-flight suburbia had been, despite its genesis in post-WWII tract housing and G.I. Bill cash. By the time our greatest of societies emerged, cash not-in-hand, knowing the exact location of a .45 caliber hand-rifle proved evolution's hot existence, time and again. And colloquialisms die much harder deaths, ladies and gentlemen of the pages' jury. Pigmentation aside, economic factors could have pre-determined a variety of similar outcomes. If only we truly could have "... all pulled together as a team." Perhaps some pockets did ride the gravy train, as it were, but as Hopi quickly agreed, unless people behave, self-interests will always seize each and every day. Chris then made an analogy of how different molecules are able to melt into nearly translucent glass, in most cases, and how crystals, in the right sunlight, emit magnificently brilliant rainbows–acting as prisms often do. Also how it's odd that a populist did not rise from JFK's ashes, even if not a mystery within many intellectual circles.

Truth, however, always being stranger than fiction, if such a populist candidate could have entertained an electorate crowd with visions of gaffe elimination and models of scaled-efficiency, game theorists could have eaten out even their own hearts as an appetizer to a main course of beef chow mainstream.

Think of this, easily, or hardly at all, but if non-taxable perishable produce and commodities represent a family's third biggest expense, behind only housing and clothing (and cold-fusion technologies can somehow, in the near future, win the day), educational and health expenses could easily be divided among derivative markets, world-wide, and coupled with economies not reaching rates of diminishing returns, service of most excellent quality and care could be shared among many. The trick is taking that long-shot, dark horse called community–each being within shouting distance, of course. There lies the truest of truths. Communities must be capped by size, and weight. Caucus, anyone. Iowa?

"United we stand, divided we fall. Right?" Jaime let out, now upright, as well.

"No. Not at all," Chris disagreed adamantly. "Only the pink flamingo and occasionally, a sand hill crane, use the deception of one leg as strength. Its prey believe it to be hobbled and thus not a threat. But most animals prefer at least four legs, some six... or eight–land and water. Look at your centipede."

"Right now," Jaime asked, almost whining.

"Do what?" Chris asked, sincerely bewildered.

"Oh, you mean a real one."

"A real what?"

"Centipede," Jaime said.

"They make decoys?"

"Do what..." Jaime pondered in Chris' direction, but not exactly.

"Ah, neva-mind-it," Chris slang. "Listen, you know angry birds...right?" he asked, unapologetically. "Angry birds...? On your phone...?"

"Not personally," Jaime replied without a smirch. "I don't own a cell phone, but I have heard before that a lady, one from way back when was–and quite the bitch, at that...based on the story I heard anyway."

"Which lady? The centipede?" Chris asked.

"I don't know... Johnson, maybe? From Texas. Do you remember from history?" Jaime attempted to shed light upon.

"No... well, yeah, maybe," Chris gave up. "Hey, hear about the half-price shoe shine boy?"

"For reals?" Jaime said, most unfortunately.

"Yep," Chris said, without more.

"No," Jaime finally broke the awkward lull.

"Yes sir, 'he said,'" Chris began the joke at last. "The first one's half-price, but the second one's twice as good, but at regular price. And you'll never be able to spot a difference...promise."

"Who couldn't?" Jaime questioned.

"The guy having his shoes shined, dummy," Chris laughed.

"What?"

"Eh... oy-vey," Chris said, carrying forth his grandmother's expression.

Secretly, Chris lit a candle each and every Friday night–just as his grandmother had done. He didn't know it symbolized the flame of Judea and Yahweh. Still, he kept his grandmother's memory alive through the practice. It became a sanctimonious occasion he never failed to keep.

"You're sorta quick on the defensive," Jaime noted to the Hopi called Chris.

"Yeah? You really think so?" Chris wondered.

"I do," Jaime confirmed. "But I really do not think anyone sells plastic, or otherwise, centipede decoys."

"Well," Chris stated slowly, with deliberation. "They should. They really should. I know a boat-load of Filipinos that will pay top dollar. Just sayin'."

Jaime nodded affirmatively.

Chapter 12

Mariella Holbrook, Jaime's mother you'll recall, slept well at night, knowing full-on well, she fought the day's good fight, and fought it hard. Her son, on the other hand, found life with Chris the Hopi quiet educational, exciting and yet also, somehow, relaxing. Thus, reaching Woodward, Oklahoma, and its nearby painted buttes, Jaime literally fought back tears upon realizing he may never again see Chris the Hopi. As it is with hitchhiking, some good-byes are more difficult than others.

As proof to this tid-bit of road travel, Jaime Holbrook's next driver, who sported a nice Buick Riviera–sorta souped-up, whitewalls and leather trim...the works, in some circles. Its owner, however, lay decapitated fourteen miles east in a shallow, red-dirt grave. Not that he didn't full-on have it coming to him, mind you.

A feathered-dream-catcher swung from the rearview mirror. But smooth skin can travel only so far. Sadly, Jaime Gabriel discovered this soul sore, three point four miles too late.

"Don't you tell me to slow down, Mr. Mr.! I've been driving this car since I's fo-teen," Tashinga jangled. "Mo-fo tell me summin'!"

"Are you part Indian, by chance?" Jaime gambled, as his first request died rapidly–more than can be revealed about the recently deceased, former accomplice, Crazy "Big Mac" Donaldson. (His actual birth name, minus 'big' and 'mac'–honest))

"Part Indian...?" she chuckled. "What part Indian? East Indian? You see a fuckin' dot on my head? Mo-fo...do I look Indian to you?"

45

"Your skin is so smooth, beautiful..." he stated.

Had the beast been tamed?

Ay?

Ay...

"You fuckin' with me?" Tashinga yelled, yet somehow sincerely.

"No," Jaime insisted.

"Indian...?" Tashinga then laughed heartily.

It would be the last laugh she would share for a long while, despite a hefty repertoire of laughs–the best being one which rises from her belly and exits through her large nasal cavities. It's truly a sound to behold, yet as just mentioned, many years will lapse before it will ever happen again. That Jaime Gabriel Holbrook eluded conviction like a cheap suit's tailor, remains a mystery even to the arresting officer. It could be described as especially mysterious, in fact, to the involved, arresting officer, except that he's seen it before–too many times, really.

Technicalities are neat, but fires stink eventually. Smoldering rot. The worst. What's worse, po-dunk counties do not necessarily require back-up governmental records. Not all, at least. And when the volunteer fire department, accidentally (uh-hum) floods the county-seat's basement during its nearly heroic efforts toward saving the courthouse, all told, some defendants did walk.

"Skip to the Lou, my dear," Jaime could be heard singing all the way to Wichita, a few even claimed. Hello Greyhound Express. Didn't someone mention hard habits before?

"Express my ass," Jaime complained in his dreams, just six and one-half hours later. Then later he would wonder why a dream-catcher, one of any color, decoration, design or otherwise, would be round. He fancied a triangular shape should perform more efficiently. Not necessarily a right triangle, either. No...definitely not right he thought making him feel confused as he sat in 23b. He always hoped for 23b's availability. It happened about half the time, so it felt good this early evening to find it.

"Eldorado is a state of mind," a strange voice swiftly whispered from 24b.

"Do what?" Jaime shot back.

"A state of mind," the voice, female, said matter-of-factly, speaking up. "Eldorado is a state of mind. The Conquistadors believed it to be somewhere in South America."

"Yes, Peru," Jaime said, knowingly.

"Oh, you've heard of this, then?"

"I have," Jaime said, refraining from utilizing an open moment for ripe sarcasm.

"Well, they too were wrong, and twice," the feminine voice continued.

"Do tell," Jaime smiled, simply enjoying the pleasures held within the pitch of her voice.

"They believed Eldorado to be a place of buried, perhaps even in the open, treasures. Gold and silver, of course...I mean, you said you know of them."

"Yes, treasures... ornamental armorticte'-horse ships-with-no-names—like from the gilded age," Jaime said, now with biting sarcasm, unleashed. "I know of the Conquistadors."

"Well, they later believed..." the raspy female voice went on, unwavering, although she leaned forward slightly, now, just into the light coning on the shadow of 24C. "The treasure was a spiritual one—like Eden. And they were right, to that point only. They were conquerors. Did they deserve good karma? They did not," she answered herself, rather rhetorically.

"They don't at all," she reiterated, a slender, almost gaunt cheek exposed. "Never-the-less, their location was their biggest mistake."

"Location?"

"Yes, mister 23B...Yes, location," she repeated demurely, leaning back into her darkness.

Jaime's mind drifted to South America, lush and fertile, with wild rivers and even wilder animals. Mile after mile of open spaces, towering rainforests and monkeys. He still liked monkeys from trips to the zoo with his mom, on Saturdays when his dad had to work. They seemed so free in some weird way to his mind, able to swing and climb and roam, always in the moment. Balls exposed.

He dozed asleep for just a minute, the idea of a jungle bungalow and hanging vines lulling his senses. But it couldn't last as a feeble man making his way to the rear restroom rocked into his cheek with a sharp elbow, not anticipating a sudden lane change.

"What the hell?" Jaime let loose.

The old man simply sneered and grumbled past.

"Did you see that?" Jaime questioned the woman who spoke of conquistadors.

But she only smiled and shrugged.

Disgust filled him, naturally. Damn Greyhound! And he closed his eyes searching for South America, again, but couldn't find it, or sleep, for the next two hours. He decided two hours after that, that he'd just rather hike.

Chapter 13

"Dollar bills, if folded exactly in half, not easily accomplished, mind you, are the exact length of a standard-sized cigarette," Jaime's next driver stated. "Is that coincidence? I don't think so."

That he happened to be deputy sheriff of which-ever county seat they happened to be circling leftward around a marble-based courthouse, would not be known to our thumb-dependent friend, dear readers, until another fourteen and one-half miles, precisely, as it goes.

"Or fasting as a cleansing agent for the brain. Like a poop, ya know. But for the brain," Harold proposed, offering an honest smile. He feels most comfortable in his officer's uniform. It allows his kind, nurturing nature to shine. Only during after-hours, dressed in his 'civvies', do his troubles percolate and sometimes boil over.

"Silence is golden," Jaime mimicked.

"Indeed," our newest driver agreed, whole-heartedly.

That a dollar bill might even be close, cut in-half, to a cancer-stick's height, might be coincidence? Or not.... Only engineers truly know.

"Don't let the search for yesterday's truths ruin your tomorrows," Harold added as they at last broke right, escorting Jaime Gabriel Holbrook of Los Angeles, California northward out of Dodge.

"Who said that?" Jaime inquired.

"I did," Harold chuckled.

"I know, but originally, I mean," Jaime said with a tilt.

"I don't know? Some Warwick witch, I think," Harold shrugged. "You know, I do haul some of you hikers to jail."

"I'm sorry," he pleaded.

Harold eyed Jaime carefully, then told him it would be alright and stopped his cruiser just past a county-line sign.

Ten Best Peters

1. Saint Peter (Heaven's doorman. Need more be said?)
2. Peter Sellers (From Lolita to Pink Panther with Dr. Strangelove to boot)
3. Peter Lorre (The Maltese Falcon & Casablanca, just for starters)
4. Bernadette Peters
5. Peter Pan (Makes time stand still)
6. Peter the Great (Brought enlightenment to the Caucasus)
7. Peter Townsend
8. Peter O'Toole (phallic double-entendre alone earns spot)
9. Peter Rabbit
10. Peter Gabriel

Ten Worst Peters

1. Salt Peter
2. Soft Peter
3. Short Peter
4. Leaky Peter
5. Peter Rose
6. Scott (and/or) Drew Peterson (close enough)
7. Peter Principle
8. Peter Piper
9. Skinny Peter
10. Peter Griffin

(If you're not too petered out, please proceed to next chapter....)

Chapter 14

LA and our Milky Way necessarily go together....do what? Oxymoron, much? Darkness offers the clearest glimpse of light–whatever the spectrum. Jupiter serving as our solar system's liver, swallows whole most menacing comets and larger meteors. Without its catcher-mitt mentality in-play, earthlings possibly might never have reached its heights of human accomplishment, not-the-least of which for western culture stands as public and higher, continuing education–the least of which being imperialistic zealotry. Let's not digress, though, please.

As leading teachers of the world, however, many fail to recognize the inherent fallacies within empirical science. Hypotheses become theory, only to be debunked centuries later. What popular scientific 'truths' might fall from grace many years from now? Dark matter? Parallel universe? Spiritual matter's non-existence?

Reaching heights along the Arroyo Seco trail north of metropolitan Los Angeles, one can obtain a far fairer view of our galaxy's offerings. Wild cougars have proved fatal, though rarely, to hikers along Seco's 'dry-stream' paths, however. Gazers beware! But it offers much better sights than from the concrete gullet of Los Angeles' River, for instance. And any reports of a devil's face existing upon the facade near Seco's dam, are greatly exaggerated–beauty lies within the eye of a beholder.

Cougars of a different sort, however, and often much less tame, in fact, roam other boulevards famous to the strip of sunsets–its fallen prey most gullible just before midnight, when ladies appear flat if not taken. The term 'taken' must be considered with a grain of salt, mind you, dear reader. For whilst their purest desires are of a submissive nature, the game played well still leaves the ball squarely in an aggressor's court. Young men of Hollywood need look no further than to one said, Jaime Gabriel Holbrook, who waits facing the sun just west of Pueblo, Colorado, once again. He intended to head east from Dodge City, Kansas, but once again set out the wrong direction.

Having located Chris the Hopi through a short series of questions posed to certain folk who walk southern Pueblo's dusty streets, Gabby learned that his *feng shui* could only be found after he faced the sun for a total of 40 hours within 90. During summertime, one might finish such a feat in four days' time; even three, if said combatant's physique can endure and they don't forget to bring along an adequate stick of lip balm. Winter months in the northern hemisphere require five days' time to accomplish such a feat but typically provide a more suitable climate.

Despite that blizzard conditions only pay visit to the south-eastern plains of colorful Colorado about once or twice in a decade, a storm this afternoon trapped east of Walsenburg and north of Trinidad, dumped a hardy load before traveling toward Amarillo; yes, just by next morning.

Jaime, being one not inclined to carry hand-held computer technology, could not have guessed two days into his journey somewhere east of Pueblo, that the pursuant afternoon would turn much colder, wetter, and oh-so much more difficult. Although, briefly, he did find fascination in the beauty of a flake feathered upon his tattered coat sleeve. But similar to that of a cougar's tactics, a fine southern breeze may lure the unsuspecting soul with feelings of warmth and security, however temporary. (and men always know–it's just for kicks) Why climb that mountain, right?

So to believe that Jaime's frost-bitten fingers needed more than a cliché for heat, is to know why Chris earlier suggested he had more to learn before his true calling would even consider picking up the phone.

"Flint, anyone?" Jaime could maybe be heard had another set of human ears been anywhere even remotely close. They were not.

By sunset that rather prescient, as it will turn out to be, evening, and just shy of nine hours remaining for success, Jaime began his trek west for shelter. Darkness could not hide amidst the stinging ice crystals. He collapsed nearly unconscious within three hours, just short of 8:00 p.m. mountain standard time, his solar friend pacing ever westward, perspective considered.

Across the desert floor, farther east, Chris traced white plumes of smoke rising gently from a fire flowing within the confines of a rust-hued chiminea. Perhaps Chris' vision can be accounted to pinion wood, or else, but he sensed danger; particularly, a subtle stinging sensation racing northward along his spinal vertices.

"Jaime," he let forth, placing his bottle of Choc ale upon the dirt.

"Jaime?" the high priestess naturally questioned, but too late, Chris' ignition already having turned over positively.

Nearly an hour later, Chris discovered a freezing, wan Jaime. Too large and heavy to haul, Chris ascended a nearby rise in hope of spotting an elk or antelope. That he did so within ten minutes may only be attributed to ancient buffalo gods, whom sometimes reign outside their genre. Chris gutted the doe within fifteen more minutes and spent close to another half-hour sledding his kill down to Jaime, whom he expediently placed inside the moist, but warm carcass.

"What the...?" Jaime gasped, awakening a few minutes later to the power of two of dried blood, wild game and fur, with just a hint of excess cacti.

"In a little while, once you are warmer still, we will make it back," Chris informed Jaime's amazed stare, illuminated by small firelight, reflecting tartly in his pupils.

"You are an angel," Jaime whispered.

"No, but now you know what it means to know a three-dog night; although, tonight could really have worked with just two," Chris added, alluding to the lore of a kill's protection from a bitter mother nature. A dingo or two to huddle tightly, also counts.

"Ya know that Bob Marley song, 'Stir It Up'?" Chris asked from far left-field.

Jaime managed to shake 'no'.

"Well, it doesn't matter.... You really don't? Anyway, it's just that if you look at that song, well, stir it up can be taken on many levels. Like, stir it up, could be the weed in your bowl that's getting clogged and needs to be stirred–it's not cashed completely. Or it could be on a political level," Chris continued, as much on a roll as trying to keep Jaime and himself alert, awake.

"Like MLK or Malcolm X. They stirred it up, although at different angles."

Jaime nodded 'yes', a little less gingerly.

"So, then on its deepest level," Chris continued, "it can be a metaphor for the shape of galaxies–a swirl, ya know..."

Jaime agreed, physically more.

"That's all," Hopi said. "It's just a metaphor for life. That everything works on three levels, all connected in an upward, swirling fashion."

And with Jaime's next nod of affirmation, now even more pronounced, the two slowly stood.

"You can make it," Chris stated. "It too is a metaphor–a metaphor for all mankind."

Jaime wondered how a transplanted, Pueblo Indian might be so philosophical, but then recalled a palm reader from LA who turned out to be an Indian–which tribe, Jaime could not even pretend to know. It didn't matter. She also spoke eloquently and in a sagacious manner. Maybe the fact that these ancestors of any particular group from anywhere in the Americas, endured for at least 20,000 years, if not much longer, explains more than Harvard's Dean of Political Science can recite. American Indians have long known the lay of the land, and then some, let's just say.

"One small step for man," Chris laughed....

"One, giant, step, for Jaime," he smiled in return.

Certainly, Indian societies are not without fault, then or now. But let northern European descendants not be the first to cast a tomahawk. Indians valued the circle of life most of all (buffalo not excluded). Everything needs each other, optimally in-balance. Warring can be attributed to achieving more equity–at least over the course of time. And any accurate test must begin with just that–time, and as much as possible, if handy. Many of the American Indians lived harmoniously. And as Mayan history seems to indicate, for some, in large, congested city-states. Only the greed and avarice of conquistadors spoiled the show–damn their lust for loot!

In present-day Pueblo, pine's high-oil content still lends to crackling, rousing flames. Just the sort to keep a safe man too far from a heat's best warmth. Yet, within thirty minutes, Chris' indoors chiminea let loose a blanket of comfort that permeated clear down to the morrow of our duo, wrapped in rustic potato sacks, adorned with interwoven, turquoise colored embroidery. Circular philosophy eat your ever-lovin' heart, clean. Triangles rule!

"Do you like green Chiles?" Chris asked, standing next to Jaime to help rearrange coals inside the chiminea.

"I think so," Jaime replied, teeth still slightly chattering involuntarily.

"Well, they contain a fat soluble molecule, capsaicin," Chris explained. "It also fights back cancer."

"Indians don't die of cancer?"

"We do," Chris the Hopi confessed, "but not stomach or pancreatic, nearly as often."

Medical journals aside, Chris once more rattled cages of science, not necessarily popular. And cancer, not to be out done, holds nothing on super nova black holes. Three to the third power equals twenty seven. At the risk of string theory hypocrisy, note how many western musical icons choose this number as their 'x'-'y' point of departure; lends many to find "Fascination Street" a much more indicative song of our time–that being anything post 1975, a powerful year in any historians right-mind. As "White Christmas" scratchily belted from the in-static Saigon Hilton, west-minded conservative hawks openly plotted an end to domino horseshoes. Thatcher fans and Reaganites can at least boast Iran knew the score. (444)

That there must be a winner, as many now decry, cannot pull the wool over every fool's eyes, however. As the Theory of Cubism (Chris' phrase, dear readers) exposes, look deeper–there you may find a better question. A better question usually leads to deeper truths. To handle that, however, places many a tush too far below, or above, their level of expertise–akin to the more widely-accepted, 'Peter Principle'. Of course, experience is the 'real' mother of invention, and we all need change to remind us just how very alike, indeed, we all are.

Chapter 15

Proteins build from amino acids; is this correct, dearest readers? Touché'. Let's proceed.

Chris suggested Jaime Gabriel Holbrook should attempt something sincere–in place of his failed attempt at facing the sun for 40 of 90 hours. Like acting, he then mentioned.

"Did you say, 'acting'?" Jaime asked, sensing a notion more to his liking.

"Yep."

"I need to be in New York, like, tomorrow," Jaime emphatically stated.

"Scorpions cannot fly. Duh," Chris laughed.

"No. No they cannot, indeed. But they can hike!"

With that sequitur, Jaime left Chris the Hopi once more–smiling this time, however, and rather widely, at that.

How he could encounter Tashinga's cousin, forty miles out of Dodge City, will remain a mystery for all times. (To most, anyway.)

Chapter 16

"Journey of Death"

The Santa Fe Trail (basically the same as Kit Carson's) follows a natural route, as any anthropologist worth his sea salt will agree. Ancient migratory animal trails' follow a path of least résistance...like water, electricity and ninty-two percent of all humanity. Small game for dinner, anyone? Christopher Houston 'Kit' Carson blazed a trail...but, to live up to his father's grizzled tales of fighting in the American Revolutionary War...well, who's to say who or which accomplished more. Seems to be the plight (Sigmund Freud, not-with-standing) to many a man's life. What his mother, Rebecca Robinson, might have been able to know, one can only speculate--she bore ten children by Chris' father, including Kit. Yet, five other off-spring came first for Kit's father from another wife, who passed during that last effort. Rebecca, on the other foot, must have possessed at least an inkling of strength. Speaking, dear reader, of charged particles and an easy out, our hero has a new question for Tashinga's cousin, somehow driving that same souped-out Buick Riviera through south central Kansas, not too far from the original Santé Fe Trail.

"Why you guys keep hittin' them Dollar Stores?" Jaime Gabriel asked, innocently enough, a few minutes into the ride.

"Who you talkin' bout, nigga?" Loretta asked. (recall Tashinga's genetically maligned ancestry, if the name 'Loretta' seems out of place)

"You said it," Jaime stated, staring out into the brown horizon.

Enter brakes heaving!

"Get the..."

Jaime beat her to the punch. Hello blacktop.

Squealing tires and gravel spitting cannot deter a professional, Jaime reminded himself as he truly assessed his "Dollar Store" target theory. Do they see the retail trinket outlet as an Evil Empire? Evil, in that it saps poorest of alls few dollars. Cheap shit doesn't last, as most trinkets are assembled at the hands of unskilled foreign labor and as thus such products often are not prepared well enough to even make it back home intact, let alone out of the store. Add the fact that such stores must keep cash on-site, as the majority of its customers do not qualify for credit. Brothers hanging 'round conspire this seminal truth and seek vengeance. They rationalize a stint in the sit-house, at worse—ignoring peripheral dangers—police bullets, jail-house cuisine, jealous wives noticing new jewelry on the missus down the street who keeps comin' round, etc.

Liabilities don three colors: *Black, Unexpected (karma); *Blue, Unfortunate (coincidence or random order); *Red, Expected (you had it coming and you knew it was just a matter of time). Like a polar bear's spirit, snuggled in fur and fat, wistfully wiling the day beneath yellow-green petro layers of wispy breath, within there lies security—minus numero uno's (man's) under-lying threat, liabilities reign supreme. The past haunts the present, as many, many before have ascertained.

Bob Dylan eat your cue cards. Hop goes the rabbit. Dig! Dig, all say. Tombstones near Glenwood Springs, Colorado claim Wyatt Earp's final resting place (puhlease!) Yet, tourists flock accordingly, some even traversing said trails overlooking the city to visit possible alternate grave sites. Others seek the spring for its mystical, naturally flowing, warm mineral waters. That a train route from Chicago to LA lie 160 miles south, did not pose enough distance to prevent even FDR from sending ailing grandchildren there in search of relief.

Mineral Wells, Texas developed into a proven haven for

Hollywood types. Combined with a dry, central-Texas climate, the mineral-rich water from shallow aquifers were, and still are, believed by some to ail anything and everything from foot fungus to alcoholism. Trace amounts of arsenic promote healthy blood and tissue, the story goes. Sodium alleviates arthritic symptoms. But FDR couldn't risk even a semblance of connection to those left-coast liberals. They really couldn't hold a candle to right-coast lefties.

Under a bridge somewhere among the rolling 'flats' of central Kansas, Jaime finally drifted to slumber, soon to literally dream of an east coast, Woody Allen film set–it tickled his inner funny bone, in a dry, sorta way. Hopi, back in his adobe home in Pueblo, dreamt of buffalo eating Jaime for breakfast, with white corn tortillas and salsa verde, to boot. Juices everywhere!

Unattended, Hopi's fire this evening died an hour before he fell asleep. Shortly thereafter, his sonorous snore could almost be heard echoing off canyon walls in neighboring states, but not quite. Jaime awoke desperate, inclined to carry on–the most essential step in hitch-hiking adventures.

So it was, that near Blacksburg, West Virginia, Jaime encountered yet another representative of authority. And once again, a jar-headed officer retracted his square jaw and took a shine to our protagonist. Jaime felt flattered. Not every hitcher finds such gratitude. Jaime Gabriel Holbrook felt confident the foot hills of the Jefferson National Forest stood as a threshold to his ultimate, successful acting career. Jaime may not have mastered an academic subject, but he did remember well stories of his favorite Founding Father, Thomas Jefferson–most impressed by Jefferson's insistence on separation of church and state, as well as the genius of differentiating powers vertically among federal, state and local governments. Only a localized municipality can govern itself without self-preservation as its chief operating component. Doubters to this hypothesis, please click your red-heeled shoes three times while repeating 'Military Industrial Complex', and see if you're still in Kansas any longer.

Mankind needs trash removal services and people create a lot of trash (although most unfortunately and un-necessarily so).

Likewise for education, whose ripples affect all of society–but that black hole issue must be diverted, for now.

Jaime felt it divine to enter this protected land of West Va. Perhaps something good might happen, after all. Tracking north eastward along I-79, just shy of Salem, almost to the Roanoke cut-off, Officer Hamilton allowed Jaime to ride un-handcuffed and shotgun to the county line. Authorities grow bored, too, after all. What occurred next nearly gave Jaime his first experience with sudden cardiac arrest.

"I've changed my mind," Officer Hamilton announced, breaking a brief lull in the ride out of town.

"About...?" Jaime cautiously began to wonder aloud.

"I'm going to give you a ticket, after all," Hamilton answered before Jaime could finish.

Jaime's heart visibly palpitated.

"Take it easy," Hamilton switched tone upon seeing Jaime's fluttering tee. "I meant it good. It's just a lottery ticket, for good luck, ya know."

Hamilton laughed lightly, hoping to entice Jaime to do so.

"Oh shit, you really scared me," Jaime wailed.

"That's it!" Hamilton said with raised voice, dramatically swinging emotions, again.

"What?!" Jaime cried.

"Nobody curses in my cruiser," Hamilton stated, piercing eyes through Jaime's bewildered forehead.

"I'm kidding you," Hamilton croaked a few seconds later. "Psyche. Gotcha!"

"Sorry," Hamilton added, handing Jaime an Atlantic Seaboard Powerball lottery ticket. Hamilton's cousin, Leon, had purchased it for him recently while visiting Jersey's finest shoreline resort host–Atlantic City. Hamilton found gambling to be sin in Holy eyes. He found this moment perfect to pass along to Jaime this chance in a billion to win millions–technically he would not be gambling, as Jaime, himself, had not risked money on the play.

"You're okay, kid. Good luck in NYC," Hamilton said, gently depressing the brake pedal of his 2010 Ford LTD cruiser. "I'm sure you'll find a role."

Jaime eyed the lottery ticket, unbuckling the seatbelt to step out onto I-79 once more. It would take 'til Broadway, W. Va. (no relation to Jaime's eventual destination of nearly "off" Broadway, New York City), just northeast of Harrisonburg, while catching a break in a cross-town bar, that someone yelled aloud, breaking a creaking silence in Fred's Bar & Grill, as a television screen's bottom news ticker scrolled–"'winner' takes all $143-million of Atlantic Seaboard Powerball Super lotto."

Minutes later a bartender, actually named Sam West, read aloud the seven numbers, ending with Powerball '18'.

"Powerball 18," a customer, nearly flopped at the end of the bar, shouted, shaking his head with disgust, "I had '17'. Figures!"

"It always does," Sam consoled. "It always does. You had all the other numbers, though...right?"

The louse dismissed Sam's sardonic jest with a wave.

"You need another one?" Sam asked with sincerity, turning to Jaime.

"Can only afford this one," Jaime admitted with open disappointment.

"Okay," Sam smiled, toweling the water ring left beneath Jaime's empty mug.

Jaime sighed, unsure where he'd sleep later this evening. He asked Sam for a glass of water, pulled out his five-spot to pay for the one beer, and watched his lottery ticket he received from Officer Hamilton drift down to the floor like a freshly fallen leaf. The guy at the end of the bar, two stools removed, waited in anticipation to Jaime's response; which he shortly did, turning it over but noticing only the last number—Power Ball 18.

"Did you say the power ball number was '18'?" Jaime asked Sam as he delivered the glass of iced water.

"Yep," he replied, plainly.

"Oh," Jaime said, emotionless. "Well, do you know what the other numbers are?"

"Let me see," Sam indulged him, walking back to look at the television, luckily still scrolling the winning numbers along the bottom of the screen. He copied them down to a piece of paper and returned to Jaime.

"Here you are," Sam offered and walked back to tend to the customer at the end of the bar, whose attention continued to aim solely upon Jaime, impatiently waiting for him to confirm his ticket to be a winner or not–as if it being the one might turn some profit for himself. Desperation oozed from his being like a toupeed patron seated close to a dance stage in a dank strip club.

Jaime's body drew still, perfectly motionless, for a long three seconds. He held the ticket up, then quickly retrieved it back into his fold. He turned to see the drunken man at the bar's end eyeing him so closely, and rapidly turned back away. He motioned for Sam's assistance.

"I think I have a winner, here," Jaime whispered, leaning as far as possible from a seated position across the bar's surface.

"Let me see," Sam whispered in return. "I'm not gonna steal it from ya. Geez."

Hesitantly, Jaime relinquished his ticket to the stranger named Sam West, who read the numbers aloud, quietly, checking each one against the sheet of numbers he had just prepared.

"Holy shit," Sam whispered.

"What?" Jaime snapped. "What?"

"Kid, you're the luckiest man on the face of the earth at this very moment," he stated, delicately handing it back to Jaime's waiting hand.

"You mean...?"

"Yeah, no shit," Sam reiterated.

Jaime patiently re-checked the ticket's numbers against the ones written down by Sam. As he reached the last one, his life very nearly flashed before him. He couldn't decide what should happen next. He wanted to scream aloud, naturally, but wisely he didn't want to alarm other people in the bar or bring more attention to his situation than necessary. One valuable lesson he knew all too well from consorting with hikers and other transient types–don't brag about money, particularly unexpected windfalls of cash that others surely will guilt you into sharing, if not just slash your jugular.

"It's found money," they always say, or something essentially the same. "Easy come, easy go."

Gush, gush.

"No thanks," he learned to reply, a while back. "What's mine is mine and what's yours may soon be too, if I decide to take it, mo-fo!"

Jaime contemplated returning back down I-79 to share the loot with Officer Hamilton, or maybe even attempt to somehow locate Hamilton's cousin. Next, he considered hopping onto the next flight back home and pay a visit to his mother, whom he hadn't even had contact with in so long he couldn't really remember.

"How do I get the money?" he asked Sam, taking an intermission in his decision of what to do next.

"Well, I believe on these big ones, you've got to go to the state capitol. It should say so on the back of the ticket," Sam noted, pointing to the ticket itself.

Jaime read the back and sure enough, he needed to report his winning ticket at the capitol, instructing specifically in font, shout serif: DO NOT MAIL WINNING TICKET.

"What's the capitol of West Virginia?" Jaime asked, looking a tad embarrassed at his ignorance.

"Charleston," Sam rattled back, minus even a whiff of condescension.

"Oh," Jaime exclaimed. "Charleston. Where is it?"

"About two hours southwest of here," Sam answered, watching for Jaime's reply.

Jaime's downtrodden expression rapidly revealed the pain of living on the fringe.

"You know what..." Sam began, intuitively. "I know someone who's headed down there tomorrow morning."

"Really?"

"Yep, no kidding."

Jaime felt like leaping across the bar to hug him—a man who somehow seemed to have no hidden or ulterior motives. So unusual, he thought. Or have I become jaded, he worried, momentarily?

"I don't really have a place to stay tonight, though," Jaime admitted.

"Sorry, I can't help you there," Sam shook his head, then turned to a new group of customers taking three stools to Jaime's right. On cue, the intoxicated, droopy-eyed man from the other end, so intent on honing in on Jaime's scene, left his stool to take a stand adjacent to Jaime's back.

"I gotta a place with an extra bed," the man offered. Jaime's eyes showed fear, wrapped so tightly in loneliness as to seep real desperation.

"Well, I guess so," Jaime hesitatingly agreed, curious how the strange man knew to offer.

"Let me pay up," the temerarious man stated eagerly. "Sam, here you are." He placed a ten dollar bill on the bar and eyed Jaime to follow. Jaime felt an odd, awkwardness of emotions overtake him. His instincts belted a reprisal of Three Dog Night's *Momma Told Me Not to Come*. Reluctantly, though, he started to follow the slender, blotchily dressed stranger.

"Oh wait," Jaime remembered, turning back to wait for Sam to finish tending to the newest drinkers. "Let me ask Sam what I should do for tomorrow."

Sam instructed Jaime to simply meet him back here at the bar at ten the next morning. His buddy always has two bloody Mary's before making his semi-weekly trip to the state capitol. Jaime agreed and turned back to the stranger, feeling somewhat less apprehensive, trying to muster courage and confidence, to thwart timidity attempting to surface and make it through just one more night of uncertainty. This latest in the never-ending string of Jaime's acquaintances went by the name of Jim, although his actual birth-given name read Jeremiah Washington–no middle name. Jim found the name Jeremiah too formal and reminiscent of a mountain man, whose stereotype Jim despised like an educated Texan dislikes being labeled redneck. Obviously, mountain men do reside in West Va., as well as more than four million bigots calling parts of Texas home. But Jim turned out to be an ex-marine with an attitude to boot. He also knew exactly whom Sam intended Jaime to catch a ride with to Charleston the next morning, and Jim held every intention of preventing that from ever happening.

"His name is Leon Hamilton," Jim explained, pouring a cup of herbal, green tea, piping hot for Jaime's night-time nook. "And he's a madman."

Jeremiah Washington kindly informed Jaime of Leon's history. Not until the middle of this explanation, however, did Jaime connect the dots to realize it possibly to be Officer Hamilton's cousin and gracious source to the lucky, winning lottery ticket, in the first place. Jaime could not immediately reveal this fact, he knew. For Jim clearly despised this Leon, whom he deemed a "top-secret" bastard.

True enough, Leon Hamilton had recently gained employment via the United States Federal government. He worked as a data analyst, combing through countless reams of information delivered to him through a network of NSA handlers. Leon's military background and family history of police work made him a perfect candidate for this position. Of course, thousands of others perform the same job for the Fed, an array of out-sourced intelligence analyses conducted in secretive fashion, as part of the US government's on-going, never-ending, battle with so-called extremists from around the world and within.

Thus, and with merely a hint of reservation, Jaime set out the next morning to hitch his way back to Fred's Bar & Grill to meet Sam and possibly 'top-secret' man, Leon Hamilton. Only a few miles away, Jaime still opted to leave by nine, just in case. How situationally ironic, he thought, that I must still use hitch-hiking as a means of transportation, all-the-while possessing a multi-million dollar escape hatch. A bird in the hand is worth two in the....but he couldn't remember the rest, knowing only that his ticket was just that until he actually made it to the capitol. And even then...?

Morning commuters are not typically inclined to suspend their race to beat the clock to support a thumbs-out walker. So Jaime felt proud to have left Jeremiah's place early enough to have time to walk the entire way, mostly along West Va.'s I-79, spoiled with typical stray pieces of broken glass and aged liter. Jaime's usual disgust with society's sloth-like nature consumed his thoughts as he avoided a shattered automobile window along the road. He made it early, actually, quickly becoming worried someone might grow suspicious of his loitering. But Sam pulled into the parking lot ahead of 10 a.m., and he allowed Jaime to wait inside for Leon. He even poured a tap beer for Jaime to nurse, needing to bleed the keg lines, anyway, he explained. Had Jaime decided how to spend his money, Sam asked?

"I'll give some to mom," he conceded, "and I've got some ideas and all, but I really don't want to jinx this, if you know what I mean."

"I gotcha kid," Sam nodded, looking as if he really respected a guy in Jaime's situation who would be so humble as to not immediately expand with arrogance.

"You know, you're right," Sam added a few minutes later. "Don't let the money change you. You're absolutely right. Dead on. I mean, you should get a car. A nice one, ya know. But don't let it change you, man. Be different."

Leon entered almost on cue as the digital clock above the bar read 10:18 in red l.e.d. dots (bar time almost always displays a quarter-hour fast). He took the same seat at the end of the bar where Jeremiah Jim had been the night before. He acknowledged Jaime's presence and quickly reached inside a windbreaker for a bill to pay in advance for his usual two bloody Mary's. Sam didn't immediately mention anything about providing a ride to the capitol for the guy down the bar, here. It worried Jaime, suddenly–as if it might not be a sure thing. Or maybe Jeremiah Jim had been right. Perhaps Leon indeed worked as some 'top-secret' agent and should be feared more than appreciated. Jaime eyed them closely, now, careful not to let on, looking for clues within Leon's demeanor for a trace of fear, or even trepidation. He didn't seem to be afraid, though, Jaime thought after a few minutes of watching. Maybe he just wanted to allow the vodka to first do its trick.

Sure enough, Sam stopped his morning bar prep and began talking with Leon. Jaime felt better when Sam motioned his way, and Leon turned to notice him again. Jaime quickly forced a smile, to which Leon nodded, then stood to make his way to Jaime.

"Leon Hamilton," he said extending a hand to shake.

"Hey, Jaime Holbrook," he returned greetings.

"So, Sam here says you might have a winner," Leon said to the point. "You need a ride to the capitol?"

"If it's not too much trouble," Jaime replied, wanting to exude his graciousness.

"Not at all. Not at all," Leon grinned. "I won't even charge you, either. Hell, I don't pay for the gas anyway," he bragged.

Jeremiah Jim might be right, Jaime thought. He felt it prudent at that moment to hold off relaying the information of Jaime's having acquired the ticket through Leon's cousin, Officer Hamilton. Leon might not feel so charitable, if Jaime mentioned its geniuses, and Jaime already felt a twinge of guilt. But he wanted to be able to thank this man, wholeheartedly. What would Hopi do, Jaime then wondered, for some reason?

"Okay, well, we'll leave here in about ten minutes," Leon finished, lifting a hand to trigger Sam's mixing skills.

Leon Hamilton drove an oversized, GMC suburban, silver with tall wheels and running boards, decked to the nines inside and out. Jeremiah Jim might be right, Jaime thought. He knew the federal government purchased these by the fleet. Not that every GMC on the road belonged to a government official, but what were the odds of Leon driving one and it not being a company vehicle. Hadn't he said the gas was paid for?

"So Sam says you hitched your way here from California, or something," Leon started not twenty seconds on the road.
Jaime confirmed Sam's information, adding that part of the journey came via Greyhound and how utterly despicable so many of those fellow passengers could be, let alone the depots and all those fucking stops. Leon shot him a look at that notion, though. It said, doesn't that really make you part of the despicable ones, and then with a squint of the eyes, Leon's face said, "I don't like hypocrites," the stench of self-importance filling the truck's cab.

"I mean, not everyone, you know," Jaime quickly added in response. Leon's face revealed a blend of being impressed at

Jaime's ability at picking up on body language, with it's a good thing you're not being hypocritical. "Just some, you know."

Leon nodded, agreeing. They rode the next several miles in silence. Jaime noted the hills flattening to a rolling terrain, lushly green and nice, just the same. He wished a John Denver song could play on Leon's radio, stealing glances at him when he could. Jaime desired to not rustle this possible top-secret man's feathers. He found him to be a bit unsophisticated. His forehead ran too high, his eyebrows too bushy and cheeks far too round. He seemed like some throwback from a *Dukes of Hazard* episode, and not in a good way. At 11:00, Leon promptly turned on the radio to an A.M. news station. No "country roads take me home." The radio man's fluid voice instead announced a report of new terror threats; Leon turned swiftly toward Jaime.

"You believe that?" he asked.

"I guess," Jaime uttered. "I mean, it's hard to say. You?"

But Leon only scoffed. Jaime didn't know if he had done so toward his answer or at the notion of terrorists, real or conspired. Jaime suddenly grew anxious. A notion of his own fear swept across his brow. Was he being played? Perhaps in a few more miles, in some even more remote, more rural area of West Va., Leon would pull along some dirt, country road, claiming he needed to whiz, or something, and Sam, and maybe Jeremiah Jim, too, would all be lying in wait to clip old 'off' and high-tail it to Charleston, where they'd collect Jaime's loot and never think twice about any part of it all. Of course, Leon had purchased the ticket, originally, but he didn't know that. Or...did he? Jaime thought back to the night before. Only Sam and Jeremiah Jim really knew. He wanted to trust Sam, though. He had to. He winced back at Leon, who now seemed to be studying Jaime up one side and nearly down the other. Say something, he thought.

"I know," Leon finally broke the uncomfortable lull. "I know enough, anyway. More than most, ya know."

Jaime nodded in acknowledgement of Leon's superiority. He wanted desperately to check the hidden, inside chest pocket of his pull-over hoodie, but thought it unwise to reveal the ticket's location or appear nervous. His agitation only subsided when Leon began spilling his beans, as it were. For the next twenty minutes, or so, Leon explained how his stint in the Marines led to a post in Washington with the Department of Defense, and from there to a private-sector firm that subcontracts with the Department of Homeland Security to analyze piles upon piles of data collected in volumes through various listening devices, to then be utilized by National Security Agency officials throughout the planet.

Leon stated that at first, just after 9-11, everyone he worked with felt completely gung-ho about their efforts. Within a few months they helped locate a cell in Yemen, or somewhere, and high-ups from NSA paid regular visits, even calling Leon out, specifically, once, to acknowledge his work, he claimed. Lately, though, he carried on, the work had become much more mundane. The better people left the force and some were even beginning to openly question the necessity of its own continuance. Such forward thinking! As Leon droned on, it increasingly occurred to Jaime that Leon associated not even an inkling of importance to Jaime's existence.

How could he, Jaime questioned? How does he not know this whole lottery ticket deal, the 'I need a ride to the capitol,' isn't some semi-elaborate ruse to trick him into exposing national secrets. At the least, its practices. Look at him. He's telling me everything. Maybe he's only actually sharing what's already public? He doesn't seem guarded, Jaime thought, growing more exasperated by the second.

"I've got big balls," Jaime interjected in the midst of Leon taking an inhale of oxygen.

"I like to think I do too," Leon chuckled, sticking out his lower lip in some expression of humility–faux humility, Jaime thought.

"No, I mean, I literally have oversized testicles," Jaime attempted to clarify. "I used to be a porn actor, but I'm heading to New York City, soon, anyway. To be a real actor, ya know."

Leon said nothing for a long moment.

"What sort of actor?" he finally asked.

"Dramatic," Jaime answered, matter-of-factly.

"Yeah, but on TV, theater, movies, ya know?"

"Well, I haven't really decided, I guess," Jaime had to admit. "It doesn't matter, really. Anything that doesn't involve sex, ya know."

"How big are they?" Leon almost screamed, having lowered his window as they started to exit the highway.

"Are we here?" Jaime asked, ignoring Leon's query.

"No. I just need to piss."

Ah shit! Jaime stiffened. Alas, however, Leon wheeled his silver suburban into a Shell station. Relief flooded Jaime's central nervous system. Jaime exited the vehicle, too, just to stretch his legs and look around a bit. He made his way from the side of the station to the front and as a customer made his way back to his vehicle at one of the gas pumps, Jaime asked the man how far to Charleston? Not far at all, he answered, pleasantly.

And so, only fifteen excruciatingly long minutes later, Leon steered his large vehicle into a parking lot at the state capitol of West Va., advising Jaime to watch his back because you never know who might be coming 'to get ya.' Like yourself, Jaime scoffed to himself, but thanked him again for the ride, recalling the fact of Leon's having indirectly contributed to Jaime's bounty. Only later did Jaime feel so utterly foolish at not having gone a different direction with concerns to not expressing his gratitude–for as the ticket clearly states right on its back, the representative at the West Va. capitol explained, the ticket must be redeemed in the state in which it was purchased. Dear readers of good memory will recall that to be the swamp devil locale of New Jersey. Mother f*%#+^!!!

Chapter 17

With a look reserved for those needing to know a lover's heart, Jaime Gabriel examined his next ride-provider's eyes.

"Hello," Sharla said, simply. Grin.

"You have a great smile," Jaime let out, snapping the seatbelt's buckle with a click. His reply caught even himself by surprise. It just came to him. Only later will he learn how much a girl adores honesty, not to mention compliments. It would require far less time to realize his love for Sharla—another five weeks after that to act on this truth.

As for leaving Charleston, West Va., Sharla dropped him right back in Blacksburg (mildly ironic, yes... but it turns out that Sharla lives in Blacksburg. She was just returning from Charleston herself). Any of the reading crowd will be pleased to learn that Sam West connected Jaime once again with a ride, and in the proper direction this time. Thus, by that very night, he landed in Trenton, New Jersey. The odds!

The problems we receive when lest we make not even a single attempt at deception. If only....? The state of New Jersey, budget-short fallen and currently under federal investigation for pilfering state pension funds, informed Mr. Jaime Gabriel Holbrook of the four- to six-week lag time legally allowed by a state before becoming obliged to cough up $143 million, minus taxes, naturally.

"Legally?" Jaime questioned aloud.

"Yes sir," Ms. Bland robotically confirmed, further explaining how all such information is published on-line, as a matter of public record, she added, unable to guess or care that he might possibly have only limited access to the world wide web, hitch-hiker extraordinaire, or not!

"There's just no way around it," she reiterated in a pit of kindness, hoping to quell Jaime's look of exasperation. He immediately reflected on a memory of southern California gangstas, rappin' hard beneath a full-blown mast sail, giant Pacific orange ball aglow, tipping beyond the sea-green, convex horizon. Roll with the flow, Jaime. Roll with it.

Amazing how little an uncollected, multi-million dollar ticket can do to alleviate frustration of having traveled more than one-hundred miles the wrong direction; particularly, when that traveler owns no means of transportation—not yet, anyway. Such negativity must emit an aura, for Jaime could not convince anyone, or even luck into a single ride to cross the river into the big city. He opted instead for a jump-start, and luckily for our protagonist, Spring would rush ahead of schedule in the upper, mid-Atlantic region, with low temperatures hovering in the mid-40s. Ill-equipped, though, Jaime's mind boggled at the notion of the night's primary obstacle—attempting to make it successfully through the chill of the dark, lodged only beneath a bountiful collection of gaseous lights, shimmering from far and near. He shivered through the hours.

Having provided Fred's Bar & Grill's address for the glorious State of New Jersey to deliver by certified mail the check of his winnings, Jaime needed only to kill a few weeks in the Apple, and find a ride in-time back south by southwest to Blacksburg. Among the ways he spent taking a hatchet to time, while concentrating on not becoming another homeless, Washington Square chess master, or being lost in the myriad of architectural awe afforded on the rectangle of Manhattan, Jaime plotted the spending of his windfall. A trip home to visit Mariella must definitely be first, he decided just after encountering a clean, Frank Lloyd Wright vision of modern design. Strange how lonely a city of eight million people can be.

When, at last, the knock on Mariella's door occurred, (his return to Blacksburg was mostly unremarkable, receiving a check cleared for $73 million left him speechless, of course, minus the paperwork at the Bank of 'Yes!'), having not phoned ahead in attempt at surprising his maw, she didn't answer. Not for being at work, or out shopping, or under a flowing hot shower. She lay in a Xanax-hangover fog, refusing to remove herself from under down comfort. By that afternoon, though, she felt her knees buckle upon sight to her baby's beautiful glare.

"What are you doing? Jaime! Get in here. I've missed you so much. What have you been doing? Where have you been?"

To these and many more questions, he provided adequate answers. When a moment for him to inquire opened, eventually, he grabbed a framed photograph of Mariella, pictured in the arms of a man not his father.

"Who's this?" he naturally demanded.

At the end of her scatological, excuse-laden explanation, Jaime opened a dormant bag that would alter the course of their small-town history. With a touch of subterfuge, Jaime ignored the fact he'd not be seeing his father that evening and broached a subject to mom; isn't it odd, to his mind, he added, how big his own feet and hands are, and his head, and, well... you know. In comparison to dad's, he continued, only alluding to exposed evidence.

"Why?" she replied.

"Well, I mean, it's just unusual, isn't it?"

"He's not your father, okay," she let out after a quick look of dread.

"Do what?"

"I'm sorry. It's true. That's all I can tell you, okay," she wailed, turning to retreat to her bedroom. "I should have told you sooner, I know. But..."

Half an hour later, Mariella apologized in full, followed by how it all has become far too complicated. Maybe someday she'd be able to tell him more? For now, if he wanted to see the man who raised him, the one who he knew as his father, he would need a plane, maybe two—Adrian Holbrook currently resides in Peru, Mariella confessed with a shrug of 'ya-know'. Of course I don't, he wanted to yell!

"And you might have been able to afford to find him there, had you not ran away from that very lucrative film career in California," she further wailed, unaware of Jaime's true purpose for having returned back to see her.

Jaime very nearly re-thought the notion of sharing his booty with her, but decided the possible guilt of wondering whether he had made a mistake would outweigh the slight. And thus with little pleasure or fan-fare to be had in giving away two hundred thousand Benjamin's, he informed his mother of his most fortunate turn of events. The photograph of her new 'friend' somehow soon had a different spot for display–in her private bath. Jaime was still happy to leave the next morning.

The chief export of Peru being minerals, Jaime's "father" had set out for the Port of Callao, he learned from a man Adrian Holbrook had worked with at the car-body repair shop. Hadn't the conquistadors already looted the Peruvian people of its largest deposits of gold and silver, Jaime asked this same man?

"That sound's right," the man tried to agree. "I don't know for sure. I guess they have found some new mines, maybe? Copper, maybe?"

How exactly he would be involved in minerals, the man couldn't say. Fortunately for Jaime, more than one airline offers flights to Lima. He had only to choose between which major airport he wanted to make that leap from. Not that it matters, in the end, and he found only the take-off and especially landing over the turquoise hues of the south eastern Pacific to be enjoyable. Finding Adrian would not be as easy, he dreaded. Hailing a cab in Lima turns out to be more than uncomplicated, however, and now having cash always in-hand, he simply hopped a ride for the 15-minute skirt to the port and sought the largest mineral exporting company he could find.

No one he spoke with there, however, had any knowledge of a Holbrook, employed or otherwise. Jaime meandered along concrete barriers of the port, watching seamen shape bows or guide a crane operator loading a freighter's hull with large, metal cargo bens. The men worked steadily, not necessarily exerting great effort or energy, but standing firm and healthy. He could envision Adrian doing the same. He would always be his real father, he told himself.

Glumly he continued along the water's boundary, now eyeing ahead at a gathering crowd near a bobbing fishing vessel roped to an anchor on the seaboard. Smaller totora boats jostled alongside the bigger one, with frayed ends of reed at the point of each. It reminded Jaime of the Peruvian hats that almost everyone donned.

Personally, he couldn't choose between the derby fedora or granola toboggan ones. The yarn tassels might grow old, he laughed. Broken bits of Spanish were catching his ear, here and there. 'Gringo' littered some conversations. Grande! Grande!

But search after search netted no sign of Adrian. He had hit every cargo company he could find. Every day became progressively better, however. He decided on a derby, a metallic-rust job—only eight sols! Farther off the coast, Jaime discovered taco carts on the streets of Lima. They offered carne tacos and pork, plus more variety of potatoes and corns, hues matching all the different varieties of colors of the derby hats—dark purple, popping oranges, even blue corn.

Spanish began to roll in his ears, now. Salsas flavored with mangos and purple eggplant topped the tacos. At a four-corner intersection, just outside a fresco café, a man with facial lines of fifty, maybe sixty years, painted impressionistic-styled day scenes— oil on canvas. The painter's eyes and still-dark hair, revealed a hidden youth. It reminded Jaime of tales of treasures buried beneath the falls of Lake Titicaca.

He couldn't prevent a grievous chuckle at the idea of one of his LA films being set at Titicaca. And then a notion came to him, suddenly, like a kernel of purple corn bursting out an iron kettle— he could produce. All it takes is money and a flare for the dramatic. Thanks to lowly New Jersey and color-filled fashions of South America, he could do it right here. Why not, he said to himself? Why not, indeed.

Although mining industries definitely spur heavy industry, apparently such doesn't translate to heavy make-up. Jaime's first leg to the journey of becoming a Peruvian film mogul, began with learning its film-industry history. A curator at a Lima museum took less than two minutes to summarize it all. La puerta es abierto. Muy abierto, he said.

The skies, however, closed tightly, just after dos, unleashing a torrent of rain drops the size of large insects. The deluge did not ease until next morning, leaving deposits of tan erosion sifted throughout narrow allies and by-ways leaning to the port. Limans seemed unimpressed, taking the nature of it all as a good omen for late-Spring harvests. Had Jaime realized he would not see winter again for seven months, he might have delayed his search for Adrian. Jaime despised severe heat. He watched noon-day sun slowly eat away morning's wispy, pinkish mist of clouds rising with the tide.

Jaime sought a Ms. Sanchita, who he was told operated Lima's only reputable modeling agency. Sustantivas, actresses, almost always supplement theatrical careers by posing for still-photography shots. The stone archway to Ms. Sanchita's bore a turquoise and silver framed mosaic that spelled out Sanchita Modelo. Perfect, he thought, until not four feet inside the pock-marked building.

Photos hanging in the small, dusty room serving as a lobby, seemed little better than Polaroid quality. A shabby table supported a black, thick phone—like from the 60s, and some of the women pictured appeared less than glamorous, in Jaime's estimation. From behind a curtain of beads in the next room, a ladies voice stated: Abuela Sanchita says, "Yo como las manzanzas." Eat your apples, I say!

"Ola," Ms. Sanchita greeted Jaime, who returned hello in English. After a hardy laugh, Ms. Sanchita invited Jaime inside, past the next room, to what he guessed must serve as the studio. A half-broken set-light leaned against well-worn reflective panels. A computer monitor idled black-screened, nestled in a back corner on a stool. Its legs rattled as Jaime walked through the room waiting for Ms. Sanchita to finish boiling a pan of water on a portable gas stove. She retrieved lemon slices from a dorm-style mini-fridge and asked

Jaime if he minded his sans sugar?

It tasted nice, Jaime thought, with a nod, sipping the steaming brew, very fresh. In choppy English, but with a delightful tone, Ms. Sanchita explained most filming in Peru to be done by foreign gringos in documentary form. Some film Machu Pichu, of course. And journalistimos form Geography de Nationale regularly retreat to Lima from jungle or ocean expeditions, usually in search of a lost tribe or footage of Indians speaking even rarer languages–Quechua, or other Spanish off-shoots, tracing lineage to Incan ancestors.

Ms. Sanchita suggested Jaime seek out such a project and first learn more about the country and culture. These people would have contacts and wisdom, she added. Peruvian citizens certainly respect elder generations, Jaime noticed. They prefer a camp-fire story to a western soap opera, and French reggae to Jamaican. He tipped his derby and thanked her for the most delicious tea he had had since entering this mystical land.

Exploring more back alleys, heading downhill toward the port, once again, Jaime contemplated all his options. A romp along an Andean highland ridge sounded adventurous, especially in contrast to boarding a sea-bound freighter or tuna boat. Just being near the sea, with its lurching boats, seagulls screeching, Jaime wondered how sick it might make him out there? He wiled away that afternoon with no definitive response, pining for Sharla, of all things: But beautiful women in Lima and the port, were bountiful.

Next morning, buckling his belt around his jeans, he noticed he had gained a notch. Fish tacos! He purchased a top-of-the-line Sony digital video recorder in Lima. He wanted the advice of Ms. Sanchita on sea sickness, (why her?) but a sign hanging from the door read: Buscar en hora. Jaime knew he didn't have ten minutes to waste if he wanted to hitch aboard with a tuna captain. Dirty cabs stringed along the roads. He nabbed one whose driver's derby almost matched his color, and the middle-aged man who spoke broken English informed Jaime that tuna boats stay at sea working for three days, minimum.

Not willing to risk his well-being, Jaime asked the driver which boats, ones not sewn together from reeds, might work for just a day?

"Rent," the man replied, turning back to look Jaime in the eyes.

"Rent?"

"Rent," he repeated.

"How much? Tu se'?"

"Forty sols," he answered, assuredly.

But he couldn't go alone, Jaime explained. He possessed no sea experience, other than floating. The cab driver removed his deep-red derby, and took his eyes from the road, again, as he brought the cab to a stop in the right lane. In earnest like an undertaker consoling a young widow, he said his son to be an excellent sea captain. He knows every part of Callao, he said. Only twenty sols!

A wave of adrenalin tickled Jaime's toes from inside. His head tingled. It felt like sparklers danced a jig in his ear canals.

"Si'. Okay."

The cabby wheeled a u-turn in unison with on-coming cars, seamlessly gliding ahead through traffic. The salty wind cleansed Jaime's lungs. Had he ever felt so alive?

Chapter 18

Jorge, the cabby's son, took less than two minutes to gather a back-pack and pair of lengthy bamboo poles, which stuck out of the rear passenger window nearly as far as they were inside the car. A small circle of men, all smoking anxiously, gathered on a rectangular pier, north of the more industrialized section of Port Callao, where Jaime had started his search for Adrian Holbrook. Hatched-hut villas dotted the tan beach just farther ahead. Jorge followed one of the men from the short pier. The father handed Jaime two poles, tipped his hat and shooed him along.

Having been part of almost fifty southern California film productions, low-budget as they were, one would believe such experience to teach the importance of having charged batteries ready for a digital camera, particularly a new one to be used at sea. One would be wrong on this day, and thusly the first day of Film Producer 101 became a trial and error practice run. It's what makes being a movie producer so difficult—the details.

It didn't bother Jaime, though and certainly not Jorge, now looking forward to another day's pay. Sols abound, right. As they motored over coral beds adorned with more colors of fish than might be seen in a Lima harvest parade, Jaime could not know how the evening's exploits would lead to a 200-kilometer journey up the Andean steep. Had Jaime remembered to wait a day to have time to charge the battery, he would have captured a bright beginning to his efforts. Working ad-hoc, as it were, the loss will surely not be recounted campfire-side. Still, it could have been something, albeit somewhat conducive to motion sickness.

In addition to the necessary tackle, Jorge's back-pack revealed four bottles of water, two cans of sardines, two green bananas, a filet knife and an A.M. radio. The static crackle of lively Spanish guitars broadcast all morning made the experience, Jaime thought in a swaying daze.

By afternoon, he wished Jorge's father had mentioned unquenchable thirst. Not even a day at sea, baking sun unrelenting, Jaime knew he'd never last at any job on the big water. He envied Jorge's endurance, who didn't seem bothered, finding something new to point out or explain every few minutes. Never a sign of thirst. Jorge's bait at the end of his bamboo also consistently snagged fish, while Jaime's remained the same–baited hook. Maybe it was just the sun, Jaime thought, wiping sweat from his brow, turning red.

Not since the late 1800s' "War of the Pacific" did a foreign invader cover so much ground, so rapidly, as when Jorge finally docked their rented fishing boat that afternoon and Jaime high-tailed it up the hill to the first hotel in sight. Sols make chilled air and iced water. Jaime placed the digital recorder on the night stand and collapsed on the still-made bed 'til late that evening. He found the hotel restaurant closed by the time he made it out of his room in search of dinner, but a bar just off the lounge area remained open.

"Are Lima beans from here?" Jaime asked a young matronly-type foreign visitor seated at the bar to break the ice.

"I think so, but not just from here, you know," she replied in-differently.

"Oh," he said. "It just occurred to me."

"You should ask someone who might know better," she continued. Her eyes were peaceful, he noticed.

"Like who?" he asked a minute later.

"Him, for instance," she quickly answered, pointing to a man sipping a whiskey by himself at a back table tucked in a corner.

"Why him?"

"Him? Because," she said, adding nothing more than a wave of her dirty blonde hair.

"Yes...because...?" Jaime prodded a moment later.

"Because he is a bean farmer," she said with a tone of insistence, as if to scold Jaime for brandishing such temerity as to doubt her validity. "I didn't tell you this, though," she tacked on, shaking her head.

Why would she want to hide such a fact, he naturally wondered? Or was he ashamed of being a bean farmer? Jaime studied him. He didn't appear sullen in the soul. The man's teeth looked long and thin. His face taut, lightly whiskered. Then Jaime noticed a hat rack between the bar entrance and where the man sat. Jaime waited to see if he would look at the hat on the rack, now, also. But Jaime turned back around before seeming more suspicious. He offered a smile to the girl. She had light green eyes and sat upright, head high, self-satisfied, erudite.

Jaime turned back around to see the hat rack once more, just in-time to watch the thin man leaving. He took the hat. Jaime couldn't make out its exact color–less light from the bar made it back that far. A moment later, Jaime left to follow the possible bean farmer. He didn't know what prompted his curiosity. A sun-washed fragment of light cast rays of fuchsia seeping through an alley across the street where the man walked through. The hat was rose. A dark red rose. Jaime sprinted a few paces to gain ground.

He thought he lost him, though, when the man turned a corner exiting the alley and as Jaime did, he couldn't find him. He ran again to the next corner, but still didn't see him. He hustled back the other direction, up another corner. Giving up, Jaime noticed a door closing along the street and thought it might have been him. Everyone seems the same given enough distance. Jaime waited a half-hour to see if he'd re-appear. Sounds of various music poured out of upstairs windows nearby. Jaime had forgotten what day it was. It felt like Friday, he decided. The rhythmic beats continued to flow freely, but the man didn't show.

Jaime returned to the hotel bar, but the girl already had left. Another couple smoked at a table, with slender, square-edged rum & coke glasses–red skinny straws sticking out. Jaime bought a beer and took a table one removed from them. He could hear the man talking to the girl with a serious tone.

"It's killing the water. Where are the anchovies?" the man said raising a hand.

Ms. Sanchita had told a story before as they drank their hot tea about British influence in Chile, many years ago aiding its war to possess islands rich with guano deposits that the British crown desired in order to make better war, among other things. Feasting on ancient anchovy abundances, centuries of bird droppings saturated these undisturbed islands. Inca fertilizer, the Spanish had labeled it. British chemists transformed its nitrates into ammonia-based explosives. Not until 1909, when Fritz Haber perfected a process (still in use) to expunge nitrate from the atmosphere, did Britain's bird-crap hegemony expire.

Modern industrial applications of the Haber Process today assist in the annual production of more than 500 million tons of commercial nitrate fertilizer, helping to increase farm yields to meet the nutritional demands of seven billion hungry human beings, let alone the feed for animals traded in any commodities market around the globe. But the continuous drainage of nitrates saps water of oxygen throughout the web of waterways, small and large, particularly egregious upon oceans near a river's end.

Meanwhile, back when, German military scientists utilized the Haber Process to rapidly produce ammonium-nitrate-based weapons of mass destruction. One could argue minus Fritz Haber's scientific prowess, Germany's war machine could not compete with Europe's more established powers and World War I doesn't occur, which means no Treaty of Versailles, thus removing the impetus to World War II and its insanity. Such speculation can lead a lad to madness, though, as there's really no end to how far back to say what led to what. Here we are. Where are we going? How will we get there, successfully? These are questions to which good answers seem to remain mostly elusive.

"Electrolysis," the man two tables over stated, then promptly stood to leave. Jaime eyed his exit, then went out behind him, though not to follow. And he wouldn't need to, for the man with the rose-colored derby from before walked back up the street, just now. Jaime cracked up. He waited to see if he planned to return to the bar, but he passed by continuing up the avenue. Jaime trailed him again, for a minute, and then sped up to close in on him so he could seek his possible bean expertise. The man stopped, suddenly, sensing Jaime's presence. His body language made Jaime nervous, and he couldn't muster the right words.

"I just wanted to...to ask you a question," Jaime nearly stuttered. The man returned a look almost a snarl. Jaime panicked, telling him never-mind. The younger man who had just left the bar, speaking of anchovies, or lack there-of, ambled up the hill himself. He recognized Jaime from the bar, making eye contact.

"Que pasa?" Jaime offered.

"How are you, my friend?" the slender man returned with a broad smile full of teeth.

"Okay," Jaime said, relieved to be freed of the bean farmer's surly demeanor. "You fish?"

"Not much, anymore," he waved up the hill, but meaning beyond. He wore a terry-cloth, off-white shirt, its buttons half opened from the top. Unusual style, for a Peruvian, Jaime thought.

"No?"

"No," he reiterated, continuing his march up the street.

Jaime followed, asking where he was going? Another bar, he pointed across the way before them. Jaime wondered where the girl he had been with had gone? Many drinks later and a couple of hours spent, Jaime and Romero boarded a bus bound for higher elevations. Having already wanted to take in the Andes, coupled with whiskey-backed courage, Jaime completely blocked out previous Greyhound experiences. But such psychological trickery wouldn't be necessary this evening in Peru.

Riders tonight were either extremely sedate or just the opposite, revelry ruling the bouncy ride. In no time Jaime noticed almost everyone on the bus singing, laughing, stories of glory on the exchange. Jaime's tales of southern California exploits brought the scene to a hush, peppering parts of his tale in Espanol, before unleashing, "Bodacious! Bodacious!" Heaving his chest in triumph.

Not until the bus driver screeched the tires, also caught up in the party atmosphere and not paying enough attention to the road, along one of 22's increasingly sharp curves as they climbed toward LaMerced, did a lull finally settle over the rowdy collective. After everyone took a breath to give the driver peace, Jaime noticed how dark the skies had grown outside the bus. He pressed his cheek to a pane, peering into the black night spotted with what seemed like a million stars. So near, he thought, harping back on Chris the Hopi Indian and that first night with him in the southwestern desert. He wished he could be with him now. As soon as he finished his journey here, he vowed to himself, he'd return to share the wealth with Chris. And with that thought a sudden wave of sadness filled his heart–he hadn't come close to locating his father, Adrian. He longed for him. Why now? Through the front windshield Jaime thought he noticed lights on the horizon. Sure enough, around the next corner, the bus slowed a bit, coming to rest shortly.

"This is us," Romero said, breaking the silence.

Half the passengers exited at LaMerced.

"Where are we going?" Jaime asked Romero, who seemed to know as he stepped off the bus quickly into a line forming to go somewhere.

"We'll sleep this one off in one of the picker's camps tonight," Romero answered, motioning up ahead of the line of bus riders.

"Pickers?" Jaime repeated somberly, the festive mood from the trip having completely dissipated.

"Sí. Pickers," Romero confirmed. "Where did you think we were going tonight? Do you not remember from the bar? You said you wanted to know more of Lima beans. Well, now you will."

Jaime could only nod in seeming acknowledgement. He turned back to where the bus had dropped everyone off, but it had already departed. He had a nice room back at the port. Air conditioning, ice and a bar stocked with nice things to purchase on the cheap. Sols abound, he mumbled.

The line of apparent bean pickers, mostly men but some women, continued along a narrow dirt path, winding up an incline toward a thatched-roof canopy, overlaying rows of cots. Only now did Jaime notice blankets being toted by most. Romero left his side and was now speaking with a burly man who seemed to be in charge. Romero pointed to Jaime. He instinctively waved, but the man didn't respond.

"We're lucky," Romero said upon return. "He has extra blankets for us."

Within minutes, nearly all the cots were occupied by the pickers bedding down for the night. What had he agreed to? And yet, what did it matter? Here he was. The day at sea and wild evening suddenly caught up to him. Before he knew what else to question, he watched himself in a dream stretched out fully on a hammock under one of the beach huts he had seen that morning. But a swarm of mosquitoes began biting and all the swats he could muster did little to thwart the attack. He took refuge in the ocean, but long strands of sea kelp entangled his efforts, forcing him to abandon that for the beach. He rolled around in the dirt to protect his skin from the still swarming mosquitoes, to which he'd respond by going back into the water, where the whole cycle repeated itself.

Just as someone standing on a distant pier, who turned out to be the blonde girl form the bar, noticed his struggle, he awoke in a damp daze, parts of his undershirt soaked with sweat. His head ached. For a moment, as he tried to gather his wits, he couldn't recall why he should be waking up in a cot surrounded by twenty others doing the same. Romero then sat up and it all came back to him—lima beans. Today, I am a picker.

The man in charge might have had blankets to loan for the night, but he didn't have any hats to share. The other pickers, prepared as they were, each sported large, loose hats of woven straw. While certainly nothing of fashion, they were all Jaime could think of as the noon-day sun wreaked havoc upon the back of his neck and forearms. The air was lush with moisture. In the distance Jaime could faintly hear the sound of moving water.

He thought of simply giving up the labor of picking beans, desiring instead to explore the sounds of the nearly jungle-like terrain surrounding the acres of bean fields. No one else seemed to have a care in the world, though. A few even sang right out-loud, and others hummed along. A grumbling from his belly reminded Jaime that they hadn't eaten any breakfast or dinner from the night before. The sun shone straight overhead. As if on cue, the picking crew began standing tall, taking notice of each other, then started exiting the field. Jaime followed, last in line.

At the end of one of the rows of vines, three large picnic tables were covered with sheets. Large bowls of rice and something else, Jaime couldn't tell, were passed around as the pickers all took a place at the benches at the tables. The other bowl contained beans. Lima beans! How could they, Jaime wanted to shout? But juicy chunks of seasoned ham filled the dish and carafes of tea, though warm, also were passed around. Rice and beans never tasted so good, he thought. Warm tea never quenched a thirst so well.

Just as the meal was being finished, Jaime felt a great urge to climb atop and recline fully extended on one of the tables being cleared by young girls, the man in charge's daughters, Jaime guessed. But the pickers, without word, obediently returned to the field, each going back to where their bean sacks lay, somehow knowing just where they had stopped to break for lunch. As the day wore on, Jaime's thoughts ran wild. His back began to ache and his scratched-up hands were starting to itch. Why did he continue this? And yet, any time he looked around at the others, no one else seemed affected as such. They pick without wavering. Even Romero seemed unfazed.

At last the sun began its decent behind the sinking horizon, yet no one showed a sign of letting up. Only just before the last minutes of light remained, did Jaime notice the man in charge standing back at the tables where they'd taken lunch. The pickers moved to him, unloading their sacks of harvest into a bin hauled on a trailer behind an old truck, painted in aqua sea-green. After dumping off the beans, the pickers formed a line before one of the lunch tables, where the man in charge now doled out sols for the day's work. From there, most of the men and few women returned to beneath the canopy and laid down on their blanketed cots. Jaime found Romero there waiting, but he hadn't taken to a cot.

"Well?" is all he said, at first.

"Wow," Jaime could only reply, exhausted. "I'll never take a bean for granted again."

Romero nodded, agreeing.

"Don't they eat dinner?" Jaime asked, next, sensing his appetite coming on like a freight train.

"They will later," Romero answered. "Siesta, first, though."

"They will?" Jaime lamented.

"You don't want to do this tomorrow, right?" Romero shrugged.

"Not particularly, no," Jaime concurred.

"Right. I didn't think you would. That's why we are taking one more stop up the road," he said. "Come on, the bus will be here any minute."

Romero collected their pay from the farmer then quickly headed back down the trail to the LaMerced stop. With an underlying reservation as to what Romero had in mind, Jaime followed him. Sure enough, in only moments the same bus and driver from the evening before stopped. A pair of elderly women, who looked like they might be sisters, exited first. More pickers then stepped off the bus before only Jaime and Romero climbed back onboard.

"Where are we going?" Jaime finally asked as they took seats near the middle.

"You will see. You will see," is all Romero provided.

Chapter 19

The next stop up from LaMerced left them in the middle of nowhere. And as the dead of night arrives much earlier in such places, Jaime wondered what in hell lie in store? Romero explained plainly that they'd make camp at a spot he knew of just up the trail. Jaime noticed he held two blankets as they started off. Where did he get them? Wild animal cries already echoed in the distance. Any hope of eating dinner seemed a farce. The sky grew darker quickly as Romero's pace quickened. Jaime lost sight of him but could hear the steps and sense of him just ahead.

In a while they came to a small clearing and Romero stopped. A sound of moving water seemed close, but Jaime couldn't decide how near and wondered if it could be the same source of water he thought he had heard near the bean field. Romero stopped, checking familiar markings in the dark silhouette of moon-lit tree tops. Then he tossed out the blankets and simply laid down.

"Buenas noches, amigo," he said after fixing his bedding for the night. He rolled to a side facing away from Jaime. This is it? Jaime felt to cry, then thought to scream. But again, what would be the point? Ten hours of crouching and reaching under a sun showing off lends to good sleep.

Sore from neck to toe, belly aching, he awoke the next morning excited for the day. To see where they are? Where they'll go? Romero's blanket lay rolled and tied. Where is he? Maybe to wash in the water? Two bright-yellow canaries French kissed on a branch of a flowering aphranda. The air tasted sweet, Jaime thought, standing to stretch. A layer of dew lining the ground cover glistened.

A rustling sound of leaves sounded to his right. Jaime tightened. It moved his way. A machete hacked through a hanging mangrove vine. Jaime ducked, quickly dropping to a squat, then kneeling low on one knee. Another whack!

"Wait..." the man wielding the machete warned, holding the blade high in a hushing signal. Had he been detected? Jaime slowly crept down to lay belly first.

"I think I hear one," machete man then stated.

Silence.

"Tally-ho," he then let loose like a musketeer but in a hushed whisper.

Swoosh...swish. Then a cadre of swooshes. What were they after? Jaime could now see several people trekking through knee-high water, apparently not twenty yards away. A mix of light-skinned white men and women waded along, formed in a jagged line, trailing the brown-skinned leader.

"I'm glad you didn't alert them," a voice quietly offered from just behind his left ear. Jaime whirled back, flailing an arm, nearly striking Romero, forced to react quickly to avoid the blow.

"Oh, it's you" Jaime let loose.

"Yes, it's me," Romero said. "Who did you think it was?"

"They're after monkeys," he then spoke softly, nodding toward the passing eco-tourists.

"Monkeys?" Jaime repeated, falling back on an elbow. "Wait...they're going to kill them?"

"What? No, they just want to see some," he said. "These groups of gringo eco-tourists get back in here from time to time."

"Where are we, anyway?" Jaime asked, sitting up.

"The jungle, *pendejo*," Romero answered. "Jeesh! Are you ready?"

"For what?"

"Adventure, my friend. Adventure," Romero reiterated, extending a hand to help hoist Jaime to his feet.

"Here we go," Romero said wasting no time. "Grab that blanket and stay close. Stay alert, too."

"Alert?" Jaime asked, growing slightly alarmed.

"Just stay close," Romero said, dismissively.

And so they went, off through the semi-dense jungle. They seemed to be following close to a river bank. When he could gain a glimpse of the water, however, it didn't appear to be moving. Jaime couldn't decide if it wasn't some sort of jungle marsh, instead. The terrain began to flatten. White, fluffy cumulous clouds towered in the western skies, Pacific moisture rising along the build of the Andes.

A memory of his father came to him. Adrian had wanted to get Jaime out of the house and deciding every kid loves fishing, once drove them down a remote dirt road to the crest of a ridge around a bend where it opened up to a half-acre stock tank. They fished from the bank, catching mostly small sun perch that they only threw back, but an image of that afternoon remained. The towering clouds and clean moist air must have sparked the memory, Jaime thought. How would he ever find his father? What of eating again? Or water to drink?

Romero trudged onward, only occasionally glancing back to make a check on his partner. Jaime imagined it as a hunt for monkeys in the wild. A myriad of birds now littered the skies and trees. Jaime thought he saw a pair of Scarlet Macaws, though they flew off quickly upon hearing thrashing sounds of the two trouncing through thick switch grass. A diverse concourse of smells also kept Jaime's attention keen. At once a powerful stench of dung would spoil the air, then only a few yards later a potpourri of flora perfumes would sweeten the lot.

But even this diversion soon fell way to pangs of hunger reaching from inside his empty stomach. Onward they trekked, though, the thickness of the grass gaining gradually. Jaime's mind began to sway with the tops of the grass drifting with the wind. Hopi had said the sun's greatest trick upon man is the illusion of time. Only the now actually exists. What's gone is gone and what will be always remains in a future of which light particles have not yet reflected to anyone's conscience, so it doesn't exist either. Each moment to moment is all that counts. Each step. Each breath. Horrific screeches of animals suddenly rang out from high and far.

"Are there many monkeys back in here?" Jaime asked, breaking their long stretch of silence.

But Romero whipped around to shush him, saying they were getting close. Move as soft as possible, he ordered. Jaime grew tense again. Who could hear them over the jungle wails of wild? What could they be sneaking upon? Snakes? Were they after jungle pythons? Jaime stopped momentarily to look behind them. Could he find his way back out if he had to? He couldn't, really, he thought. And besides, what would Romero do if he did make a break for it?

Jaime continued on, blindly following Romero, trying to just be in the moment. Their trail turned sharply and then Romero broke off from the water's edge and started up a heavily covered incline. Jaime stopped for a second and waited. But Romero looked back and motioned him to follow. Why couldn't he talk aloud, Jaime wondered again? The cover became difficult to maneuver, various vines interlocked, twisting opposite directions, creating natural slip knots that tightened with every pull.

Beyond the top of a small hill the land swept down to a covey-like den, guarded by rows of mature junipers, spider-moss spanning throughout vast branches. Then seemingly out of nowhere, a slender, meagerly dressed man approached Romero. They exchanged a quick, quite greeting and without giving notice back to Jaime, Romero followed the man as they walked into a shanty-styled hut, corrugated sheet metal supported by rotting shanks of lumber. Jaime waited just below the crest of the hill. Minutes later, Romero came from the hut hauling a burlap, potato sack over each shoulder. Romero handed off half this bounty without word to Jaime as he passed following the same path back out.

"Potatoes, huh," Jaime eventually offered with a forced casual tone.

Romero laughed, leading forward like a leopard on the take. Around midday they reached back to the bus stop. A teen-age girl whose round face shined in the high sunlight waited quietly by herself beside a lonely sign pole. The wind from the open windows felt fine, Jaime thought once inside and headed back toward LaMerced and then on to Lima. As the bus picked up speed, every few seconds broken dried bits of grass blew off them forming small eddies of swirling debris in the isle. They were both too spent from the journey to care. Jaime's instincts propelled closed lips to the whole scene. He'd depart from Romero back in Lima. The cabby's son would be available for tomorrow and he'd probably know about anchovies and what-not. Jaime would be prepared this time, too, he told himself.

At the LaMerced stop more than a dozen new riders waited. Jaime enjoyed watching them all board. Such gentle people. It eased his mind, until the driver closed the mechanical door behind the last two. They took isle seats apart from each other two rows behind them. Jaime looked to Romero, but he seemed in a trance. Conversations among the other passengers filled the air, shortly, breaking the spell over Jaime's nerve. But he could feel the presence of the two rough looking men from behind them.

Jaime shifted in his seat to gain a better angle to spy them. But they both noticed his move and eye. A scorpion's image filled his imagination. He re-settled back toward the window, and didn't look elsewhere until they reached Lima. As passengers began making their way to the front of the bus, Jaime quietly informed Romero that he had to get back to his hotel, immediately. They'd wonder why he hadn't checked in from the night before, he offered. Romero shrugged his shoulders with indifference, grabbing both sacks and blankets.

Jaime glanced back at the two men finally. Glinting glares shot back at him. He stopped to allow them to pass first, but they did the same, forcing Jaime to exit behind Romero. His senses heightened. It felt slower. As Romero took the last step off the bus, three more men waiting in the street closed in on him.

Romero ditched the sacks, somehow breaking between two of the men attempting to apprehend him. Jaime watched momentarily in dismay, then thought to leave, aiming to turn the opposite direction. As he did, though, one of the mean-faced men from the bus grabbed his right arm, squeezing forcefully.

"Adonde vas?" the man said briskly.

"Do what?" Jaime shot back.

"Where do you think you are going?" he clarified in broken English.

"What are you talking about?"

Jaime could hear sirens now, growing closer with each wail. He didn't know if it pertained to this situation, but they must, he thought. Then crashes like commotion came from just up the street, the direction Romero had fled. Out of nowhere, the dirty blonde-haired girl from the bar and his dream from the night before, suddenly appeared in the mix. Had she been there all along? She told the man holding Jaime that he was alright. She repeated this information in fluent Spanish then flashed some sort of identification to the guy, but Jaime couldn't see what it showed.

Whatever it revealed worked, because the man relinquished his tight grip on Jaime and walked away to join two other men just up the street. Just like that.

"What's going on?" Jaime implored of the young woman who had cleared him.

"Come with me," she only replied, swiftly leading them away from the ordeal.

"Is Romero okay?" Jaime then asked, despite real concern to the contrary.

"Maybe not," the woman stated. "But you don't know anything. I know that. You're lucky I recognized you from the hotel."

"Why? What's going on," Jaime questioned.

"Cocaine," she said. "Really just the paste, but it's all the same."

"I had no idea," he implored.

He turned back around and thought he could see someone with a knee to Romero's back as he lie at the corner just up from the men he broke through.

"Really? Cocaine?"

"Afraid so," she said plainly.

As they made it to the end of the block, she led them again, around a corner, then stopped. She wanted to know what Jaime was doing in Peru? He explained the search for his father, or the man who raised him as such, he added, and then told her about the idea to do a documentary on the depletion of anchovy fisheries. She wanted to know how he would pay for all this?

"I won a lottery," he smiled.

But she seemed unconvinced and suggested Jaime wrap up the visit and be gone as soon as possible. Authorities might have allowed him to go free today, but they'd be watching him closely, now.

"But I haven't done anything wrong," he belted.

"It doesn't matter," she insisted. "They've got their eye on you, now. It's not like you're here with family or a new wife. You stand out, being alone. If they want, they can make things very difficult for you. They have their ways."

"But..."

"Listen," she interrupted, "I've done you a favor, here. Don't push your luck, pal. Go!"

Bewildered, Jaime slowly made his way back to the hotel across from the beach where the rented fishing boats dock. The warming temperatures lured more tourists to the beaches. In the distance he could see a crowd gathered around one of the fish-taco lunch boats. The young woman had said to leave, but he wasn't ready, he tried to convince himself. If he left now, would he ever see his father again? What of the anchovies' film? What of seeing more? He needed a drink, he decided. He needed Ms. Sanchita.

At a small grocery mart, he picked-up a six pack of Peruvian beer and a ham and cheese on fresh buns. It felt good once the sandwich infiltrated his emptied stomach to have pushed so long without food. It tasted as the freshest food he had ever had. A sweetness to it all. He opened a beer and proceeded back up to Ms. Sanchita's model studio. She wasn't there when he arrived, though, so he strolled along the street to kill some time, casually keeping an eye for Jorge's father's cab. The air of the afternoon seemed listless. Nary a soul appeared. Jaime finally took a seat on the sidewalk, leaning back against a building that provided shade. He drifted off for a few moments, snapped back to reality as two older ladies shuffled in front of him along the sidewalk in rapid conversation with sing-song voices.

He tried Ms. Sanchita's again. An assistant let him inside this time, but informed Jaime that her boss had traveled to Mexico City for business. The young assistant seemed nice, Jaime thought. He told her what had happened with Romero and of the lady who saved him's warning. It all sounded possible, she said. Many men, who struggle because of depressed fishing or other lost opportunities, turn to other means of making quick money. And authorities are just as corrupt, she went on. He could always come back at a later time, she suggested.

With that, Jaime concluded all signs pointed to his departure. Off to New York, he said with a raised finger. The assistant's smile seemed forced. She was lovely none-the-less, he thought. Despite having only just met, he decided he would miss her, too.

Chapter 20

He had to wait two days before he could arrange for a flight direct to New York. The forty-eight hours were excruciatingly long. He thought it wise not to tempt his fortune any further, so he languished inside his hotel room the entire time. In comparison, the plane ride, though long and cramped, felt enjoyable. He liked watching the earth below as they flew along. For miles the rain forest stretched on and on. How many Romeros were out there, he wondered? How many monkey-seeking tourist clans?

As they made their approach to JFK, it occurred to Jaime that he'd be missing winter again. Being mid-March, Spring stood poised. Thus, only he grinned when the pilot announced they'd be circling in a waiting pattern before landing due to runways being jammed at the moment with planes in-line to be de-iced.

"Did he say 'de-iced'?" Jaime asked a young woman next to him just to hear it again.

"He did," she answered. "Can you believe it? Winter should be gone by now!"

His smile widened. She gave him an awkward look in return. I missed last winter, he explained, but it only increased her hunch to his oddity. She nodded and turned deliberately away. He didn't care. He felt a warmness swelling inside. New York waited just across the river and acting waited there. Real acting. His excitement nearly boiled over, until he saw the line through customs. Four hours later, he wished he'd never left Peru.

But his sense of anticipation returned once he navigated the concourse and endured the cabby-line (another 45 minutes). A twinge of apprehension paid a last brief visit when the cab driver asked where he wanted to go. Where to begin, he suddenly wondered? The cabby repeated the standard inquiry, not hiding his impatience.

"Times Square," Jaime blurted at last, failing to think of anything better.

"Just right in the middle?" the cabby said with a sardonic snicker.

"That'd be fine," Jaime answered, curious as to what he might have said wrong. Welcome to the Apple, only now slightly in decay.

After finding a new jacket to purchase at inflated prices in a nearby retail store, having been unprepared for winter, Jaime stepped back out into the madness of Times Square bundled tightly. He watched in awe. The lights. The bustle. The swarms seemingly oblivious to the biting north-east winds howling. A Holiday Inn would have to serve as his first point of no return.

"How much?" he uttered with his jaw hanging low.

"Two eighty-five per night, sir," the clerk repeated, stone-faced. "You're lucky, too. We're usually booked. I think the storm has led to a few cancellations."

"Is this a standard rate?" he pleaded.

"Yes sir. For Manhattan, in Times Square? It's quite reasonable."

She paid little interest to his story of Peruvian hotel rates. Sols abound, yes, but these are US dollars. A line now formed behind him. He had to act, in oh so many ways. But where to begin?

The room, though small, smelled clean and its view faced directly into the square. He could watch for hours on-end, he thought. But destiny lay somewhere midst the sky scrapers. He had to find it. And the next morning, at least, he would begin. For this afternoon, a bout of jet-lag left him sinking and the flakes of white whipping against the rapidity of neon-lit background mesmerized him. It quickly soothed his weary mind to a dull numbness, alleviating the throbbing behind his eye sockets. By night, his attention wandered to television. It didn't take long to remember why he hadn't missed that. The next morning felt more promising. Sunshine shot through his window as he pulled apart the heavy curtains. Particularly bright streaks reflected from short stacks of snow plowed to the curbs, unsoiled along its highest points. A concierge suggested he grab an issue of *Village Voice*–Jaime might find acting auditions posted among its back pages.

"Do I need a résumé?" he asked.

"Not generally," the clean-cut attendant answered. "Just bring some talent. Oh, and some thick skin."

Sure enough, he found two auditions listed for that afternoon he thought seemed promising. It took the remainder of the morning to find the first theatre, despite its proximity to mid-town. The Bleeker Street Theater's doors opened at two for auditions.

He passed time meandering Canal Street. Tempting as it may have been to purchase faux-brand items on the cheap, he hadn't brought much cash along for the day's outing, and so settled on the luxury of people watching. When he tired of that, ducks hung to dry in front restaurant windows on the Chinese side of Canal provided brief interest. The dark sheen of blood slowly drizzling underneath to where it didn't show. A stare he couldn't avoid. The rawness of the scene suddenly flashed his mind to his Arizona bovine killing spree. At least duck meat doesn't lead to cancer and other ills, he decided, turning north off Canal onto Mulberry Street, quickly enthralled how suddenly a neighborhood could change locale. A stout man donned in a pen-stripe suit waited outside a small pizzeria. Jaime couldn't help gazing at his white-wings of hair slicked back and the strings of small flickering Christmas lights outlining a first-story eave behind him. It reminded him of an Italian restaurant in southern California.

"You need sum-tin?" the man suddenly stated with force, pressing out the cherry of his spent cigarette beneath polished wing-tips.

Jaime feigned ignorance, looking around as if he may have been speaking to someone else.

"Yeah, yous," the man said, taking a step his direction.

Jaime offered up-turned hands in nothing-here fashion,

speeding up his gait to gain distance. Just ahead a cabby waited atop the hood of his yellow car, perusing a newspaper. Jaime opted to climb inside before he encountered any more trouble.

"Bleeker Street Theater, please."

Before stepping inside the theater, Jaime admired gargoyles jutting out of the building's facade across the street. The theater's lobby was dark and damp. He questioned if he had the right place. He stopped to listen, but couldn't hear anything. He waited longer, then thought he heard movement inside. Opening a door to the actual theater, he could see the lighted stage. A skinny young man with thick black frames, holding a clip board asked for his name and motioned Jaime to follow a side-isle down the slope to a side-stage entrance.

"What part are you here for?" a slender woman asked, waiting at the base of stairs at stage-right.

"Well, which ever one's right for me," Jaime replied.

Her forced half-smile suggested her impatience.

"Sir?" she insisted, tapping a pencil to her clipboard.

"The lead," Jaime finally answered, unsure what else he could say.

"That part isn't up," she bemoaned, fingering through pages held on the clipboard.

"No? Oh, sorry," Jaime winced. "Well..just give me...."

"Here," she snapped, handing him a page. "Just read this one."

But he couldn't see it in the low light of that part of the theater. A dozen or so other hopefuls stood waiting before him. He could see that more light would be available the closer he got to his spot, so he waited to look over his lines until then. The guy in front of him was reading through his. He wore a yellow and green plaid scarf. His curly blond hair sat tousled on a slender, triangular-like skull. Jaime towered above him. He noticed all of the others waiting also were much shorter than himself. It made him feel confident, for some reason.

A middle-aged woman stepped out to the stage to read her lines. Her voice carried out loudly, filling the theater. She performed passionately, Jaime thought. She stopped, appearing to listen to

101

instructions from someone seated in the theater. Curtains and stage lights limited visibility out to the seats. She then repeated the lines, varying the read by reducing the force of her effort. When she finished, a red light atop a pole at the side of stage left flashed on, and the woman abruptly exited that direction. The rest of those auditioning moved up one position.

Jaime could make out the lines on his page, now. The title of the play spanned the top–*A History of American Sexual Prudence*. He read the first stanza of words. They portrayed a man justifying exploits of colitis. Jaime's spirit fell to the floor.

"Isn't this the audition for *Mary's Attic*," Jaime asked the slender man waiting one spot before him.

"No. That's the play running here now," he sneered. "This is for the upcoming show for this fall."

"This fall?" Jaime stammered.

A roll of the eyes served as the man's reply. The next to audition began; another short man, young and somewhat stocky. Jaime could now see on his page that he was reading for the part Jaime was given.

"They don't call me Gene, for nothing, darling," the man read with a cheesy smirk. "I'm not like the rest, doll. It's worth your money. Believe me. You won't be disappointed."

"No. No. No!" Jaime shouted, throwing his page to the stage. Everyone froze for a flash. Jaime fled.

Once back outside, he felt faint. What had just happened? Real acting. He wanted real acting. He needed another copy of the *Village Voice*. He started back uptown, turning west a few blocks farther. At the next corner he stepped inside a store. Racks of publications were just inside and he purchased another copy. There it was. The Bleeker Street Theater auditions were for next Fall's upcoming feature–*A History of American Sexual Prudence*. How had he not noticed before?

He continued north two more blocks, then turned toward Greenwich Village, though Jaime was none the wiser. Maybe he could find someone there who could help him. Spotting an unoccupied park bench a block ahead, he stopped to wait and collect his thoughts. Passing people varied so much, he noticed. At once, a pair of young ladies wearing stylish heels and fine fashion, then a hefty woman, alone, toting two sacks of groceries. Her face revealed lost hope; a life reduced to mere existence. Next a trio of men of Latin decent strolled up, flashy hip-hop types, with expensive sneakers and over-sized gold necklaces bouncing on their chests with each step. He took care to not let them see him looking.

He moved on minutes later, pledging to himself to have more conviction for his dream. He liked the atmosphere of wherever he was. It seemed friendlier, though he couldn't decide why he should think so? People were no less strange; no more inclined to offer assistance. He found a small bistro with alfresco seating, although empty this afternoon. He bought a coffee and bagel and sat at a seat next to the glassed front. From watching his waitress interact with other diners, he thought he might be able to talk with her. She smiled openly and seemed nice.

Kendra, he learned upon asking, came to the city from a small place outside Detroit. She also came to act. She had been here already for more than a year, she said, having landed only two minor roles. He should try the Cherry Lane Theatre, just around the block, she added.

"They're not so bad," she said, "Not like most of the rest."

The dimples in her cheeks deepened when she smiled a certain way, Jaime noticed. He took three more cups of coffee, stalling for inspiration. He liked watching her move about the tables, light on her feet, airy, an aura of innocence exuding her being. When only he remained, he left for the Cherry Lane Theatre. She wished him luck through the entrance as he closed the wrought iron fence gate that surrounded the patio.

A line of about thirty had formed outside the entrance. The would-be actors reminded him of the audition from earlier–mostly under five-foot six and varied in shape and form, yet somehow similar–though he couldn't decide exactly why he found them all as such. They looked like actors, or at least bad ones. A few appeared to be waiting with someone they knew beforehand, but most stood silent and sullen, bracing the chill in the wind.

After more than two hours, his turn on the hardwood stage lasted less than two minutes. No one provided any explanation. Another red light simply came on, as it does for most. And nothing more. At other theaters later that week, some auditions ended with a word, or two. Give NYC its due–she can chew 'em up and spit 'em out as quickly and efficiently as any other man-made machine.

Ever since Lenape Indians abandoned the mouth of the Hudson for a thousand dollars' worth of marked-up trinkets, the island of Manhattan's natural beauty, save three interior square kilometers, has succumbed to an onslaught of man's appetite for destruction and construction. Lest, Jaime's acting aspirations took a figurative rest; for how long, one can only speculate, dear readers. Odds makers would place the chances of his ever breaking a leg on stage right at greater than a thousand-to-one.

Albeit, such forecasters have no knowledge of Jaime Gabriel Holbrook, let alone his hopes and dreams. Also not in actual possession of any working crystal balls, soothsayers could not know that Jaime will return to NYC and will land a role that shall place him, however temporal, in the midst of the city's thriving arts scene. For the time being, though, our protagonist decided his efforts at achieving a successful audition failed because some cosmic energy has taken cause against him. Why such a force may be working at his artistic demise, Jaime cannot begin to decipher. His best prognosis leads him to believe that his lack of any formal 'thank-yous' for his recent financial windfall may be spinning karma his direction.

Thus, a return to West Virginia must occur. Not wanting to embark upon another thumbs-out deployment and coupled with monetary freedom, Jaime opted to take back to the friendly skies–first class! To his pleasant surprise, he found Fred's Bar & Grill just as he left it. Sam even recognized him–always a boost of self-esteem, even if motives in such situations are typically ulterior.

"What's new?" Jaime asked of Sam.

"Same 'ole," he replied, but shortly amended the clichéd response by telling of Leon Hamilton's latest exploits. The big shot currently sits in the county jail on a half-million dollar bond for attempted second-degree murder, Sam explained. Jeremiah Washington, local rumor mills had it, became infuriated at a New York Times' article relating how the federal government began sifting through each and every digital transmission in the world more than ten years earlier.

Having nowhere else to unleash his angst, Jeremiah focused on the one person he had convinced himself represented a real-life big-brother, Leon Hamilton. If not for Hamilton's advanced military training, he may not have reacted so swiftly to Jeremiah's sneak attack. And only because detectives discovered Jeremiah unarmed, did they level charges against Hamilton.

Had he stopped before fatally stabbing Jeremiah; had he not inserted his six-inch buck knife multiple times; and particularly, had he not stomped on his grizzly Adam's face repeatedly, his lawyer claims he could have argued for a case of self-defense. But whether or not this might have held up before a jury, no one will ever know. Boot prints don't lie.

The news, from Jaime's perspective, rapidly altered his effort to relate appreciation for his recently-acquired fortune. Even contacting officer Hamilton now seemed un-appealing. Needing to express gratitude of some sorts to someone, Jaime recalled Sharla. And perhaps even more random than taking possession of a winning, Garden State lottery ticket, Sam also knew Sharla.

"She doesn't come in here too often," Sam said with a slight shake of the head. "But I'm pretty sure she plays beach volleyball at a place over by the river."

"River?" Jaime said.

"Yeah. The Woods."

"Oh yeah? The Woods?" Jaime aped.

"The Woods. Right."

Jaime left Sam a twenty for tip–a start to recovering good mo-jo. And sure enough, that very evening, Sam's usefulness proved itself invaluable, once more. Jaime indeed found Sharla ankle deep in beach sand and looking even better than he had remembered. Chalk it up to Jaime's natural good looks, or to his semi-tout physique, or maybe the Fates can be said to have played a part (despite that we know better), but something clicked.

Within two weeks, Sharla's inner-adventure-seeking fancy tickled at the notion of traveling with Jaime to find Chris the Hopi. Southwestern desert colors always look so mystical to her mind. To have someone who can foot the bill and is easy on the eyes, just makes too much sense. Pueblo prepare!

Chapter 21

Love being in the air, and what not, Jaime at last decided to let loose on part of his fortune and make a significant purchase. Had he known how much enjoyment could be gained simply from shopping, and had he been made aware of how much pleasure appeared to come to Sharla, simply by being part of the car-buying process, he might never have embarked on destination NYC. The having-money scene was still all so new.

An all-terrain, four-wheel drive vehicle made the most sense. It just seemed to invoke adventure. The "Explorers Sport" package even included a dashboard compass. A nice touch for himself, Jaime laughed inside. Despite the buy not scratching the surface, really, of his total bankroll, a twinge of guilt still flashed through him as he signed the check, paying by cash of course, to save money in loan interest. He'd never even had a real job and he just paid cash for a real-life Hotwheel. They left Blacksburg in a giddy state of bliss.

Conversation along the way to Pueblo flowed as easily as butterflies are light on their tips. With each stretch of miles, a connection between them deepened. By Saint Louis anticipation of physicality precipitated goose bumps. Nothing in the human experience quite compares to the warmth that envelopes a heart in the midst of fresh love. The sun's light appears brighter, breath sweeter, sensitivities keener, and a simple touch along skin pure pleasure.

At sight of the Arch, they exchanged a look, each reading the other's mind. Their first all-the-way should occur at the height of the Gateway to the West's apex. When they discovered the narrowness of the observation look-out area and complete lack of any hidden space inside, however, they realized it couldn't happen high over the southern banks of the Mississippi. The hotel room that night couldn't diminish the passion, though, let alone Sharla's delight when her fingers cupped his magnificent pair.

"Oh my," she whispered softly into his ear. "You're quite the man."

Blush. Blush.

Their making of love left both drunk on endorphins. They peacefully slipped away to a sleep so deep the Mariana Trench would be envious. Sharla dreamt of Russet potatoes. The next morning felt like the sun had risen for the very first time. After another round of raucous intercourse, they took a late start westward, not minding the least to take another night's stop before arriving the following warm afternoon in sunny Pueblo.

But Chris could not be located by that evening. Luckily, Jaime remembered a restaurant specializing in green-chile recipes. Sharla's first bite cast a spell of taste-bud euphoria saturating her mouth and upper intestines.

"I've never had anything quite like this," she confessed. "So delicious. It just warms you up all inside.

"It's the way they lightly roast them, I think, that makes them so good," Jaime said, almost boastfully, as if he had some hand in their preparation. "Chris says they ward off cancer, too."

Sharla nodded in mild amazement. She grinned from ear to ear later that night back in the hotel room. Jaime also fell to slumbers in a world of emotional Edenistic revelry. Nothing before in his experience could compare to the sense of security swimming gladly throughout his being. If only time could freeze right here in this moment, he wished. Behold, it did not. Could not. Will not.

Finding Chris the next mid-morning, though, eased this truth.

"What's this?" Chris the Hopi asked upon sight of the new Land Rover.

"Our adventure mobile," Jaime gleamed. "I'm itchin' to try out her four-wheel capabilities. What do you think?"

"I know just the place," Chris responded.

He further suggested they take along his camping gear and take in a night beneath the stars. For old time's sake. Sharla agreed the notion sounded grand, and off they went. Jaime waited until they made camp that night to reveal news of his winnings. To his surprise, Chris seemed less than excited upon hearing this. Jaime couldn't understand? Shouldn't he be happy for him? Sharla was.

Not having any background to Chris and Jaime's previous outings, aided only by campfire light, Sharla could not detect Jaime's consternation. She found Chris the Hopi particularly contemplative but assumed it only to be a natural trait among his people. She further believed her assumption correct when he stirred the conversation to philosophies on time. In truth, Chris understood money to be a trap, its influence a major distraction from the more esoteric and deeper understandings to be gained through life.

"Kant offered that time is not an illusion," Chris said. "But an Eternalist begs to differ."

Harping back to the first time he and Jaime spent a night in the desert, Chris alluded to time's existence also occurring at three levels. On the surface, he explained, time certainly moves in one direction and must be of at least some consequence to one's life. There are places to be or other people to meet, often scheduled within the confines of a certain time frame. The sun, likewise, from a person's perspective on earth, creates a sense of time as it appears to travel across the sky, eventually giving way to night. But on the deepest level of existence, a spirit out in the universe will encounter timeless existence. The art of life is to achieve such understanding in this conscious state.

"It is only each moment that matters," he continued. "For most people, worries of the future, or lamenting over past transgressions, consumes too much of their mind, leaving them dead to any moment. It is this sense of time, like a mighty river, that washes away each moment. Unable to escape past regrets, or too concerned with what the future may hold, most people fail to capture the simple beauty of any given moment at hand.

"Only when one attempts to begin to comprehend eternity, can he, or she," Chris said, turning his eye to Sharla, "realize, even if only in a minimal sense, how time doesn't matter. Let go of time. Time is like a yoke on the soul, always pulling one back, or straining to lead it forward."

Chris the Hopi's words, coupled with the hypnotic flicker of live flames, worked like a séance. Spellbound the three sat, captured by the possibilities of existence without the constraints of time. Indeed, as they were in this moment, it seemed to at least slow its pace, or produce the appearance thereof, Chris' theory notwithstanding. When their collective introspection broke, Jaime lifted an arm to show skyward. A smile crept across Chris' gaze when Jaime rightly pointed out Orion's belt to Sharla.

"The question is not how far," Jaime said, further spreading Chris' upward turned lips. "The question is how near? How near."

"I see what you guys mean," she replied, picking up on Jaime's knowledge of this having origins in Chris the Hopi. "In the vastness of the universe, the stars we see here are relatively close. Still, it's quite a distance."

"It is," Chris jumped in, "until one appreciates the freedoms to be had minus the shackles of time. Without such limitations, what matters of distance? All is one. One is all."

"Interesting," Sharla commented. "I suppose in the big picture, molecularly, all could be constituted as one. The trouble I see lies with the modern condition. For far too many, the expanse of technology permeating nearly every aspect of life leaves them void of any connection to all this. Or anything of consequence, for that matter."

"All this?" Chris sought.

"Just the greater galaxy. This...like you said, a sense of being a part of it all, of having a connection between one's self and the cosmic forces. I don't know," she added. "It's hard for me to put a finger on it, exactly."

"I think I know what you mean," Jaime interjected. "Nature. Being part of the natural world is what draws us closer to that connection. It's lost on most in the modern world."

110

"How will you spend this money?" Chris asked, switching subjects without warning.

Jaime paused, pondering the question. He didn't know, for now, he admitted. The talk of time and space and bigger ideas, left him searching for a deeper cause. Maybe it was the decadence of his southern California experience. Maybe it was his travels. Something. Something inside stirred to the notion that the money must be spent with purpose. Nothing frivolous, he demanded.

"What do you know of anchovies?" Jaime then inquired of both.

"I know they're horrible on pizza," Chris quipped.

Sharla laughed in agreement. Then Jaime joined in.

"I've never even had one," he further laughed, explaining to them his reason for asking.

"They are like the buffalo were for the American Indian," Chris offered. "What can be done?"

"That's what I'm after," Jaime belted. "This could be the cause, no?"

Chris looked to Sharla, who pursed her lips in a show of 'perhaps.' With this, he stood, stating the fire would need more wood before too long. He'd be back shortly, he said. Jaime also rose, momentarily giving thought to joining him to gather wood, but then decided it would be better to not leave Sharla all alone.

"It's nice out here, huh..." Jaime said, moving his fold-out chair closer to Sharla's, who nodded in agreement.

She possessed a smallish frame, equipped with like features–slender, skinny fingers, joints, even her skull was rather slight. The last of eight children, Sharla entered the world six weeks prematurely. Her body never quite seemed to catch up. And though not always apparent, particularly to the casual observer, to those who do know her well, her spirit more than compensates for physical slightness. Which is not to say she lacks overall strength; at least not for her size.

Not only does she represent the last of seven brothers and sisters, but her closest sibling is ten years older. By the time Sharla came along, her parents were weary. The better part of rearing responsibilities were left to the next two youngest siblings, a brother and sister, whose attempts at structure and discipline lacked significance. As a result, Sharla at times could be impetuous. At earlier times in her life, this trait could lead to trouble, though not in any terrible sense. More along the lines of taking up with a boy who might be, or not sticking with musical lessons long enough, or not caring strongly about grades in school.

At home, however, love abounded and various friends and family routinely circulated. From such an environment Sharla excelled socially. She blended easily, laughed heartily and rarely blundered with a trip of the tongue or glare of the eye. Thus, when Chris returned with arms full of dried pieces of timber and Jaime proposed the three of them make a southerly trek to Peru, Sharla did not immediately reject the idea. Chris wanted to at least sleep on it, first, he said.

The clear, crisp dark desert air offered a spectacular vision as the Milky Way and its cohorts rotated through the night sky. Sharla snuggled tightly in the sleeping bag and slept soundly. Minus four walls from which to bounce, Chris' snoring innocently drifted out into the vast expanse of desert, barely competing with crackles off the campfire. Jaime's excitement at the possibility of venturing back to Peru in the company of his two favorite people, kept his mind percolating. He didn't drift away for more than two hours. His soul, while very much alive, felt still, at peace. His entire life, it seemed, had led him to this point. To this moment. It felt nice.

The next morning, Chris related that maybe it *was* time for something new. Not since leaving Arizona had he really traveled any distance.

"Mexico is dangerous," he added, though, as Jaime shoveled dirt on top of the last embers of the night's campfire.

"Only at the border towns," Jaime said, matter-of-factly.

"Maybe?" Chris questioned.

"We'll go right through that. We'll find remote areas and camp, just like last night," Jaime said.

"The whole way?" Sharla wondered, bemused.

"Well, maybe not the entire time. It'll work out, you'll see," Jaime pleaded. "We'll get rooms, too, along the way" he added, sensing their skepticism.

They spent that afternoon and night in preparation, mapping out possible routes, checking off lists of things they'd need for the journey. By next mid-morning, they were on the road. Sharla rode shotgun, weeding through unappealing radio stations. Making good time, they took a slight jaunt to be able to take in lunch in Taos, walking off the calories afterwards by mingling through a few art galleries.

South of Albuquerque, they took off from the highway down a dirt road just long enough to be out of sight and set up camp amidst the scrub brush and scattered firs. By next afternoon they crossed into Mexico at Palamos, on Highway 24, wanting to avoid possible violence at Cuidad Juarez. A few hours into the country, they found another side road to take, escaping civilization once again.

Chris the Hopi thought it impossible to gain a better view of the night sky than from the deserts of the southwestern United States, but upon sight that first night in Mexico, he amended his consideration, stating stars appeared brighter here than he had ever recalled—as if someone had taken Windex to the atmosphere.

"See how they sparkle," he said, gazing in awe.

"What about the southern cross?" Sharla voiced. "I've always wanted to see that."

"Not until Peru," Chris informed her. "You have to be south of the equator. Well, to gain a good view, anyway."

"Oh," she uttered. "I thought we were close."

"Not really," Chris said, plainly. "But we will be."

Chris expanded on this subject by explaining how the Incas' symbol of the Chakana originated through visions of the Southern Cross. The stairs of the Chakana star are like the levels of existence. There are three, he proudly noted. The four exterior sides represent the four basic elements of life—earth, air, fire and water. Through the circular center of the Chakana, shaman transport spiritually to experience the depths of our galaxy, Chris further stated.

"When they return, their soul will have encountered ancient star dust, which holds wisdom and purity," Chris went on. "Maybe when we get to Peru, we will find a shaman."

"Maybe," Jaime joined in, as they fell into silent contemplation. "Maybe....?"

The farther south they made it, the safer they felt. Still they preferred to stay on the less-traveled routes. Near Vera Cruz they decided to spend a few days exploring pyramids of the Aztec. The Votive pyramid at La Quemada impressed Chris the most. It's galactic accuracy further proves the astrological acumen of these original human beings, he proposed.

By the third day, and having spent each night at a camp since entering Mexico, Sharla easily persuaded Jaime to spring for a room at a beach resort. The flow of hot showers can never feel as soothing as after being deprived of its elixir-like powers. Sharla spent thirty minutes under the heated cascade.

As she entered the room with her hair and torso covered in pink towels, shoulders ruddy from the water's heat, Chris forced himself to look away. Just the smell of clean, feminine skin proved too much for his manhood. He would not even consider the idea of intruding upon Jaime's domain, but the warmth of her freshness permeated the air, forcing him to retreat to the balcony overlooking the Pacific. Maybe he could find a companion along the way, or in Peru, even.

They gladly slept late the next morning, reluctantly fastening seat belts to continue south. Shortly, though, being back on the road loosened their mind-set. They camped again that night, and by next afternoon made it to Guatemala. At the Nicaraguan border, Jaime had to bribe an officer to let them continue. Crossing into Costa Rica brought much relief. When Sharla mentioned she had a friend who took a white-water river adventure here, Jaime and Chris agreed they needed some excitement to relieve the tension of passing through Nicaragua.

In San Jose they found a four-star hotel that catered to gringo tourism, American and Western European. A concierge readily connected them to a river-guide outfit. Why Jaime insisted the three of them not be teamed with others during the float, only he knows. Before they entered the water, Sharla entertained the idea that Jaime had become possessive of her body and simply didn't want any other men close to her water-soaked figure (aside from Chris and the guide, who upon accepting a two-hundred dollar bribe to let the three of them in one raft, demanded that he at least be in the raft, also.) He refused to rent them one, otherwise, he stated. After the day, Sharla wondered something else entirely.

A tropical storm two days before dumped nearly twenty-four inches of rain upstream. The river was running at flood-stage proportions. All were warned to be vigilant in following any and all instructions from guides. Only Sharla's nerves were peaked initially from the severity of the speech. Upon entering the first set of rapids, however, Jaime and Chris' attitudes quickly tightened.

Due to the grade of decent, what lie ahead could not be seen until almost entirely upon it. About thirty seconds before reaching rapids, a low grumbling roar would begin. A sense of power by mere volume, alone. Massive power. Near ten seconds before, the noise became so strong that when Jaime excitedly shouted to Chris, "Can you believe this?" Chris could not hear the words. Only because he could see the motion of his lips did Chris even know Jaime attempted to communicate.

Inside the rapids, the violent churning of twenty-five thousand cubic-feet-per-second of moving water evoked so much adrenalin, the overwhelming sounds became an afterthought. All of one's senses focus squarely on balance and the oar and voracity of the moment. Of survival. Each successive set of rapids grew in size and magnitude of intensity.

Between each bout of severe white water, a feeling of accomplishment produced smiles and giddy laughter, subsided momentarily by hints of relief, only to repeat the cycle upon hearing the next roar of chaos coming nearer. Six teams in separate rafts all stopped midway for lunch–a meal the crew had prepared and brought along to serve to the paying customers. Why Jaime failed to securely buckle his life vest afterwards, not even he is sure? How the guide failed to notice this and still allow them to embark on the afternoon's rapids as such, also qualifies as mysterious.

Whatever the reasons, at the second set of afternoon rapids, a large dip and subsequent swell sent Jaime spilling over their raft. The water's velocity almost instantly robbed him of his unfastened vest. The current conveniently swept Jaime a tumble midstream, free of any protruding boulders. As the river carried Jaime along, it nearly dragged him under. All his energy went to keeping his head above water. The guide had Chris and Sharla rowing frantically to reach Jaime, but they couldn't get to him before he would encounter a lone rock jutting a foot above the surface. Jaime paddled his hands beneath his back to steady himself. He raised his feet just out of the water in anticipation of the rock he now realized he would not be able to avoid.

His feet caught a flat angle of the rock as his momentum propelled him upright. For a long two seconds he maintained his balance, erect on the rock with open arms like the statue of Christ the Redeemer. But inertia didn't let up and another second later he splashed face first back into the water. The guide finally directed the raft close to Jaime. With Chris pulling, Jaime managed to climb back inside.

The guide's instincts prompted him to cancel the remainder of the adventure, but they were now a ways back of the other five groups and it would take hours to walk the bank dragging their raft along to meet the others downstream for the return bus ride back to base. Reluctantly, he allowed them to continue.

At the next set of rapids, their rubber boat rammed a protruding boulder, sending the raft askew, before it rotated one-hundred eighty degrees. They soared through the rest of the white water facing upstream, crossing at its end beneath the remnants of an old rope and timber bridge. On the right bank just beyond the bridge, as it were facing backwards, an Indian sat rigidly on a rock's surface with a fishing pole in-hand, line stretched tightly into the moving water.

Just as they passed the stolid-faced Indian, the view of his image silhouetted against the outline of distant mountains, caused a memory from Jaime's youth to race out of the depths of his mind. As part of his "special educational needs," Jaime had been required periodically to meet with a psychologist provided by the state. During one particular visit, the doctor had Jaime complete a set of six small drawings designed to enlighten both patient and examiner to the inner workings of a patient's psyche. Six equal boxes on a standard 8 x 11 rectangle of paper contained predetermined prompts, which a patient would then complete by adding as much or little to the original shapes provided.

In the upper right box, box two as it were, with the paper turned lengthwise, the starting shape consisted of a horizontal line with a symmetrical half circle that dipped precisely in the middle. Jaime turned this into the profile outline of an Indian fishing in a mountain river. As the doctor explained, in addition to the other five boxes whose shapes were said to reveal short- and long-term goals, self-identity, feelings on death and one for creativity, box two contained insight to one's guardian angel.

In truth, it is how a patient speaks after the doctor stirs the conversation to each of the box's insights that reveals what the doctor wants to explore. But as the patient is never let on to the actual purpose of the drawing exercise, in Jaime's mind at that moment on the river, he thought back on this Indian he had drawn as his guardian angel. And so it was, that at the second their raft passed facing upstream and this same image that he had drawn years before became reality, he turned to Sharla.

"I just saw my guardian angel. I just saw my guardian angel," he repeated from excitement.

Having no background to any of this, Sharla offered a smile as sincerely as she could muster. Jaime knew she could not know and that it must sound, at the least, a little random. The beginning roar of the next set of rapids quickly rendered the situation moot. Jaime's heart being in a flutter with the recognition of the possibility of a guardian angel, he smiled at Sharla in a show of gratitude for not being overly judgmental, and then did the same at the guide in appreciation for his being part of the overall experience.

The guide's return look, not a smile, even minutely, but one of seriousness and focus, snapped Jaime's spell of mystical reminiscence. The next set of rapids, the last of the day, were more potent than even the experienced guide anticipated. No amount of paddling or stirring could control the raft. It roiled through the turbulent ferocity of foaming waters, careening off extruding rocks, until at last finding the top of a boulder the size of a mini-van.

A thin sheen of water passed just over top of the large rock, but not enough to float the raft or propel it forward. The three waited for word from the guide, but he too remained speechless. The swell just beyond and beneath the boulder dropped at least fifteen feet with an eight foot lip curling back at end. At last, the guide screamed that they had no choice but to push over.

Using the ends of their oars, they each pushed against the rock's surface just beneath the streaming water, inching the raft slowly ever closer to the edge. When they finally freed themselves, the raft plunged into the enormous swell and then straight back up the lip, sending craft and all four hurling into the air. They each landed head down facing back upstream.

Chris, Sharla and the guide, Andy, quickly resurfaced aided by their life vests. Jaime did not. The hydraulics of the water crashing over the large boulder, sucked Jaime to the river's depths. Upon first feeling the bottom, Jaime kicked up and away from where he thought to be the swell. But his feet quickly touched the sandy floor again.

Familiar with the hydraulics of water falls, Jaime knew the situation to be serious. He kicked off from the bottom once more, but with extra force and kicking harder. Only seconds later, though, he felt the soft sand of the river's bottom again. He opened his eyes momentarily, but the water's murkiness offered little vision. The force of churning water bubbled over his forearms and face. It seemed unreal, for a second; as if this were maybe only part of a theme park ride and in a few seconds the ride would be over, everything peachy, calm.

Back at the water's surface, Andy managed to secure onto the raft, now floating upside down. A rope fastened through loops along the raft's perimeter allowed him an easy grip. He spotted Sharla and Chris and they swam to him to grab onto the rope. As they each regained their bearings, they all quickly began scouring the water for Jaime. Tears already started to swell from Sharla's eyes, as the emotion of the moment overcame her.

After the second attempt to push and kick to the top, Jaime waited a few seconds, standing back on bottom. This can't be how I go, he told himself. Not drowning in Costa Rica less than three weeks after receiving so much money and after falling in love for the first time. Sharla and he hadn't actually exchanged these words, but being stuck and frightened, the fact that she would enter his mind and how he felt for her, he knew it had to be love. His fear faded to sadness, though, thinking how this could be the end, unsure how it wouldn't be.

And then he heard a voice.

"Grab your oar."

But in his panic and already becoming depleted of oxygen, Jaime didn't fully comprehend what he thought he heard. The voice repeated itself, somehow knowing Jaime's lack of recognition.

"Grab your oar," it stated with clear pitch, not warbled as a person's voice typically sounds when spoken underwater.

My oar, Jaime woozily repeated to himself. My oar? And then it occurred to him, finally. My oar. Yes! If I'm being held down by hydraulic forces, maybe my oar also is. A surge of adrenalin kicked in. He began moving his arms and hands, swirling them in search of the oar. And in only a few seconds, he felt it. He stepped to his left and used both hands, and did it. He secured the oar. It was there!

He squatted low to give one more push at freedom, one hard, strong kick, sensing this would be it, otherwise. With extra strength, kicking madly and now aided by the oar, he could feel himself break free of the hydraulic. Bam! He broke the water's surface, quickly gasping for precious breaths. Forty yards or so away he spotted the overturned raft, the three of them still clinging to its side. They didn't see him at first, though. So he swatted the river's surface with the oar's flat paddle, splashing frantically.

They saw him moments later, quickly splashing with their free hands. The river widened, flattened and calmed. A few yards farther it made a sharp left-hand turn, forcing the current wide, allowing a shallow pool to form along the left bank. Tears of joy now fell from Sharla's face. Chris hugged him, forcefully. Andy patted Jaime's back, relieved not only for Jaime, but for himself and the ordeal it would have been to have to report a drowning under his care on the river, let alone the guilt. Not wanting to return to the water, they walked the half mile to where the others rafters waited to ride back.

"You really scared us," Sharla said as they took a seat at the rear of the bus.

"Yeah. That was bad," he agreed. "How long was I under?"

"I don't know...five minutes it felt like," Sharla said.

"Who told me to grab the oar? Was it Chris?"

"Do what?"

"To grab my oar. Someone said, 'Grab your oar.'"

"No. We were past the falls," she said. "Way past. Besides, how could you hear us below the water?

"But I heard him, or someone. Grab your oar. That's what someone said. Grab your oar. It's what saved me," he whispered gently, insisting.

Sharla shook her head, with that same half sympathetic, half patronizing smile as before when he spoke out about seeing his guardian angel.

"I was stuck, you know," he pleaded. "The hydraulic held me down."

"I know," she said. "We thought we lost you."

"That's so weird," he cried. "But someone said, 'Grab your oar.' I definitely heard it. And the voice was clear, almost. Not like you'd expect under water."

"I don't know," Sharla offered.

"Chris?" Jaime said across the aisle, seeing that he was hearing the conversation.

"It wasn't me, man," Chris offered, though, softly.

"The guide?" Jaime asked.

"No," Chris replied. "He was right there with us. We all just looked and waited. I thought you were a goner. I think Andy did too."

"Huh?" Jaime wondered.

No one said more.

Chapter 22

That night at dinner, a strange air settled in among the three. Hardly a word was spoken, yet no one felt it awkward or odd, this silence. Rather, it felt appropriate. Death's reaper remained near; its pall spread beyond them to permeate the restaurant. Each table's patrons looked sedate, solemn. The light within the restaurant appeared muted, somehow, as if cast from a shadow. Jaime couldn't decide how it could be true, or if it just appeared this way through his perspective? Costa Ricans are soft spoken people, as it goes, but this was more, he thought.

As Jaime eyed the check and removed cash from his wallet to leave on the table, the mood shifted upward, just a bit. But everything seemed to be moving a fraction slower still. The air felt thicker. Heavier. The drive back to the hotel proved the same. Inside the room, having already showered before dinner, Sharla and Jaime promptly climbed into one bed, and Chris tucked himself into his. No one said good night.

Jaime fluffed two pillows and turned on CNN International, which upscale foreign hotels around the world all seem to carry, but it just served as background noise. After a while, he realized he hadn't really listened to a single word the news reader had said for quite some time. He couldn't stop thinking about those three words, 'Grab your oar.'

Then it occurred to him—the guardian angel. That had to be it! He had been right there just minutes before. Jaime had drawn the very image he saw, many years before. It could not be coincidence. Coincidence doesn't exist. He had been right there! His guardian angel saved his life. Just as they're supposed to, he laughed, momentarily, but then felt guilty for doing so. The angel hadn't been laughing. He didn't even smile. He didn't even move, Jaime recalled. Maybe he couldn't move? Maybe he just appeared for the few seconds that Jaime laid eyes on him. Had the others even seen him? He rolled his head to ask Sharla, but her eyes already were closed.

He watched her for a few seconds, but her eyes didn't flinch. He looked across to Chris the Hopi, but found him doing the same. At least he wasn't snoring. Jaime turned off the television, spilling a darkness throughout the room. Amazing how black a hotel room can get so quickly, he thought, drifting fast asleep with the other two.

The next morning, any remnants of the pall seemed to have dissipated. The sun was bright and they all agreed it best to take an early start to the road. Chris said he had talked with one of the hotel doorman, and he recommended strongly that they stay to the main highways once they reach Colombia. No dirt roads or side streets, he added.

"Dude said if we don't, we'd wish we had all drowned," Chris further stated.

"You told him about the river?" Jaime said.

"Sure. Why not? It's quite the story," Chris grinned.

"I guess so," Jaime chuckled. "Why not... By the way, I figured out who told me to go for the oar. It was my guardian angel."

"Your who?" Chris asked, leaning forward from the back seat.

"My guardian angel. You didn't mention it?" Jaime questioned Sharla, who shook her head no.

"Just before that last set of rapids, the one we all spilled on, I saw my guardian angel. I mean, that's what I think, anyway," Jaime said, with a touch of apprehension.

"What guardian angel?" Chris asked.

"He was an Indian. Sort of like you, but different–bigger and not the same tribe. I don't know why I even think that?" he hesitated. "It doesn't matter."

"Okay," Chris uttered.

"Did you see him?" Jaime asked Chris. "He was on the right-hand bank, just after we passed underneath that old rope and board bridge. The one we went through backwards. Remember?"

"I remember going through the next to last set backwards, but I didn't notice any Indian. Sharla?" Chris said, placing a hand on the back of her seat.

"Maybe. I can't really remember for sure," she admitted.

"You didn't see him, either?" Jaime asked with surprise. "I thought you did."

"I sorta remember...maybe. I remember you said you saw your guardian angel, but we were back on more rapids right after that. You know?" she tried.

"No worries," Jaime reassured her. "No worries."

The three fell to silence for the next several hours. Lush jungles extended for miles on either side of the Pan-American Highway. They spotted a fruit vendor at a road stop by one o'clock and took a break there, eating fresh avocadoes and ripe, juicy mangos. The air was so thick it felt like it could be sliced and packaged for resale in Sub-Saharan Africa.

By evening they reached Panama City, stopping for the night. A sort of echo pall seemed to have swept back over them. They had dinner at the hotel. No one said much of anything, again. Sharla wanted to know how much farther they had to go before they reached Colombia. She asked Chris if the doorman had really advised them to not venture off the main highway. He assured her that he had. Jaime said he had planned to do as such, anyway.

And so they went, arriving late that night in Medellin. Travelling almost non-stop the entire next day, they hoped to cover more ground, but the Andes made for slow travel. They made it only to San Juan de Pasto, where they were relieved to find nice accommodations. The next morning, they awoke to splendid mountain views. Magnificently clean, the air tasted sweet. The altitude abated the humidity a bit. By breakfast, they decided any danger to be minimum. A group of Danish tourists banded off for the Las Lajas Sanctuary, Sharla overheard.

When Jaime discovered its origins rooted in legend of a young girl to whom a strike of lightning had revealed an apparition of the Virgin Mary, he insisted they spend at least the morning in exploration. The gothic structure of the Sanctuary of our Lady of Las Lajas proved Jaime's inclination on target. Spanning the canyon of the Guáitara River, with towering spires and stoned, ornate walls, it appeared like something from a German Black Forest, splendid and majestic.

Across the river on the face of the nearest canyon wall, Jaime located where he thought the face of the Virgin Mary to be. Sharla said she might see it, too. But Jaime felt she only said so to comfort his ego. For the first time a feeling of something other than utter exaltation crossed his mind for Sharla. Did she feel sorry for him? Had she found his story of a guardian angel too fantastic? He studied her from the side. He did love her. Soon he'd tell her.

Chris thought canyon walls similar to seeing faces, or what-not, in clouds–each person sees something different, sees what they want to see. It really reveals more about the individual than the canyon or what they think they see, although a spirit may choose to make a cliff face home for many, many years, he added. But why would the Virgin Mary choose here?

"Maybe she came with the conquistadors," Jaime intervened.

"I don't think she would be seen with those murderous pillagers," Chris countered. Jaime laughed. He was probably right.

"Maybe she was here for the victims?" Jaime then added.

"Yeah, but the girl didn't see her for another hundred years," Sharla interjected.

"But what's time to the Virgin Mary?" Chris shot in.

They settled on a nod of perhaps, followed with a shrug of the shoulders and found the moment a perfect cue to move on. They crossed into Ecuador early afternoon, continuing on to Quito by that night. Sensing their destination growing closer, all things considered, they left out early the next morning, hoping to make it to Peru by nightfall. They did, and it took another long day and a half before at-last arriving in Lima. The last legs of such an arduous journey are the most tedious.

"We should've flown," Sharla said as they stopped at a fuel stop just inside the city's boundary.

Jaime disagreed, but offered that they definitely deserved a reward. They booked a room at a four-star ocean-front hotel. After just the second full day of lounging beach-side, however, Jaime began growing anxious. Chris hadn't spent more than a few hours outside the hotel. He only splashed in the ocean for a few minutes when he did venture out. Indians don't do beaches, he claimed. He spent most of the time in the lobby, using free Internet researching Incan shaman.

Sharla said it didn't matter to her. They could continue to do virtually nothing, or just the opposite. Her personality really matched her delicate features, Jaime thought. He never knew someone so easy to be around.

"I've been thinking," Jaime said, late that second afternoon, as he and Sharla took refuge from the sun beneath a rented beach umbrella. "What we need is awareness."

"For...?" Sharla obliged.

"For the plight of the anchovy fisheries, of course."

"Oh, of course," she smiled sincerely. "But...do you think there's enough interest? People here really care about anchovies that much?"

"I think so, and I do. And if we do it right, it can grow," he insisted, proudly, but teetering on the edge of maudlinity.

The next morning, Chris awoke restless. He asked to borrow enough sols to last a few weeks and said he'd be back when his soul was satisfied.

"Are you going to face the sun?" Jaime asked, knowingly.

"Not exactly," Chris replied, "but you're in the ballpark."

With nothing more said, he left the room.

"He'll be okay, I think," Sharla offered to Jaime.

Jaime nodded thusly, but inside he worried a little.

After a few minutes of mulling Chris' intentions, Jaime declared the search for the anchovy museum and cultural awareness center should begin. Unsure where exactly the starting point for this should be, he opted first to show Sharla the Port of Callao and the places he had been. By noon his tour exhausted itself of anything else to reveal. They took in lunch from a taco boat and watched people move about. By early afternoon, Jaime led them back to Ms. Sanchita's modeling studio. Maybe she'd have an idea for a location? Which she did. Several locations might work, in fact, she suggested. More importantly for her, however, would Sharla be available for work in the studio, she asked Jaime? A client had a new line of American-made designer jeans he hoped to market to Lima's newest generation, young and burgeoning of style in many areas, including fashion. Sharla's delicate yet wholesome features are perfect, Ms. Sanchita explained.

"Peruvian women do not respond to overly glamorous," she added. "Natural beauty is what they like. You tell her about it today. Let me know manana, no?"

"Okay," Jaime answered.

Scouting the streets of Lima, Jaime had trouble following Ms. Sanchita's directions exactly. So many of the buildings and shops were constructed in similar fashion, red brownish stucco, indiscreet, bland. Nothing seemed particularly appealing, until within vicinity of Lima's museum district, as Bolivia Boulevard dead-ends to the triangle of FDR and Bambas Streets, of all places. They spotted a small building with a Para Arriendo sign, for lease.

Once home to an upscale, modern furniture store, within only blocks sat the Museums of Art, both Italiano and de Peru. It seemed a natural fit. That afternoon, they met with a rotund commercial real-estate man, who said his brother-in-law operated Lima's most successful advertising agency, should they want any help promoting their new business. When Jaime explained what they intended to do at the site, after shedding his initial squint of befuddlement, the man said at least the location was right. His body almost formed a perfect circle, Jaime noticed, thinking how varied a body can grow fat. For some it all goes into the belly, which then barrels over the belt line like a sack of potatoes about to burst through the bottom of its sack of flax. Women put it on around the hips and rear. But this guy's body somehow distributed its excess into nearly symmetrical perfection. Amazing, Jaime thought.

For the next two weeks, Jaime and Sharla set to preparing the inside of the store to transform it into a showcase of green baitfish. Sharla worked like a Midwestern farm girl, cleaning, painting, whatever task was needed, without complaint and seemingly never growing tired or bored. Jaime adored her. As she went about her doings, she'd lose herself in the work and not realize he had stopped to watch her. He liked how strands of her sandy red hair hung softly behind her ears. How her shorts fell loosely below her tight ass when she stood straight to stretch her back, the smooth symmetry along the back of her calves, the slenderness of her raised arms. His love was growing in ways he never knew it could.

Jaime laid out designs for the museum. A history of the once ubiquitous saltwater prey would circle along the inside perimeter, with informative plaques outlining both the evolution of the fishing industry and of its importance to Peruvian ancestry. Pictures depicting similar scenes could also be included. In the middle of the space, a voluminous saltwater aquarium would span floor to ceiling, schooling anchovies whirling inside. Or at least Jaime hoped they would behave as such.

"What else would they do?" Sharla posed in a bid of reassurance. "It's what they do. Right?" Jaime's sols were betting thusly.

In a few more days after working around the area, they found a collection of condominiums adjacent to a botanical gardens park nearby. They thought it could be perfect to move to for a more permanent space to live than the hotel. So close to the museum, they could walk between the two. But the last spot Chris knew of their location remained the beach front hotel room where they last saw him before he departed to satisfy his soul. If they left the room, how would he locate them? After two more days working on finishing touches to the museum, they signed a one-year lease for the condominium.

That night, tired once again from a long day, Sharla related to Jaime how she'd have to make a visit back home at some point. When they left, she didn't know they'd be moving for a year. He understood, he said. She could return back home whenever she liked, for as long as she needed. After all, sols abound, right, he smiled.

"They do," she agreed, but found it to be more than that. His kindness seemed rare, she thought. His sweetness adorable.

The next morning, Jaime returned to the beachside hotel to settle the bill and leave a forwarding address. The clerk said they weren't in the custom of forwarding mail. As luck would have it, however, just yesterday a letter had arrived for Jaime Holbrook. The slender attendant left for a back office and returned with a sea-green envelope.

Sure enough, it was from Chris the Hopi. His search so far netted news both good and bad. The good news: he had learned of a sacred shaman whose insights already were legendary among Peruvian Indians; bad news: he lives high in the Andes, accessible only by rugged mountain paths. More horses and mules would be needed before the last legs of the climb could be successful. Could Jaime possibly send more sols? If so, much appreciation and look for the next correspondence in two months.

Jaime found the return address curious, a trading post near Siula Grande, a mountain outpost, apparently. Could he trust sending cash through the Peruvian mail system? After some investigation, he learned sols could be wired to the trading post. He sent off a return letter to Chris, detailing when to expect the wire transfer and the new address of their condo.

Satisfied to at least now know of Chris' whereabouts, Jaime returned his focus back to the Anchovy Museum. With Sharla's unwavering assistance, he hoped to launch its grand opening within two more weeks. Plaques for display outlining the historical evolution of Peru's fishing industry and its significance to the culture would be ready in a few days. Ms. Sanchita connected him with skilled craftsmen who constructed a floor-to-ceiling, 2,700-gallon, saltwater aquarium. The three-inch thick glass required to withstand the pressure of 21,700 pounds of water arrived that afternoon. The men worked late into the night securing the heavy glass in place.

"Isn't it amazing how hard those guys work, and overtime and everything, and not one of them complain," Jaime said to Sharla as he waited in bed for her to finish washing her face for the night. He thought back on his work in southern California, lying here as Sharla now brushed her teeth. They only had purchased the bed so far, and its isolation within four walls reminded him of a film set from those awful days.

Observing Sharla climb into bed, her clean wholesomeness quickly quelled his memory's bad connection. Just the smell of her as she snuggled in close cocooned his soul in warmth. It spread through his shoulders and into is arms. This moment could not last long enough.

"I'm sorry I have to go back," she softly said.

"It's okay. I understand," he whispered in return. And he did. "How long do you think you'll stay, though?"

"Maybe a couple of weeks. I mean, if I'm gonna make the trip, I might as well stay a little bit, right?" she said.

"You should."

"See, my dad, when he was young, he was a roamer," she said. "It's in my blood, I guess. But once he settled down, he never wanted to move again. My parents have lived in the same place for forty-five years."

"That's nice."

"It is. If that's what you want, I mean," she offered. "What about you? You hitched for a while, right? Does it make you want to settle in one place, eventually?"

Jaime didn't reply immediately. He thought probably he would like to be in one place, at some point. Have a home. Maybe a family of his own?

"What about you?" he turned the question on her, instead.

"I don't know, to be honest," she said, as if she could be anything but, he thought. "I've never travelled, really, much, you know. I like the freedom. The adventure. The grass is always greener, you know."

With that his mind flashed back to Kettle County. He could never tell Sharla of that experience. It felt like such a dark moment, suddenly. At the time, it didn't. Now, though, it almost seemed like it had only been a dream—or rather, a nightmare. As if such a thing couldn't be a part of *his* history.

"We don't have to decide tonight," he said, leaning in to kiss her slender lips.

Chapter 23

Sharla flew back to West Virginia the next week, missing the grand opening of the Natural Anchovy History and Peruvian Culture Museum. Jaime felt sorry she could not be here to experience the celebration of their efforts, but it allowed him to concentrate more fully on the event, and for that he actually felt thankful. And due to the work of the real-estate agent's marketing-guru brother, local television and print media covered the event and people came in droves; mostly Peruvians, but also visiting tourists. Genuine interest among many patrons occurred, particularly with the section detailing military rivalry between Peru and Chile, Spanish Conquistadors, British intervention, the Haber process. Unquestionably, though, the centerpiece anchovy aquarium garnered the most rave reviews.

Fifteen feet high, its ultra-clear glass runs forty-five feet long on either side, spanning twenty feet on both ends to form a rectangular spectacle. Slightly tinted blue with continuous rising bubbles of O, the green back lighting creates an almost fantastic vision of iridescently scaled anchovy schools in constant motion. Young children sometimes were left momentarily catatonic, its power to mesmerize so great. Artisto, whispered lightly, gently echoed once or twice off the aquarium glass.

Three different reporters, two television, one newspaper, interviewed Jaime. Only afterwards did Adolfo Costa approach him to explain inherent danger of being too visible in Lima, especially as an outsider. He might consider a more low-key approach, Costa recommended. Upon further discussion, it occurred to Jaime how Adolfo might be of real importance.

"You sometimes work as a private detective?" he asked Adolfo Costa, ignoring his warning, instead recalling that he had alluded to such work in the course of his explanation to the pitfalls a rich foreigner in South America might face: extortion, kidnapping, the usual suspects.

"It is something I am employed to perform, from time to time. On occasion," Costa beleaguered about his detection abilities. "Now in my younger days..."

"The original reason for me coming to Peru was to find my father," Jaime interrupted, eager for his response. "Perhaps you could... I will pay you, and handsomely, if you could find him."

Combine handsome and sols and many a man of any culture will climb aboard. Adolfo admitted, however, that with only a name it could take a while. Jaime hesitated fearing his sols being taken for a ride, but he at least wanted Costa to begin the search. He gave the go-ahead. Later that afternoon, Chris the Hopi received money Jaime wired to the trading post and his search also continued to flow.

That afternoon, in fact, Chris used part of the cash to rent two horses and two pack mules. Loaded down with four weeks of food and water, Chris and two hands he hired as guides and for assistance, set off toward the peak of Siula Grande where Shaman Dondito might be located, or so locals said as much. Shaman Dondito definitely lived near a high valley of the Siula Grande, but his availability could not be guaranteed, Rafael the guide warned Chris. He is the best, though, Rafael added.

"Let's hope we do find him," the slender and long-faced guide offered, a rare sight among Peruvians.

"I have a good feeling we will," Chris stated. "I have good karma coming my way."

Eight scenic days of ascension later, Chris and his team arrived in the high Siula Grande valley. The journey itself, though slow and tedious, filled Chris' spirit. Much of the way paralleled a mountain stream. How the sound and sight of rapid water stirs the spirit as nothing else. Perhaps its movement reminds a soul of life itself, pure and powerful, unrelenting. Maybe it's simply a vivid reminder of how alive earth really is or just that it's the foundation of our existence and survival, or the basic paradoxical nature of it being so soft to the touch yet so strong as to carve mountain into canyon.

During most of the climb, high cumulous clouds slowly drifted along stark blue skies. Alpine chinchillas ran wild in borough villages at various points, their playful mirth almost contagious. Packs of alpacas, human-like smiles visible upon their faces even at a distance, grazed beneath herders' careful watch. Rafael even spotted big horn sheep along high ridgelines. Chris liked the swirl in their horns.

In the high valley lived a small collection of herders and farmers. Rafael and one of the assistants, Miguel, explained to one of the elders the purpose of their arrival. He and another four who attended the conversation with perked ears, mulled over Chris the Hopi. Perhaps his American Indian skin helped or the gentle aura his exudes, but the villagers easily bought into the cause.

At Rafael's suggestion, Chris had brought along modest amounts of meaningful gifts to reveal at introduction: wild rice, black beans, green tea and white wine. They accepted these in uneager fashion, but with real smiles of small, crooked teeth.

As the sun began to sink behind the western horizon, Mount Siula Grande's peak stood steady to the east. Rafael allowed Chris to light the small campfire, which they constructed from random pieces of timber collected along the way. Only Chris and his partners showed surprise shortly when one of the men approached the circle at the fire carrying a guitar. With their worn leather boots and weathered western-styled hats, the men reminded Chris of the sheep cowboys he occasionally encountered back home in the Rockies. True American cowboys. True South American cowboys, Chris thought. Gauchos.

After a few verses into one of their camp-fire songs, being sung in a falsetto high-pitch tone, for why Chris could not begin to know, Chris nearly cringed. They sounded so off but it didn't seem to bother a one. In fact, Chris saw joy on each of their faces. Gauchos here cannot sing, especially soprano, he laughed inside.

The next morning, Rafael informed Chris that Shaman Dondito would be available that afternoon. His home waited less than an hour's hike toward the peak. A few from the camp-fire the night before would join the party. Using only one mule for hauling supplies, Chris, Rafael and four more began the climb to Shaman Dondito. The men helping Chris were so real, he thought to himself as they hustled the mule and themselves up the trail. They carried no masks, no weight on their souls. It showed in their eyes. He wished it could be as such with men elsewhere.

Within an hour, Rafael and one of the locals entered the Shaman's tent first to explain their arrival. Shortly, Shaman Dondito appeared and greeted Chris warmly, smiling broadly. Rafael translated that the Shaman admired Chris' determination and sacrifice to travel such distance to find him. Let them first drink tea and dine on wild rice and goat's head soup to commence the occasion.

After the meal more song, and even dance, if it could be called that, followed. Then Rafael informed Chris that Shaman Dondito would soon be ready.

"My hope for you," Rafael whispered into Chris the Hopi's left ear as they approached Shaman Dondito's space, "is that your heart is true."

Caught off guard by his candor, Chris stopped before stepping through the folds of Shaman Dondito's tent. He turned to look at Rafael, having always been so light and genial. His eyes were deep, locked in such seriousness as to cause Chris concern.

"Don't worry, amigo. My aim is pure."

With that Rafael nodded in affirmation and Chris the Hopi entered Shaman Dondito's domain. Inside the tent, decorations were sparse, as Chris anticipated. But the *chi* was so warm it felt as if he had just stepped into a perfectly ripe bath. He felt at once his soul elevate. Dondito waited seated cross-legged on a intricately woven rug, a pattern of the Zia visible along the edges. Light, earth, fire, water wind, Chris thought to himself, pleased. Dondito gestured for Chris to sit to his left. Once seated, the Shaman brought forth a small cloth bag, spilling its contents onto the rug before them.

Chris recognized the claw of a bear, amorist, crystals, jade and the beak of an eagle, he guessed. Also now at his lap, an amulet of a tooth, but Chris could not decide from the jaw of which animal. A wolf, perhaps, he thought. Dondito lit a candle and placed it onto a nail just protruding through a carved wooden holder. Dondito used the flame of the candle to ignite a stick of incense, never once after signaling Chris where to sit did Dondito look directly at him.

The Shaman soon began to softly chant. He waved his right hand through the stream of smoke rising from the incense. After a minute or two, the level of his voice rising slightly, Dondito the Shaman reached for a crystal among the items on the rug and held it extended toward Chris. The rhythm of his chant slowly increasing, he waved the crystal through the smoke, a flavor of cinnamon and allspice from the incense now filling the tent's close quarters.

Dondito placed the crystal back down, replacing it with the deep green jade roughly shaped in circular fashion, the thickness of a button. This he placed in Chris the Hopi's right palm, instructing him to gently fold his fingers around the piece and to close his eyes, now, also. Dondito lifted his right hand to Chris' forehead, just shy of contact. Chris could feel an energy moving from the Shaman's finger tips near his skull envelope him.

Shortly, Chris felt as if his spirit began to drift, slowly lifting. Soon the speed began to increase. Within a few more seconds it seemed his soul to be in flight. Silver streaks of distant specks of light appeared to be racing past. Or more accurately, he then recognized, it was he racing past the endless stream of pin holes of far off light. On and on he soared, the Siula valley seemingly millions of miles beneath. His mind afloat on a swaying surface of thick air, the speed of the passing light gaining further still. Light appeared like beads of water flowing along a thousand strands of infinite glass fibers.

Still drifting aloft, the sense of it racing past stopped. A more prominent light appeared, not close but near enough, gentle, ever so slightly pulsating. Chris the Hopi sensed a communication, although not through voice but more simply spirit. The message was unclear, like a greeting of some sort, of place and time. In this state of suspension he remained for a while.

Then the light simply wasn't there. It hadn't disappeared, just moved on, but undetected. Chris now felt to be falling, though not quickly to invoke fear, only sliding. The Shaman's soft chanting came back into focus, as if he had never stopped. Chris opened his eyes. Dondito gestured to hand the button of jade back down. He replaced it with the claw of bear.

"To protect," Shaman Dondito offered with a nod, the first words he spoke in English.

"Thank you."

Dondito blew out the candle and snuffed out the incense in the dirt of the tent's floor just beyond the rug. He signaled for Chris to stand and then nodded once more. Chris returned the nod, then stepped back outside, the sun's brightness causing him to squint his eyes at first. It felt as if a good deal of time had passed, yet to his mind it hadn't been more than ten minutes. He wasn't sure. Rafael came toward him, observing him. Chris nodded to him and walked past to where the others sat in a circle.

They each briefly checked Chris up and down, almost as if they had never laid eyes on him before. It then came to Chris, this feeling of newness; as if even he had never known his own self like this before. A tingle spread through his arms into his fingers. The dust of stars stirred in his soul. How far he must have travelled, he thought. How far. And yet, how near, he suddenly laughed. How near.

Back in Lima, Chris turned the key to open the door to the museum. Pride swelled within him like a carnival parlor balloon. This is good, he thought. I have done something well; perhaps, for the first time.

The number of visitors the following days didn't match the grand opening, but people were still coming. The donations-only entrance fee didn't hurt that effort. The operation overall could not be said to be less than successful. It suited him well, too, the day-to-day happenings of running a museum. Jaime spent much of the time watching the reactions of visitors, occasionally sidling close enough to a couple or family to be within earshot of conversation. His Spanish had become nearly fluent enough that he could hear their observations, their discoveries.

He didn't need Spanish to translate the words of Mika Codsworth, though. Her English conveyed just fine her sentiment.

"This is very exciting," Mika offered to a muscled-out Brazilian beefcake. "Brave, even. But I really wish it went deeper, ya know."

Beefcake agreed, although Jaime sensed he only did so out of obligation. Unable to restrain himself, Jaime begged to inquire.

"What's missing?" he exclaimed.

"Pardon?" Mika asked.

"You said it should go deeper. Do you mean... are you referring to the history of the Peruvian-Chilean conflict?" Jaime wanted to know.

"No. Well, yes probably that too, but no. I meant the section on the influence of the British Empire, mate," Mika explained. "It's good to see an American so interested, I must say."

"Well, I am. I should be," Jaime snorted. "I'm the owner."
"The owner?" Mika said with surprise.

Jaime nodded thusly.

"Of this museum?"

"Yes."

"I am impressed, now," Mika expressed.

Had she been blowing smoke up my ass before, Jaime wondered to himself.

"You're so young, too," Mika commented.

"Well, I am lucky," Jaime returned. "I have big balls."

Beefcake glinted his eyes at this.

"Indeed you must," Mika smiled, a twinkle in her eyes. "Indeed. I'm Mika Codsworth."

"Jaime Holbrook. Nice to meet you," he said, now hearing the British accent in Mika's speech. "You guys are British, then?"

"I am," she said. "Enrique's Brazilian."

He extended one of his large palms for Jaime, and turned his lips up plainly as they shook hands.

"Well, I am truly interested," Jaime said. "Could we talk more? Have you guys had lunch?"

They said they hadn't and agreed to join Jaime, although he could tell the notion didn't sit well with Beefcake. But he came along. An odd sight, too, Jaime thought–Beefcake a step behind him and Mika, trailing like a wounded child enroot to a parent-teacher conference. As it turns out, Mika's historical knowledge of British imperialism more than captured Jaime's attention. By the time they finished the ceviche, he offered her a consultant position. She could have free reign over that section of the museum. Mika agreed, but noted that she'd only be available, at least for now, for a few weeks. Her punk-rock nostalgia band would be leaving soon for a tour of Argentina.

"It's like the Ramones are the only band that ever was, there," she laughed with a sardonic sneer.

"How long will you be gone?" Jaime only asked.

"A month, or so," Mika replied. "It won't be too long."

Mika indeed slapped bass for Senomar, a band that blasted out countless renditions of classic British and American punk standards, more heavily on the distortion than the right chords–but that ultimately only seemed to add to their authenticity, particularly in the eyes of their novice fans. They even employed a bleached-out blonde screamer, whose head-to-toe collection of radical tattoos and silver choker chains complemented nicely the band's deliberate image.

But Mika's historical knowledge of British imperialism did not find its footing in E, B, D chord progressions. As so often occurs, adults of indulgent life-style choices grew to be as such from roots of wealth and assessability. In Mika's case, access to pricey private education during the course of which she did steep herself in history of British imperialism, specializing in the vagrancies of imperialism's closest cousin–colonialism.

Thusly, with great ease Mika created an extended display in the museum outlining some of the more atrocious aspects that can be named in any thorough conversation of British imperialism. But for the sake of time, dearest of readers of any lineage, let us simply surmise the addition as thus: rape, pillage and plunder. Ironically enough, the title of Senomar's most well-known original.

Jaime worried that the newest addition to the museum might offend some visitors, but in the end, he decided, the truth should not be veiled for more than two centuries. Britons of yore be damned! Viva el Peru!

Yes, all and all, Jaime found life to be on a roll, the likes of which he had never experienced. Sharla would even be returning from West Va. in three days. Oh how his loins ached for her, needed her. His oversized pair even felt to be swelling in anticipation of excitement. He could swear he caught Mika's eyes drifting southward in his direction. Perhaps she wanted to know if he had meant it literally before, or maybe she couldn't help herself as his bulge did even feel more robust than usual.

And as is also so often the case, when life appears to be a big bowl of cherries, watch out. The next step often comes covered in grease. Enter el telefono. Ring, ring ring.

On the other end–Adolfo Costa.

"I have news on your padre," he said right out of the gate.

Jaime's heart began to pound. The proverbial cherry on top.

"Yes?" he implored, already beginning to grow excited at the anticipation of finding his father.

"Well, it's sort of...how do you say....good news, not good news," Adolfo said, thinking his beating-around-the-bush tactics to be a form of politeness.

"Oh," Jaime responded, his spirit falling flatter than Donald Trump's hair in a steam bath in the rain forest. "Just tell me."

"Well, like I say, the good news is I have found your father, but the not so good news is, he is in jail."

Silence.

"I might have the name of the jail, though. If you like," Aldofo offered.

"Yes, please."

Chapter 24

Thankfully, for the sake of passion, the bad news could not depress the decadence of chemical symmetry unleashed upon Sharla's return to Peru. When finally endorphins did run dry, Jaime revealed his intentions of how he planned to free his father from the constraints of a Peruvian government prison. The word jail, as translations work out for Aldofo Costa, equates to more than a local ward of concrete and steel. It means more accurately to be one of the complexes people of Peru pay to confine its most ill-revered.

The next few weeks lingered, compounded by frustration that floundered through most afternoons, leaving nights heavy and dull. Chris returned from the altitude, (to say so mildly) two days after Sharla arrived back in Lima. Even with his recently acquired universal understandings, he spent half the day trying to convince Jaime it to be too risky and with too much to lose to make any attempt to free his father, Adrian Romero Holbrook. The other half of the time he listened for holes he could expose in Jaime's efforts, obviously just another ploy to talk him to his way of thinking.

A lawyer whom Jaime paid a few sols called after a month to report details. Adrian indeed sat imprisoned, either at Canto Grande or El Frontón. He could not be sure which, he said, because he began his stint in one and had been transferred to the other. When, exactly, that transfer occurred, though, could not be determined. He did know why: one count of treason. Although, the lawyer added with a flare of hope, he could find no record of a trial having ever occurred. Apparently, he has only been charged with such.

"How long?" Jaime wanted to know.

"It's hard to say," the esquire answered. "It could be life, I suppose. If he is convicted of treason."

"No, I mean how long has he been held so far?" Jaime clarified.

"Oh, it's been more than a year."

"A year? Okay. Thank you," Jaime wilted. "I may be in touch."

"Okay. You will let me know?"

"Si, senor. Si."

The story of Adrian's demise traces its roots to decades of ruthless labor practices by the ownership class of Peru. As with all societies, some within have, most others have much less. The balance of that scale notwithstanding, it remains a fact that Peruvian have-nots often endure their battles against foreign-born haves, and this truth creates a particularly vitriolic scorn to course through the veins of natural-born citizens. Peruvian blood has been used on more than one occasion to clear acid from car battery posts, as just one example.

Be it Chilean, Spanish, British or elsewhere, exploitation seems always just an ocean voyage or mountain passage away. The most recently organized attempt at combating these nemesis gained traction in Peru around the time that British wigs felt it necessary to remind Argentina how proximity to home does not always determine what belongs to whom. The Movimiento Revolucionario Túpac Amaru, deriving its name from the last indigenous leader of the Inca tribe, sought to rid Peru of what it deems the shackles of foreign-influence elitists upon the common men and women. In more rugged terrain and within certain pockets of society, the MRTA held sway for some years.

Just as the government began to increase the veracity of its efforts against MRTA, however, a citizen of America from north of the equator found herself incarcerated, accused of aiding an attempt by MRTA guerrilla fighters to play the Ace of Coup de Tat. And while dynamite certainly can be an agent of change, six thousand sticks stored upstairs in an affluent Lima neighborhood where MRTA activist did call home, significantly bolsters evidence that more than peaceful demonstrations were in the works.

Adrian Holbrook never armed himself of these affairs, unfortunately, and as such he did not realize the ferocity to which the Peruvian government would combat any attempts to organize miners, be it coal, copper, zinc or gold. That Adrian made this move with the assistance of some of the last participants within the MRTA, also did not bode well for his plea of merely wanting to raise the standard of living among the many whose toils of labor create so much wealth for a handful of others. It could have benefited Adrian to have learned that the small percentage of wealthy mine owners feed the coffers of the politicians who enforce the ways and means.

Alas, he had not. He did not. It made the minutes of his being locked in a cell all the more sufferable. For it is one thing to serve time knowing justice to have been involved, quite the other to truly believe in one's innocence. Attempts by Adrian to educate himself to the recent history of MRTA activities also were impossible, as such incendiary "propaganda" does not reach inside such places as Adrian now resides. Jaime, on the other side and with much counseling from Mika Codsworth, now knew enough that he decided a small portion of the museum should come to include information on comrades Rolando and Evaristo, the two most infamous MRTA radicals.

"Isn't this risky?" Sharla let loose. "What, with what you want to do about your father, and all..."

"But see," he quickly shot back, "he isn't actually my father."

"According to medical records he is," Sharla noted.

"It doesn't matter," Jaime insisted. "We are talking about a museum. It's like art. One does not censor art!"

"Well.." Mika begged to differ.

Ah, the censorship of art. Nazis theft and wanton destruction of western European collections can only be usurped, most likely, by the practices of extreme Islamists at many junctures during the last seventeen centuries. But an actual Marxist might argue that most forms of art are suppressed by degrees in so much as the ability to freely express one's self is never truly allowed to blossom, particularly among the proletariat. But even bourgeois befuddlement puts a damper on creativity, Ingles once bragged.

"Yes," Sharla spurred Mika. "Tell him."

"No," Jaime beat Mika to the punch. "Save your breath. I know, its unwanted attention. But it doesn't matter. It's a part of Peruvian culture and it goes. Will you help me Mika?"

The rebel within certainly could not resist. Within a week, the Natural Anchovy History and Peruvian Culture Museum contained yet its latest addition. Within a week of this, Jaime began to notice during his day-to-day meandering, certain plump-cheeked Peruvians who came across as far too serious. The gestures upon their round faces were more than keen curiosity, Jaime felt. They appeared more like that of a cat closing in on the mouse. But the final pounce did not transpire immediately.

"Perhaps we should visit Quito," Jaime soon proposed to Sharla over dinner.

"Why Quito?" Sharla naturally inquired.

"I think Mika can help us make a connection there, to help spring my dad."

"How's that?" Sharla again naturally wondered.

Jaime's explanation lasted into the early hours of the following morning; the condensed version revolving around an idea that Mika's cousin, who works at the British Embassy in Ecuador, has access to the left-leaning premier who might be persuaded to shed light upon the plight of Adrian Romero Holbrook. And if enough pressure could me mounted, the Peruvian presidente may allow a pardon to ensue.

"I'm not sure why the president of Peru would do as such? He's being arrested in the first place by the government. Why...? Sharla posed.

"Political pressure," Jaime countered. "There is an election next year, and the people in many of these countries down here are gaining more and more power. Look at Venezuela. Or Bolivia. And here, even."

"This is going to take some time, too," Sharla added.

"It's the best we have so far," Jaime insisted.

"I guess," Sharla conceded. "We should keep thinking, though."

Jaime agreed. Alas, circumstances did not. For the next morning, awaiting Jaime's arrival to open the museum, two armed agents of the Peruvian government stood at the front doors.

"We'd like to have a few words, senor," one of the men said quietly to Jaime, motioning him to follow the two to a waiting van painted the obligatory blanco.

"But I need to open the museum," Jaime tried.

"It can open late today," the other one replied.

"And feed the anchovies," Jaime also attempted.

"They'll survive," the same agent demanded.

The three rode in silence through the streets of Peru, leaving the historical arts district for the heart of the old-town section. Jaime did not realize so many streets were lined with balcony terraces. At the Government Palace of Perú the van parked just outside the perimeters of the beige facade, so decorative it made Jaime think of a Spanish quinceanera dress. Inside the old palace, the men led Jaime to a second story, interior room where they began by relaying how much they and the government of Peru really liked the museum's history of anchovies and its depiction of the long and important role in the lives of the people of Peru.

How though, they inquired with surprising sincerity, does the Movimiento Revolucionario Túpac Amaru play a part of anchovies? Before hearing Jaime's attempt at justification, the men took turns offering evidence to the detriment of MRTA's existence. Terms such as guerrilla thugs and narco trafficking were interspersed among words like kidnapping, extortion, ransom and assassination.

"Still," Jaime begged, "it's all a part of Peruvian history. That's all we are attempting to do, you know. To showcase Peruvian history."

"Your passport please," one of the agents said in non-sequitor fashion.

"It's at my condo," Jaime whispered.

"Let's take another ride," the other agent replied after an exchange of eyes.

Again, the three rode in silence, both going to the condo and right back to the Government Palace of Perú. They used a different route both ways, for some reason, though. Jaime was glad. He liked the chance to see new sections of the sprawling city that is Lima. More balconies.

"It's really a beautiful place, here," Jaime even offered, attempting to break the drought of conversation.

The agents only nodded casually in agreement, though. Let silence reign. Back inside the second-floor room at the palace, the agents took Jaime's passport and told him to hold tight. Much to his astonishment, when they returned a half hour later, they simply thanked him for his time and reminded him to be careful. Again with the 'be careful,' he laughed inside. Too easy was his next concern.

He took a cab back to the museum. It brought back memories of his first week in Peru when he rented the fishing totora. Ms. Sanchita, he suddenly recalled. Perhaps she might have an idea? Then again?

Mika came to the museum that afternoon. She recommended Jaime get out of Lima for a few weeks. Peruvian government agents always have something up their sleeves, she said. Let them believe their intimidation tactics are working. Stroke their egos. Let things die down a bit, she suggested. Lie low. They could all go to Quito. Senomar would be hitting there, soon. Although for how long she couldn't be sure. Blitzkrieg Bop remained elusive for all but a paucity of Ecuadorians.

Still, the five of them could travel there ahead of the band. Explore what can be there. See how far they can penetrate the regime there, also. We always have fun, she threw in for good measure.

"We did hurry through there on the way here," Jaime admitted.

"Let's go for it, mate. It'll give us a chance to really concentrate on how to pull this caper off," Mika smiled. The silver rod piercing the outer brow of her left eye moved slightly with her upturned lips. Jaime suddenly realized the attraction he felt toward her. It marked the first time he'd had such notions for anyone else since Sharla entered his world. He wanted to censor his libido. But when Mika walked back to the new display on Rolando and Evaristo, he

144

caught himself eyeing her ass. It was a little rounder than Sharla's, with a plumpness that now seemed inviting.

He thought of his mother, for some reason. He hadn't spoken to Mariella since leaving her a share of the winnings. If not for her actions his father wouldn't be holed away right now. Had he judged her too harshly, though? The powers of the flesh are so strong.

"So what do you think? Quito?" Mika urged, coming back.

"Yeah, you're probably right. It would be good."

Chris said he didn't feel up to the travel. He'd stay behind and keep the museum open, he suggested. But Sharla, despite having just returned to Lima, agreed to the idea of leaving for a spell. And so they packed the Land Rover full the following morning and proceeded northward. Beefcake at last lightened up, once the four were bound together inside the vehicle. Talk ranged through a variety of flavors, bounding from the constraints of the illusion of time to how recently discovered off-shore oil fields would propel Brazil to become the next of the world's Superpowers.

Yet, only during a discourse on the influence of American Punk bands did the strangest, indeed most unbelievable, of revelations surface. And only by accident did it even come forth, at that. In a spat of naivety, Sharla had asked Mika why she considered the Ramones so important?

Mika responded by stating that if Sharla had witnessed their show at London's Rainbow Theatre, she'd understand. Sharla only nodded in innocence. But in the rearview mirror Jaime noticed an odd exchange of glances between Mika and Beefcake.

"But when did that concert happen?" Jaime then prodded.

"New Year's eve, '77," Mika admitted.

"So, you didn't actually witness it either, then?" Jaime continued.

"It was filmed," Mika stated matter-of-factly.

"But you said, had you witnessed it, then you'd understand. Right?"

"Did I?" Mika blurted.

"You did."

She spent the next few minutes diverting attention from the question at-hand like a matador's red cape to a bull—how Joe

Strummer and Johnny Rotten were in attendance that night at the Rainbow and the influence there of. Or how a section chief of the C.I.A. in Berlin helped promote the act and smuggle LPs to rile East German youth.

"They did the same thing with Bruce Springsteen and Levi's in Moscow a few years later," she claimed.

"But you said you were at the Rainbow," Jaime interjected. "If you were even fifteen at the time, it'd make you in your late 40s, now."

Awkward lulls typically change the course of conversations. In this instance, it propelled a confession the likes of which Jaime thought would make any such similar occurrence to Sharla about his previous brief stint in the adult-film world quell in comparison. Mika's explanation, in fact, would last to the border of Ecuador.

After requirements of sworn-to-secrecy were met, in addition to allusions to the sensitivities of Jaime's mission to free his father and the leverage that would afford Mika, she revealed her true age to be forty-nine. Her scientific age, as she put it, stood still at twenty-six. To say looks of disbelief spread across the faces of the front-seat passengers is to say Angus Young one of rock era's most under-appreciated lead guitarists. Jaws literally dropped.

"Do tell," Sharla said at last in a mock British accent.

A London-based research scientist, Mika began, discovered through years of trial and error how to isolate a specific gene in the DNA of lab mice.

"Telomeres, he named it," Mika said. "I don't know exactly how it works. Basically, he turned this one particular gene off, and when he did this, he was able to stop the mice from aging. It's public knowledge, in fact. There was even an article in *Time* magazine a few years ago. What hasn't been reported is that there are a handful of human guinea pigs. Well that, and the specifics of when the discovery was made isn't exactly accurate."

"Do you feel twenty-six?" Sharla asked.

"You know, that's it really. In many regards I do feel that. When I look in a mirror, the lack of lines on my face. But inside..." Mika said, "Inside I can tell it's different. Like in my bones. My joints. But it's weird, because I don't know if it's just psychological or not? And like, if it is working...I mean completely, not just on the outside, then how would I know? How would I know what it really feels like to be forty-nine? To feel forty-nine."

A contemplative silence followed. Time's illusory properties notwithstanding, the aging of the human body or mighty oak, for that matter, cannot be denied. Regardless the scale, or that this decrepitation process may occur within the framework of a 'timeless' universe, within some context a man is born, travels through stages of life, then dies, be it naturally or otherwise. And so it is also the paradox of eternal youth—if one does not physically age, one does not proceed through these stages. What of grandchildren, for instance? Or retirement? Or deep disappointment, bitterness, regrets, making up for lost time?

Mika handed Sharla a CD and the four digested aspects of all that is to the background of "God Save the Queen" and "Anarchy in the UK." The significance of the influence the Ramones handed British punk cannot be denied. And as the background image that New Year's Eve at the Rainbow was an actual seal of the United States of America, credence to the C.I.A.'s employment of western music to bolster tenets of democracy and freedom throughout the East and parts of the southern hemisphere can also be had. "I used to make a living, man pickin' the banana, now I'm a guide for the C.I.A.," Joey sang in *Havana Affair*.

"Your hair," Sharla broke the silence. "Is it turning gray? Is it also not aging?"

"I dye my hair black for the band," Mika responded. "But no, it isn't aging ither."

"No children?" Sharla continued.

"It was part of the arrangement," Mika said. "They didn't want to risk complications a pregnancy might wrought, not to mention the effects on the fetus."

"I guess so," Sharla offered.

"Do your parents know?" Jaime asked.

"Of course," Mika laughed.

"But what about your friends from back home?" Sharla

continued to inquire.

"Yeah, that can get a little tricky. I'm on the road so much, though. It is something we have to keep in mind," Mika agreed.

"We?" Jaime prodded.

"Myself and the British government," Mika answered. "They're the ones behind all this, you know."

"What do they have in mind?" Jaime asked.

"Don't know, really," Mika said. "Just to keep ahead of the curve, I suppose. I mean, it's quite the game changer isn't it."

"How long?" Sharla asked with a meekness that caught Jaime's ear. He adored that natural humility about her.

"How long...?" Mika questioned.

"How long will you keep doing it? Whatever it is. I mean, forever?" Sharla said.

"Don't know that either," Mika admitted. "Not forever, though."

"No?" Jaime wondered.

"I don't see how. I mean the idea is only to see if it can work with human beings. To see what complications will arise as a result of it, you know. It hasn't been long enough for all that to be determined, I suppose."

"But if it does work...? Who will get it?" Sharla asked.

"Well you know it'll be completely, outrageously expensive. So there's that. And you know, too, they can't have everyone living hundreds of years. What with limited resources as it is," Mika said.

"Does the soul age?" Beefcake asked, at last entering the fray.

"Interesting," Jaime responded first, after all took a moment in surprise to the sound of Beefcake's voice this exchange–a little high for a man of his muscular excess, it might be noted. "Because if the spirit is eternal, then that would mean it doesn't, right."

"It gets wiser, but not older," Sharla said.

"Yeah, it's just the sum of our experiences that marks our soul," Mika said. "If there is such a thing."

"Don't let Chris hear you say that," Jaime snapped.

"No?" Mike responded. "American Indians are really spiritual by nature, aren't they?"

"I suppose that's it," Chris said.

And so the talk continued until they reached Quito early that evening. After dinner, the couples quickly retreated to their rooms. The long ride and density of matters at-hand left them all rather spent. Could it be true, Sharla sought Jaime's opinion before they both fell to slumbers?

At breakfast the next morning, Jaime found strange thoughts circulating within. How would Mika be in bed, he wondered, bluntly? Would shutting off the telomere gene preserve elasticity and yet she'd have the experience of a mature women? He felt ashamed at the notion of his curiosity. But still he couldn't help himself. He'd only heard about the tenderness a woman of middle age brings to a party between the sheets.

They toured Quito that morning, taking in sites a little off the beaten path, thanks to Mika's experience. Sharla found the aluminum sculpture the Virgen de Quito to be her favorite. So elegant, the expression of her piety. By early afternoon they were all feeling short of breath thanks to Mika's pace and Quito's mile-high plus elevation and so left to meet Mika's cousin at the British Embassy.

"You're looking the same, as always," Ginger said to Mika upon entering the embassy lobby.

Jaime wondered if she meant it literally? They all took lunch at a trendy restaurant near the Carondelet Palace, Ecuador's seat of government. Mika outlined the gist of Adrian Holbrook's situation. Ginger said she'd see what she could do. She couldn't make any promises, she said more than once. Jaime told her he understood. They only hoped it might be something.

A burst of thunder suddenly rattled the windows of the cafe. Beefcake thought it might have been a bomb. The next bolt struck so near its charge reflected off the glass on the building across the street, leaving no doubt as to the source of power. Rain drops like small pancakes quickly began splattering the ground. For the next forty-five minutes the storm put on a show—lightning strikes sending more natural nitrates into the air than a decade worth of guano.

Only recently did science realize the chain of chemical reactions brought forth from the million-plus daily strikes of lightening around the world release literally tons of nitrates. If only they had sought the wisdom of Haber, he might of let on to Mother Nature's role in the cycle of all things biological. For as the rain falls it absorbs the naturally produced nitrates to add a boost to its already nutrient friendly ways. As such, plants small and large continue their growth and inch another step closer to death, as it were.

Mika Codsworth, much to the chagrin of Ms. Nature, might consume all the water from an Ecaudorian flash flood and its inherent nitrates and yet, thanks to her genetically altered DNA, run completely at odds with this cycle of life and death. It's enough to ponder how that excess growth gets spent? Are her bowel movements enormous? Does her pee flow like the Amazon in the spring?

Chapter 25

"Gabba, Gabba, Hey!"

Twenty, twenty, twenty-four hours to go, I wanna be sedated–blasted from the Land Rover's surround-sound stereo. Jaime thought the notion superb, if not for that twelve hour drive back to Lima. After following Senomar for a few gigs, Sharla felt a bout of jet-lag setting in, she said to Jaime. Never-mind that she hadn't actually flown very far east from West Va., or that it had been more than two months ago. She wanted to be back home. That she referred to Lima and their condo there as home was all Jaime needed to hear to be convinced. Truth be told, Sharla began to sense a strange vibe between Mika and Jaime. And now that Beefcake had allowed his personality to come out of its shell, she thinks he behaves like a reality show contestant–pretentious and showy, as if an outside audience was somehow aware. The whole scene had become annoying, Sharla said more than once.

She truly did tire of so much travel. Mika and Beefcake had the rest of the band to kick around with, so it didn't matter to them if Jaime and Sharla left before they did. Once back in Lima, they took to the rack like pieces of discarded gum to the blind soles of sneakers on a hot afternoon. Jaime awoke first the next morning with enough sleep in his eyes to construct a small sand castle and a longing in his bones aching like a half-broken tree limb creaking in the midnight wind. What he longed for, though, he couldn't name. Sharla still slept, pretty as a shiny new penny while she did. It couldn't be her. Could it be Mika?

He needed to concentrate on a better plan at gaining Adrian's freedom. Ginger's efforts already were proving futile. Neither president would risk their political necks for an American, even if he might lean left. And infiltrating any actual prison would require more manpower and time than Jaime had or was willing to give.

Yet ask, and ye shall receive, a holy rebel once said. And if anyone comes close to purity in Jaime's world, he need look no further than Chris the Hopi, who in anathema to Jaime's enjoyment surveying patrons of the Natural Anchovy History and Peruvian Culture Museum, discovered its day-to-day tending to be a smidge claustrophobic. What with his being accustomed to Pueblo life and having recently returned from his trek to the high mountain valley, he really couldn't stand more than thirty minutes. So to escape the enclosure, he closed the museum for two hours a day at lunch and began touring nearby museums of much greater magnitude.

Inside the sprawling Museum of the Nation a certain sword at last caught his eye. An idea quickly stirred within his cerebral cortex thereafter. What Jaime needs to free Adrian Holbrook is leverage–leverage against the Peruvian government and even its citizens. And while most relate kidnapping and extortion plots to those involving people, Chris would come to contend that the sword of José de San Martin could serve such purpose invaluably. And it wouldn't squeal, cry or need food and water and twenty-four hour surveillance. All they needed is the sword.

"How's security at this place?" Jaime asked without batting an eye upon hearing Chris' strategy.

"Tight," Chris responded, unfortunately for Jaime.

"How tight?"

"Let's take a see."

As with most museums, looks concerning security can be deceiving. The esoteric value of pieces on display must be minimally altered at the expense of safety from thievery. And as José de San Martin represents the bastion of Peruvian independence, all artifacts related to him are guarded closest of all in the least noticeable way possible, if being displayed within an inch-thick square of secured Plexiglas can be described as subtle. The sword also rests on a felt covered box which sits atop a weight sensitive panel of tile. If the weight alters more than three grams, a silent alarm automatically screams.

Not that Jaime or Chris were aware of any silent alarm triggered by weight. The Plexiglas bolted to the floor represented more than they could penetrate. But thanks to Jaime's benevolence, as some within the world of museums and art in Lima were coming to believe of the American who donated so much money to shed recognition on the plight of anchovies, not to mention MRTA scions, Jaime would soon have an inside track on the workings of modern museums. Stating one evening at a celebration of a new Monet collection on loan from Paris, that he worried about security at his museum, far less valuable as it overall may be, Jaime caught the ear of one Juan Gustavo, an associate curator at the Museum of Natural History. Accompanied by Ms. Sanchita as a show of having connections beyond the museum and arts district of Lima, Jaime quickly noticed Gustavo's overt attraction to Ms. Sanchita, and so suggested to give Jaime and his beautiful guest a behind the scenes tour of the Museum of Natural History, which also naturally would include the latest in museum high-tech security operations.

"Why, I'd be delighted," Juan Gustavo smiled.

Ms. Sanchita seemed far less enthusiastic. Sensing her lack of receptiveness, Jaime quickly whispered in her ear how he'd been meaning to provide her modeling studio a sizeable donation to help promote gender equality in South America. Sharla had suggested it, he added.

"Adonde es tú mujeres amore?" Ms. Sanchita asked, a smile of recognition now creeping across her lips.

"She's a little under the weather tonight," Jaime replied.

"We still need to get her in the studio," Ms. Sanchita belted.

"Yes," Jaime obliged. "She's just been so busy. But she definitely will."

"Then it's a date," Juan said with a gleam in his eye.

"Yes, for sure," Jaime agreed. "We look forward to it," he added, noting Ms. Sanchita's forced grin toward Juan.

When Jaime informed Sharla that night of the latest step in the grand plan to free Adrian Holbrook, she wanted to know why he had never mentioned Ms. Sanchita's desire for Sharla to model jeans? He didn't think she'd be interested, he answered.

"I think I'm capable of making that decision for myself," Sharla remarked.

"Of course you are," he offered rapidly. "I didn't mean anything...."

"What else do you keep hidden from me, for my own protection?" she wanted to now know.

"I don't know?" Jaime replied, his innate honesty coming forth.

"What does that mean? You don't know?"

"I don't know?" he said again.

"What's going on with you?"

"I don't..."

"Don't say it again!"

There first spat, dear readers. Isn't it just adorable?

Sharla said she needed some fresh air. She'd be back, whenever. Okay, is all Jaime could muster in response. He really didn't understand, but his lack of caring that he didn't understand why Sharla would be bothered by any of this concerned him far more. That thoughts of Mika next careened around his skull also gave him pause.

What is going on, he thought to himself? Do all men have stray thoughts of other women? Does this mean his love for Sharla could be something else? He needed some fresh air, too, he decided. He thought of the bean pickers from his initial trip to Lima. They all seemed so content, so care-free. He wondered how?

Could they really be as worry-free as they appeared? Is all of life as such–as that that appears one way actually the opposite? Are the sad actually at peace? Those outwardly giddy twisted in knots inside? The poor rich, the wealthy lonely? How can so many lust for filet mignon yet not stomach a real slaughter? Sols abound, yes, but where do I go for this?

He settled on a bench in a nearby park. The night air was still warm from the day and a mild breeze ran over the contours of his skin like the touch of velvet. How something so simple could feel so fine, he thought. Just the wind. He turned his gaze skyward, hoping for the Southern Cross, but the lights of Lima were too strong. Scarcely a star one could be found.

The park was nearly desolate, he noticed. What gives? But just then in the distance he detected someone strolling along–a small figure, slowly moving his direction. A female. A female who looked very much like Sharla. It was Sharla. A good omen. She smiled within sight. It sent a bevy of love cart wheeling through his being.

"A hottie like you shouldn't be alone at night in the park," he said.

"I'm not worried," she replied taking a seat next to him on the bench. "I'm sorry we fought."

"It's only natural," he whispered.

"It is," she agreed softly.

The ensuing kiss lit a fire inside their chests. The magic of love.

"How does karma work?" Sharla asked when their lips relinquished.

"Something bad will happen to you if you do bad," Jaime answered plainly.

"No, silly, I know that. I mean, how does it work, though? How does it know?"

"Hummm, I don't wanna say I don't know," he quipped.

"No really," she said. "Have you ever wondered?"

"Well, sure," he said. "Chris says it's an energy inside us–it gives off an aura–positive or negative. Negative energy attracts more, like a magnet, but only similar poles don't repel one another in this case."

"But is it God that watches all this, to decide, ya know?" she asked.

"I don't think so. It's more like it's just everywhere. Light and dark energy. We can't see it, of course, but somehow it can."

"Maybe so," she pondered. "Maybe so?"

"I love you," she then said after another moment.

"I love you, too," he returned without pause, followed by another long kiss. "Hey, wanna go back to my place?"

"I do," she said. "Let's hurry."

Indeed, the magic of love. And the love of love. And the chance to possess such a pair as to make the power of that love so sensual. Ahhhh, Sharla's soul purred. Hmmm, Jaime's heart fluttered.

Having reached a new, mutual understanding the next morning, Sharla proposed they get down to the nuts and bolts of how they were going to free Adrian Holbrook. Why haven't you tried to visit, she asked first, though? To avoid any link should a plan actually work at some point, he explained.

She thought the idea of holding the sword of José de San Martin for ransom sketchy, at best, she added. But Jaime countered that the power of iconic national symbols can be extreme. Think of the Declaration of Independence, he said. What if someone held it for ransom?

Apples to oranges, she replied. But both fruit, none-the-less, he offered in retort. Not wanting to spoil their honeymoon of make-up romance, they left it all be and departed to meet Chris for breakfast before going to open the museum. Upon learning of the night's previous events between Jaime and Sharla, Chris did not immediately offer his take on the merits of using José de San Martin's sword for leverage. Like a dog who cannot, no matter time or place, help himself should the need arise to sniff his or any other dog's hind quarters, when the mention of karma and its workings surface, his opinion must be shared sooner than later.

It follows as thusly: Karma works on a sub-atomic level, just as when an atom loses one electron, another one immediately replaces it, so too a man's soul emits a physical energy field that fluctuates with his state of being; i.e., if he's doing something good, something positive, in whatever capacity, then positive energy surrounds his aura, and vice-versa. And these levels of energy also vary by degrees; hence, a particularly egregious act will generate more negativity than a more minor infraction. One might argue, what accounts for a lag between action and karma? That answer becomes infinitely complex by the nature of the universe and the powers that exist within. One contention is that if a person is evil enough, he/she garners the attention of evil overlords, demons or even Lucifer himself (or whatever Dark Overlord there might be out there) who somehow can temporarily (in a geological sense of time) protect that soul from Karma's reaction...however, like all things physical, if a force acts upon another force, but is only restrained, as opposed to being redirected or repelled, then that force only increases until at some point it is released. Naturally, therefore, the longer a force is restrained, the greater the eventual release. What may confuse many unknowing inspectors will be an expectation for this balance of positive and negative energy to always resolve itself within the course of days, weeks, months, years, even a single lifetime...however, being that universal time is only a perception, the rapidity of recourse only appears consequential to those caught within the trap of time.

Equal interest may be had through analysis of Karma's opposite, for which a name has yet to be taken; yet, one instinctively understands the analogy. Throughout the history of mankind, every culture produces a lore in which exists a basic tenet–good always comes back in exponential increases. Some say ten-fold, others three or four. None, and herein lies the rub from a strictly scientific (as appalling as the use of this term here will be to some) point of view: how can positive's reward, if you will, always be greater than its initial action? One might plausibly insert here that God skews the table His direction. Whomever said God isn't going to win hasn't studied western culture very effectively, let alone the Bible; for as any literary historian should attest, protagonists always defeat their antagonist. And everyone, short of the few remaining Pygmy tribes of southeast Asia or cannibal societies buried deep in an Amazon jungle, has heard how the Bible concludes–Heaven and Hell, yo!

Not until Anthony Burgess' *A Clockwork Orange*, in fact, does one find within Western literature evil winning over good in the end. Perhaps, in reality, God enjoys continuously poking Beelzebub with His good staff by never allowing evil to gain too much ground. Of course, with only a half-hearted attempt at current observation of mankind's works of late, one could easily argue God is certainly letting those forces of Karma build, at best. Some might even contend He's taking a vacation. In the 60s, academicians could gain notoriety by contending God to be dead, with an underlying intellectual wink to their PhD brethren, that the God they refer to within their discourse never actually existed; only within the meager mind of *the common* man did they mean, and now even there, His existence is no more.

A man of the Good Book would explain at this point that the actual definition of Holy is the complete un-acceptance of sin. From here, one could argue that Karma then is only a secular version of God's innate punishment for sin. Chris the Hopi says it's all the same, which is quite literally not to evoke that trite slogan of the 90s, "It's all good." For indeed, it is not! Thank Karma for Karma.

"So in a nutshell, it's just a physical law of balance," Chris said in conclusion.

"It all works out in the wash," my mom used to say, Sharla conferred.

"Too bad something hasn't circled back to help my dad," Jaime complained.

"Give it time," Chris said, fully aware of the irony in his employment of that old cliché.

Yet as clichés go, the notion that justice eventually prevails certainly has a seat near the front whiteboard at the school of Karma. But as previously posited, clocks do not hang on any wall at Karma U. Bells do not ring to signal the end of sessions or the beginning of recess. There are no hall monitors to assist the tardy. There are, however, an array of distinguished alumni, many equipped with the equivalent of corporal punishment weapons. Among these more decorated old-school chums are some of earth's natural Bunsen burners, who work literally at great depths to achieve what occasionally amounts to a timely act, such as percolating rivers of magma that rise to seep up through crooks and crevices of bedrock, and given its due unleash forces to rip violent shifts upon our planet's crust. Earth quakes we call them.

The rumblings of one began just about the time our trio made their way from breakfast to the Natural Anchovy History and Peruvian Culture Museum. When the actual shaking started in earnest, they each stopped and looked at the other. Then the ground's dance got so jiggy, simply maintaining one's balance became priority. Chris fell to a knee. Sharla's stance got wide. Jaime took a surfer's pose.

In all, the quake lasted no more than thirty seconds, but time enough to register 7.4 on Richter's scale and send most Limans into the streets, on edge for aftershocks and to avoid crashing debris. In a flash of telepathy, Chris and Jaime suddenly locked eyes.

"The sword!" they said in unison.

So as the rest of Lima's population moved for safety outside from whatever building they were in, Jaime, Chris and Sharla hurried themselves to the Museum of the Nation where its staff currently mulled over a hundred or so early goers now gathered in the plaza just outside the main entrance. Another rumble began. The first aftershock.

"You wait here," Jaime said to Sharla. "Just in case. Keep an eye out."

As the crowd and staff grew ancy, Chris and Jaime neared the entrance. The ground let forth another jolt. A scream or two cried out. Chris dashed in. Jaime followed, moving quickly to keep up with Chris already at a brisk pace toward the front, right showroom where he knew to be the Plexiglas encasing the sword of José de San Martin, now resting slightly ajar. Chris gave a quick scour of the showroom. No one else was there. He made a shove at the Plexiglas, but it barely nudged.

"We need something," Chris said.

"I see that. But what?" Jaime pleaded.

The floor began to jiggle once again.

"Hit the deck," Chris whispered urgently.

"What is it?" Jaime whispered from his belly.

Chris motioned with a raise of an eyebrow to notice a museum guard passing from where they just came near the turn from the entrance, but he passed without noticing them. They got back up and surveyed the nearby displays for something of weight.

"Bingo!" Jaime wailed.

Across the space Jaime retrieved a bust of Simón Bolívar. With a grunt he brought it above his head, steadied himself and dashed

159

toward the Plexiglas. He did his best to hurl the bust, but it hit the top ninety-degree angle and split in two. The Plexiglas showed scarcely a nick.

"No, you've got to ram it!" Chris bellowed.

Chris picked up a piece of the Bolívar skull, backed up ten feet, then did his best imitation of a mountain Billy goat in battle for rights to inseminate the horde of waiting female mountain Billy goats. The Plexiglas cracked where the bust rammed it and at the base where the earthquake already had sent it listing.

Jaime, now inspired and with thoughts of a free Adrian racing in his brain, backed away from the sword and in a true burst of speed threw all of his own weight into the body of the Plexiglas. It popped free at last. On the floor woozy from the collision, Jaime shook his head and watched Chris grip the sword of José de San Martin. Somewhere in the museum a silent alarm wanted to belt out a high-pitched rendition of Jose Feliciano's Por Qué Te Tengo Que Olivdar?, but the quake rendered electrical power flaccid this morning. The sword was theirs!

"Here," Chris instructed Jaime. "You act like you're hurt and I'll hide the sword between us."

"I am hurt," Jaime winced.

"Then it won't be acting, *pendejo!*" Chris growled.

In a final act of serendipity, another aftershock rattled the museum once again, just in time for Chris and Jaime to hobble back outside undetected. Sharla's countenance flashed to one of amazement, easily aware of their ploy to hide the sword between themselves.

"Increíble!" she let loose.

Jaime and Chris only smiled, too anxious and focused on not getting caught to waste time on cheap talk. Quickly, like a drunken co-joined twin they moved away from the still waiting crowd in the plaza. Once far enough from the museum, Chris raised the sword high.

"En guard," he boasted.

"Stop that!" Jaime cried

"Sorry," Chris said, bringing the sword back down. "I couldn't help it."

"We need something to cover it," Jaime hammered. "Here, just use this," taking off his shirt.

Chris wrapped the blade of the sword in Jaime's shirt and placed it in the pit of his left arm. Several sirens wailed nearby. They each froze for a moment before realizing it to be only more reaction to the earthquake. They moved on back toward the condo, but when they turned the corner from across the way, they stopped. A large crowd had gathered in front of the building, with two ambulances parked with lights flashing.

They moved a little closer and could now see an end of their complex crumbled. Men appeared to be searching through the pile of rubble at the base of the collapse.

"We can't go in right now," Jaime said to Sharla.

"No," she agreed.

"Let's go to the museum," Chris offered.

"But that's almost where we just were," Jaime wailed.

"Where else?" Chris pleaded.

"No, you're right," Jaime said. "Ahh! The anchovies!"

Like a bottle rocket denied the past twelve Chinese New Year's celebrations, Jaime Gabriel Holbrook shot out in a sprint toward his museum. Sharla and Chris only watched for a minute before hustling as much as possible with a stolen, three-foot relic of sharpened steel to tote.

Relief flooded Jaime's emotions once inside his still standing four walls. The aquarium glass had withstood the quake. Or at least for the most part. Darkness prevented a more careful inspection, but the floor was dry. Parts of other displays littered the hardwood. Jaime stepped back outside to find Sharla and Chris. They were a hundred yards away. Chris moved like a wounded soldier, one arm stiff, the other folded at his waist. It caused his gait to warble. Jaime laughed at the whole notion. The sword of José de San Martin being held as ransom. He looked around to see if anyone found cause for suspicion at Chris and Sharla. They didn't. Mother Nature had the stage and she wouldn't be hitting the dressing room for at least another act.

Jaime locked the sword in a closet in the back office of the museum. Only he held a key to either door. Now feeling safe to move in public, the three made their way back to the condo and retrieved the Land Rover, somehow spared any damage, being parked in the open. They agreed the beach the best spot next, free of debris and earshot of strangers or otherwise. What to do from here? What to do, they each exchanged looks knowingly?

Chapter 26

After spending that entire afternoon on the beach grilling each other's ideas for how to exchange the sword of José de San Martin for Adrian Holbrook's freedom, a consensus could not be reached. Drink, Jaime finally demanded to break the deadlock.

"We must drink to break this impasse," his effusive voice soared. "To the bar, batman! Catwoman."

Before the bartender could finish mixing the potions, though, Sharla pointed toward a television mounted above the collection of bottled spirits. A reporter spoke into his microphone standing at the entrance of the Museum of the Nation. Jaime's fluency in Spanish was such these days that he could almost translate verbatim. In breaking news, the effete reporter stated, a theft at the Museum of the Nation was under investigation. The sword of José de San Martin was missing. Authorities believed the re-emergence of the MRTA may be at work. The bust of Simón Bolívar had been mutilated, as well, the reporter went on to add, shaking his crafted hairdo in disgust.

"Well, we've got their attention," Chris whispered after a quick search for anyone being close enough to hear.

Jaime raised his index finger upright to his lips. A light of deviousness sparked in his eyes. Sharla's brow, contrarily, wrinkled with concern. The bartender placed their drinks on the bar. Without a word, they each took a gulp.

"Okay, not a peep, for now," Jaime ordered. "Not here."

Sharla and Chris nodded in silent agreement. That night, Jaime sprang for a hotel room on the beach. Sols still abound, after all. He thought it safer than being back in proximity to the arts district. They could talk in the room, albeit quietly, he thought. Instead, they found their brains exhausted of anything that hadn't already been brought before their tribunal. Sleep could be the only answer, for now.

Jaime awoke first the next morning. The numbers seven, one and three illuminated in red from the clock on the night stand. It's little wonder man has bought so deeply into the idea of time, Jaime contemplated, thinking on Chris' theory of it being an illusion. Almost anywhere one looks reminders of that universal mouse trap exist, starting with the sun and its famous four seasons. Modern society has advanced from the sundial to the quasar time piece, accurate to the nano second and every day, roosters crow, church bells ring, alarm clocks beep, time clocks are punched, flags are raised, then lowered, tides roll in, then out. Perhaps the greatest perpetrator of this grand hoax—mirror, mirror on the wall, which tells one and any who's fairest in the land, that answer being, with the possible exception of one said Mika Codsworth and her supposed cohorts in high crimes against time, no one. Everyone, everything, grows old.

So it is, that on this partly cloudy, Lima, Peru morning, one might forgive Jaime Gabriel Holbrook for feeling his back now squarely against the proverbial face of old Big Ben. For while Chris and the many philosophers before him may be on to something concerning the bigger picture of eternity and man's perceptions of time, Jaime's father and the efforts to spring him loose certainly cannot be classified as anything short of having the restraints of time tightly cinched around the gullet. If the sword of José de San Martin can ever be used as leverage to free Adrian Holbrook, time, like a potent, erotic whiff of Channel No. 5, most definitely is of the essence.

Quickly growing anxious, Jaime opened the curtains and slid open the door to the room's balcony overlooking the Pacific. Incoming light and sounds shortly stirred Sharla and Chris to awake.

"We've got to move on this," Jaime said to Chris, still rubbing his eyes.

"The problem, as I see it," Sharla responded instead, "is how do we communicate with the government? Anything in writing will take too long."

"I agree," Chris said. "We need one of those high-tech mobile phone systems, one like those drug lords in Colombia use when they kidnap someone and call wherever to get their ransom."

"Right, but they have hideouts deep in the jungle," Jaime countered.

"So, let's get deep in the jungle too," Chris said.

"We can't all go," Jaime demanded. "The museum has to stay open. We can't all three suddenly disappear."

"Chris and I will go," Sharla offered. "They don't know me. Or Chris either, for that matter."

Jaime's heart sank to his stomach. Sharla and Chris together in the midst of nowhere for who knows how long? Such a hypocrite, he thought to himself. I drool over thoughts of Mika's prowess in bed and yet grow ill at just the idea of Sharla alone with my best friend.

"It's all we've got, really," Sharla said, moving to the bathroom to shower for the day. "You guys decide."

Jaime turned to Chris who was unaware of his hidden suspicions.

"She's got a point," Chris shrugged. "What else do we have?"

If another idea could be had, Jaime would have his way with it like a Roman soldier ransacking Jerusalem circa late B.C., but nothing came. Later that morning, they found a mobile phone system they hoped would work, paid cash for it and set out to choose where Chris and Sharla should make camp. They'd take the Land Rover. Chris could take cabs.

The next morning Chris and Sharla departed for the rain forest, destination unknown. Jaime went to the museum to begin cleaning up from the quake. Chris and Sharla would make the first attempt at communication with the government of Peru the following Monday. Goodbye between Sharla and Jaime should not run long, they decided, wanting to keep a lid on their emotions and fear of uncertainty.

Later that morning, Mika and Beefcake showed up at the museum.

"What's up?" Jaime chortled to Mika. "Same new?"

"Oh, right, right," Mika lightly grinned. "Same new. Yeah, well not for you, though, right. I read about the sword of José de San Martin. How'd ya do it? During the earthquake, wasn't it."

"Please," Jaime pleaded. "Not here. Follow me."

Jaime led them to the back office despite no one else actually being inside the museum.

"You read about it?" he then asked

"Yeah. Haven't you?" Mika snorted.

"No, I've never been a newspaper man," Jaime admitted. "What did it say?"

"Just that. That it's missing and the government's keeping an eye out for whatever, you know."

"But they are interested? I mean, they really do want to know? They care," Jaime said unable to contain his curiosity.

"Oh, it's a big deal. I assure you that," she said. "This might just work."

"I see," Jaime said, stroking like a perfunctory method actor the whiskers recently sprouted on his chin. "Are you guys busy? Can you give me a hand out here?"

Beefcake gave a shrug of the shoulders and Mika a nod of the head. As they began picking up pieces from the floor, Jaime eyed Mika bent over. He thought back to watching her perform in Quito. Draped in black and throbbing back beats, she moved on stage like a succubus, the allure of a sexual sadist to the male incubus counterpart crooning next to her. Jaime thought of Sharla and Chris off in the jungle. Was it just an excuse to lust here over Mika? This whole notion was really morphing into an issue.

"Wait!" Jaime suddenly rang out. "How did you know about the sword? Who..."

"You just did," Mika laughed.

"What?"

166

"Well, when we read about it, Eduardo said to me, what if Jaime and Chris did this to hold as ransom for Jaime's father? And I agreed," Mika smiled. "But not to worry. They don't know your intentions. So they don't know you have motive."

"Yeah. I suppose you're right," Jaime said turning away, feeling exposed like a freshly filleted tuna.

Mika and Beefcake stayed through the afternoon assisting Jaime until the last damaged display stood back at the ready. He took them to dinner for their efforts, although it took a while to find a restaurant undamaged from the quake and open. An Italian number, it turned out to be, though it tasted more like mediocre Lebanese. But a Chilean merlot and French syrah helped move the conversation along. Mika even answered more inquiry from Jaime to the static nature of her aging.

The Natural Anchovy History and Peruvian Culture Museum opened for all the next day. Jaime thought it might keep his mind from the coming unknown and Mika's forever young love canal. But scarcely a handful of visitors passed through the doors. It made for an especially long day and opportunity aplenty for Jaime's mind to wander.

He primarily pondered a point Mika raised the night before. She made mention of all the amazing, mind-boggling feathers in the cap of mankind, the ability of bio-chemical engineers to know which pharmaceutical compounds can alter a human brain and how, particularly in matters of psychotropic drugs, must rate near the finest. Yet, as clever as any anti-depressant or schizophrenic relieving pill may be, they all come with side effects, some mild and only temporary, others severe and life-long, either affecting only a small percentage of patients. This not knowing why certain side effects occur in some and not others and why they are this way rather than that in some and not others, must drive a truly caring chemist to popping their own medicine.

Thus are the masters of language and ideas, who comprise their words and philosophies so adroitly, so steeped in wisdom, as to change paths of mankind. Jesus, Mohammad, Buda, Confucius, for example. Yet, like their chemical expertise counterparts, these patricians of parables, these craftsman of the quill, these incubators of ideas eternal, seemingly also underestimate the power of will. Did Jesus know his message of love and tolerance would one day be the impetus of murderous crusaders, of gold lusting conquistadors? Did Mohammad envision the lunacy of militant jihadists, or the uber oppression against women? A fair wager might be made that they did not.

Give chemists credit. For at least they eventually recognize the need, or become placed in a legal stranglehold, to reconfigure the recipe, if not throw the whole thing away, bathwater, vats, baby, everything. Why is it then, that man holds onto words for so long, unwilling to cede even an inch? Could it be pride? Or just a simple case of not having anything more inspiring to replace it with.

The weekend passed slowly but uneventful. Jaime decided to just stay at the beach-side hotel, so much more serene than at the condo with all the clean-up and what-not still going on. Monday, likewise, came with a sense of excitement. He opened the museum at ten and kept a television in the office tuned to national news. Communication between himself and Sharla and Chris obviously could not occur. He wondered how soon before they would make their first communication?

By late that afternoon, he had his answer. All day the museum had nary a visitor–still too soon since the quake, he assumed. Yet just after four that afternoon, a slew of apparent patrons began filtering through the doors. But something wasn't right, Jaime thought. Too many were men. No one had children with them, and they didn't seem to really be taking interest in any display, or even the anchovy aquarium, attractive to the eye as it is.

Jaime felt to flee, but how? Chris and Sharla had the Land Rover. He couldn't just board a plane and leave. Then he noticed the same two plump-faced agents who had brought him in for questioning before. Something was definitely happening, he knew.

"Mr. Holbrook?" one of the round-faced men said.

"Yes," Jaime replied, like duh.

"You need to come with us again," his partner rattled.

"Ok."

Back in the white van enroot to he didn't know where, it suddenly occurred to Jaime. Of course they would come after him once the demand to free his father was made with the historical sword being offered as ransom. Mika had been wrong. If they had been able to put two and two together, then of course the government would connect the dots. Those telomere drugs were keeping her mind unwise.

All he could do is feign ignorance; pass it off as the work of some newly revised faction of the MRTA or something. The agents didn't have any actual evidence, Jaime guessed. What could there be? Electrical power had been knocked out the morning of the quake when they took the sword. There couldn't be any surveillance footage. Anyone who might have noticed when Chris exposed it wouldn't have known Chris to be able to identify him. Only because of his connection to his father did they take Jaime.

Once they began their questioning, he believed his speculation correct. They didn't possess any evidence. Not that they needed any to hold him, but unless he talked, they wouldn't know for sure. And so Jaime remained as quiet as a mouse about the cupboard, as a flower in bloom, as the moon setting beyond the breaking new day.

Agents, likewise, feigned intelligence; pretending to grow flustered, to being enraged, to having leverage beyond that neither he nor Adrian would see the free light of day again. But Jaime held tight. By midnight, the agents grew exhausted and left Jaime to the cold, rigid bed of iron within the holding cell. Ironically, Jaime slept like a kept prince, self-satisfied at his ability to keep tight-lipped and inspired by their lack of anything worthwhile.

The next day, like a play Jaime once longed to be a part of, the actors took the stage on cue, said their lines, performed their parts, rubbed their hands vertically along their faces in shows of disgruntled acrimony. Jaime, all the while, remained mum. He even added bits and pieces for affect; like he hoped whomever did have the sword because his father didn't deserve to be charged with treason, that maybe there were larger players involved here; ones who might do much more damage than swiping the sabre of José de Dean Martin.

"De San Martin, San Martin," an agent repeated in despair. "And it's a sword, not a sabre. A sabre is used for fencing. This is the fighting sword of José de San Martín."

"My bad," Jaime shrugged.

Close to three hundred miles to the east, northeast, Chris and Sharla broke camp and re-loaded the Land Rover. Convinced the government of Peru would somehow be able to trace calls from their mobile phone and track its location, Chris decided they should not stay more than a day and a night in the same spot. Sharla felt it couldn't hurt and actually enjoyed the journey and discovery.

Like a high-dollar call girl, rainforests rarely disappoint. Glimpses of spider monkeys and green leaf frogs were only dampened by dangling emerald bushmasters or sniveling capybaras. Sprawling sandbox trees rising more than two hundred feet stood like sentries, making Sharla feel humble yet somehow also free and secure.

After the fourth day of this routine, Chris and Sharla finally heard the mobile phone unit crackle with a response. It startled both of them, in fact, as they'd only placed outgoing calls to this point. The government of Peru does not bargain with terrorists, the man said with only a slight Peruvian accent. Your efforts are in vain. You will be found and brought to justice. That is all.

"Terrorists," Sharla scoffed. "We're not terrorists. Are we Chris?"

"Not really," he answered.

"But a little?"

"In a way, maybe. But don't let it bother you. They're just saying that to intimidate us. It's probably actually good. They must think we are more than we are. They wouldn't think of *us* as terrorists. We speak English, anyway."

"You're probably right," Sharla smiled, lightly.

Chris' butter melted when she did. It was all he could do to resist taking her into his arms and pressing his lips to hers. Their time together, alone in the jungle, on the move, outlaws, a duo, drew out the spark for Sharla he kept under wraps. He would never make the first move, he told himself time and again. He might not even act on the advance he still hoped Sharla would make. But it was

170

there. His attraction to her could not be denied.

He'd never been drawn to a girl not Native American. Dark hair, cinnamon skin, black eyes, these things had always appealed to his desire. But from the start, something about Sharla made him grow warm inside. Her humility, perhaps. The delicateness of her features, of her ways, of her voice. Yet she exuded strength and character, class and calmness. Stability.

"We'd better get a move on," Chris said gently.

Sharla nodded thusly. They began breaking down the tent without saying more. The game had just become reality.

Like an actor lacking empathy, or an aspiring painter without a nose for color, like a man in love with money who's always broke, or a slave to fashion with poor taste, like a womanizing misogynist or perfumer sans dramatic flair, Jaime agonized at the prospect of having poisoned all hope at freeing is father, Adrian Holbrook. They released Jaime from holding two days later. It would be two more weeks before he'd have even a chance to hear from Chris and, more importantly, Sharla.

Chapter 27

Also similar to a high-dollar call girl, the party in the rain forest never lasts for too long. And just as its name sake, the rains unleashed. A torrent began night to day, only briefly like a tuba player taking oxygen did heavy, cold rain cease, ten to fifteen minute lulls, before starting again into night. Luckily, the tent Chris set up withheld the onslaught so far, though they could feel rapid trails of water streaming beneath the plastic flooring. Condensation forming inside the tent provided drips of water splashing into collecting pools.

They couldn't shake the wetness or chill but so far had resisted using each other's bodies for warmth, although they had at last confessed that a plan B may be unavoidable. For the time being, conversation kept them at bay. But let it keep raining, Chris thought, and emergency protocol will take precedence.

What Chris liked most about the rain forest, he said, was lack of constant noise from machines in the background, both distant and nearby. In any populated city, even deep in a night there's always a low hum—a buzz of machines, computers, refrigerators, air conditioners, passing jet airplanes, diesel big rigs, mysterious waves of energy, he could not decide exactly of what, perhaps the ubiquitous flow of wireless information. In the jungle only the sounds of God are in play; be it rustling leaves in the wind to love songs of Nightingales, to screeching cries of prey.

"What I like is the purpose," Sharla added. "Whether it's a

praying mantis slowly devouring a leaf, or a string of black army ants bustling food to the nest, everything is focused on its purpose."

"Except for the sloth, maybe," Chris offered.

Sharla laughed. The rains, on the other hand, were completely serious. Chris didn't believe it could pour down much harder; fascists candidates were widely elected in early 20th-century Europe, too–strange happens. The drainage plumes beneath their tent grew wider and more forceful. Condensation pools inside the tent joined forces as one completely covering the floor. They thought to make a break for the Land Rover, but it held on to gravity by a split hair a hundred yards away uphill. They'd be drenched to the bone with shoes covered in mud by the time they could make it there, anyway. All they could do is wait.

The splatter of drops against the tent, against leaves and ground and everything were nearly like the swaying time piece of a hypnotist in jungle harmony–Count Basie jazz in a wetsuit. The longer Chris and Sharla rested their tongues, the more droopy their eyelids became. Before long, despite the wet chill and dampness of their clothes, they both fell asleep. That night they awoke simultaneously, both shivering. Instantly they shed their moist apparel and climbed into the warmth of each other. Their flesh could not resist for long and they succumb to temptation.

Back in Lima, Jaime hit the sack early, beat down to the morrow from anguish. Just as he drifted completely away an audio-nightmare seeped through the sheetrock, then came right into the bedroom. It sounded like a television from the neighboring room. Or was it radio? It sounded like television for a minute, then radio the next moment. He wanted to rap on the wall to signal his complaint, but temporal paralysis froze his intentions. The voice from the television or radio then morphed into that of a PA announcer, warning of martial law, to take cover; so real was the voice, Jaime became frightened to near terror. He desperately sought to move, at least from the bed so he could step to the window and discern it to be real or otherwise, but the paralysis continued to immobilize everything about him except the torment racing throughout his brain.

He could do nothing more but endure the hallucination, as he now felt it must be. He hoped so even more. The PA announcer stopped, but the radio began again. It sounded so real, the golden-voiced DJ, a slight crackle in the air. He tried to move again, to force himself to awaken. He twitched. Then again. He tugged at himself from within, but he couldn't budge even an inch. He tried harder. Finally, he broke free. He moved an arm only, at first. Then a leg. Then both feet moved to the floor and he went to the window–nothing. He moved to place an ear against the shared wall–nothing. It had been a nightmare. It made him think back on school, for some reason.

In middle school he had been placed in special educational classes for those not challenged by low IQs–higher functioning autistic children, mainly, or its offshoot, Asperger syndrome. He remembered one girl, in particular, whose disorder came with a side of Tourette syndrome. LaDonna would sporadically attempt to debate, if not downright discredit, even the most basic of lessons from teachers, lacing her diatribes with a host of unacceptable words. Inevitably her misplaced fucks and wayward cocksuckers would send the rest of the students into a myriad of vocal reactions, naturally somewhat abnormal as compared to the usual puerile knee-jerk commotion that takes place in conventional middle school classroom settings.

Tommy LaForge, for instance, would often begin rapidly circling about the room swiping anything and everything from desks, teachers or students. So while one teacher attempted to reign in LaDonna's filthy tongue, another would set out to gently tackle Tommy, who by Thanksgiving break became quite adept at throwing head-fakes to elude his would-be captor. Had Tommy possessed a little more speed and size, in fact, he might have become quite the high school running back. Ginny Fritz, during all this, typically would begin a bout of outrageous laughter; not so unusual except she would do this all the while following Tommy's debris trail, tossing discarded pens or pencils haphazardly into the air.

Later, once a calmness had been restored, a teacher would

almost always refer to Jaime's undisruptive behavior during the outbreak and question why other students could not follow this lead. Jaime only wondered to himself as he attempted to deflect the heap of dirty looks being cast his direction, why he had to be in there in the first place. The other students wanted to know, again, why he got a bigger desk and seat, too? Jaime adapted early on to less attention. He sought comfort in his plight being physical, in fact. But the experience to this night's struggle left in question his state of mental health. Perhaps life was beginning to overwhelm him to some degree.

Back in the jungle later that evening, a twinge of guilt settled over Chris and especially Sharla—like a blanket of molasses gradually enveloping their souls. They fell back asleep, more from physical weakness than romantic bliss. The next morning the rain finally stopped. Rising plumes of misty evaporation met columns of fresh sunlight filtering between the upper canopy of branch and leaf. It seemed divine.

"What we need are caapi vines," Chris said as they took in the beautiful scene.

"Caapi vines?" Sharla asked.

"And some chacruna leaves," Chris added. "To make yagé. We'll use it to clear our hearts of this guilt."

Sharla could only purse her lips in amazement at his forthright manner. What is yagé and wouldn't it be too muddy out there, she asked, feeling selfishly awkward for having done so? It would be, he agreed. But it would be for the next several days, too; so it could not be avoided. With that, he set out for his search, gingerly moving down the slope to where he might find a shallow marsh, habitat most favored by the Vine of Souls. Sharla quickly followed his lead, slipping along the soaked animal trail.

For more centuries than there are great Kinks songs (and to the true historian of rock music, during the Kinks' span of five decades, among their prolific catalogue of work, it is truly difficult to name more than a dozen of their numbers that are not pleasing to the ear) jungle shaman from north to south have been brewing various recipes of ayahuasca (yagé, as locals call it). Its psychedelic tryptamines allow a window on the soul to be revealed that remains otherwise covered in Tara plantation-styled drapes.

The caapi vines, yagé's key ingredient, can be a tricky find, however, as they thrive just above the surface of shallow marshes that cycle in and out of rain forests. Chris knew the previous torrential downpour episode would provide more than an adequate supply of the central ingredient; in fact, he worried it may have been too much and the sought after vines may be in a state of temporal baptism. Most jungleites employ a canoe to aid their searches. Chris thought they might just wade out into the water to recover the mind treasures.

As their hunt extended without yield into late morning, the virtual symphony of sound flowing at ease from the plethora of jungle song birds kept Chris and Sharla in awe. From ultra rapid eight-one/thirty-second-note progressions of the Kingfishers to the Mozart-like rhapsodies of the Nightingales, the realm of beautiful noises were seemingly endless.

Chris thought of the Greeks and their belief in the genesis of music deriving from the Mousai or Muses. Did song birds not exist in Greece, he scoffed? Was the isle of Cyprus bereft of Rufous-tailed Jacamars, or Guan, Curassow or Little Crakes? Surely they were not. How did they not attribute the inspiration for music from the effortless works of nature? Chris stopped for a moment to voice his query to Sharla.

"Those myths had been passed down as fact for so long," Sharla offered, "that maybe they just couldn't believe that everything didn't come from some god or another. They didn't feel they had a choice but to believe as such."

Smart to boot, Chris thought, but then turned away back in search of caapi vines, as he realized if he let this flame for Sharla grow much larger he would not be able to contain it or himself. He thought of Jaime, again. They wouldn't even be here if not for him. But on the other hand, he then contemplated, look at all he and Sharla were doing for Jaime—putting their own necks out on the line for him. He turned to look back at Sharla, as if maybe she might be having the same indecisions and could provide insight.

"Are we getting close, you think?" she asked, instead.

"I think so," he replied, but having no clue in reality.

Chris felt it a sign when minutes later they came upon another marsh and he spotted the white and pink flowers of the caapi vines. He should leave Sharla to Jaime.

"This is it," Chris said. "Jackpot."

They spent more than three hours dredging and hacking away until Chris felt they had enough for a healthy batch. They'd make enough for themselves for tomorrow afternoon, and have plenty left over to take back to Jaime. They'd need to make a trip to the high Siula Grande valley once back in Lima, Chris voiced, both to relieve the stress and as a means of hiding away. A gift of yagé to the Shaman and his people would be nice.

The haul back to their tent with their loot proved exhausting. They both stripped back down to underwear and fell asleep quickly, awaking only because of driving hunger pains a few hours later. Chris built a fire while Sharla retrieved more food from the Land Rover.

"This is about it," Sharla said, alluding to the food. "And if I don't get some dry clothes soon, I'm gonna get nasty. And I don't mean physical. Can we go back soon? Like tomorrow?"

"Can we give it one more day? I've got to brew these vines tonight and wanted us to spend tomorrow afternoon drinking some and everything."

"Okay," Sharla said. "But no more, right?"

"Day after tomorrow. Promise."

The food and night's rest alleviated most of Sharla's tension. Evaporation plumes of mist once again met the morning's rays of sun that mixed and blended in spectacular fashion. Thin rainbows flashed through prisms of miniscule droplets, lasting only seconds in any one location before appearing again a few feet or yards away. She wished she had a video recorder, like Jaime's. She missed him now more than at any time during their separation, but a sense of dread spoiled the feeling. A lie waited at-hand. She had been so upset with him for simply withholding information and now this!

Chris stepped outside the tent, also immediately captured by the beauty of the scene. Sharla liked Chris, too. He wasn't really to blame. And she certainly didn't know that circumstances would lead to what happened. Maybe Jaime would understand? Maybe truth *would* work better. She needed more time to decide. She was glad now that Chris had wanted to wait another day.

"So it's ready?" Sharla asked.

"I think so," Chris answered. "Let's wait a little while. Let our energies get going a little first, ya know."

Chris stirred the coals from the fire from last night. He retrieved more wood from inside the tent. Sharla didn't realize he had stored some in there. The new wood began to smoke, shortly, then crackled and popped. In a few more minutes a warmth began to emit from flames. Sharla moved closer to it, absorbing as much heat as she could.

"Thanks for getting the fire back going," she said, smiling lightly but careful to only make eye contact with him for a second.

"It's no problem," Chris replied, sensing her discomfort. "You know, you're right. The yagé can wait. Let's get back. I'm ready for some dry clothes, too. And some good food."

Sharla's face lit up.

"Are you sure you don't mind?" she asked sincerely.

"Absolutely," he responded. How could he not?

They broke down camp and loaded for Lima in a matter of minutes. Spirits were lifted. Heat from the Land Rover's air system felt like a sauna. Once out of the forest and back onto paved roads, Sharla broached the elephant in the vehicle. Although she felt it might be okay to let it go without a word, speaking of it could bring about a sort of closure. It should remain a secret, she said. It was only a product of circumstance and the truth would only serve to alleviate their own guilt. It would crush Jaime—concerning both her and Chris. He agreed, but a spell of sadness still replaced the deflated elephant. Chris pulled the Land Rover to the shoulder.

"What's wrong?" Sharla asked.

"Nothing. I think we should make one more call before we get any closer back to Lima. It's why we came out here in the first place," he said, moving to the rear hatch to uncover the mobile phone system buried beneath the tent and gear.

He dialed the number to the main office of the National Police of Peru, its version of the F.B.I. A secretary answered. Chris began immediately.

"The sword of José de San Martin will only be returned to the people of Peru once Adrian Holbrook's freedom is granted and guaranteed. Repeat, the sword of José de San Martin will only be returned upon the release of Adrian Holbrook."

"You know," Chris said to Sharla once he reburied the phone and climbed back behind the Land Rover's steering wheel. "It feels good to fight the man. I could get used to this."

He had a sparkle in his eyes, Sharla noticed, like Jaime had had at the bar when they first watched the TV report about the missing sword. Men are born to be warriors, she thought. No wonder wars never seem to end around the world. The drive back to Lima turned out to be cathartic. A sense of normalcy seemed to return. Sharla felt the secret between her and Chris would be safe. By the time they made it back to their condo, she felt the secret of their mobile phone transmissions also would be secure.

Upon sight of Jaime, though, Sharla instantly felt something amiss. Her stomach turned. Her throat tightened. She felt nervous and guilt flared from her bile. He barely said hello and they didn't kiss until a minute passed. When he started to explain that he had been detained, however, she thought it might only be that. But it felt like more. Then he eyed her awkwardly, and she knew he had suspicions.

"Where's the sword?" Jaime asked Chris.

"In the back of the Land Rover."

"We've got to do something with it, quickly. Like right now," he demanded.

"Let's go to the high valley," Chris said. "The sword will be safe there, and I've got yagé. We need to visit Shaman Dondito."

"All of us?" Jaime questioned.

They exchanged looks.

"I'll stay here this time," Sharla said, sensing a perfect moment to remove herself from both Chris and Jaime. "The museum needs to remain open. Right?"

"I think so," Jaime readily agreed.

"Okay," Chris said. "Maybe Mika and Eduardo should come with us, though. She'd love it."

Jaime nodded thusly. Sharla now felt certain that Jaime harbored doubts. He agreed too quickly for her to stay behind, and how would he know Mika would love the mountain? What could she do, though? It wasn't his fault, obviously. More time apart could be good.

Mika said she was free and definitely wanted to make the trip up the mountains to visit a shaman. Eduardo had gone back to Brazil, though, to visit his family. A devious twinge floated around Jaime's brain upon hearing Mika would not be accompanied by Beefcake. Perhaps limiting love to one person is unfair. Or maybe he's just greedy?

With the Land Rover already mostly packed from Chris and Sharla's trip into the jungle, Jaime, Mika and Chris set out that evening for Siula Grande. They could make camp before dark and be at the trading post by noon the next day. Mika wanted Chris to dip into the yagé that night at camp, but he insisted they wait until they could all partake with the shaman and villagers. She said they could just have a taste, but Chris wouldn't budge.

They awoke early the next morning. When they arrived just after noon at the trading post, mules were available immediately. They loaded down three. Chris would serve as guide this trip.

Chapter 28

Jaime and Mika hiked in awe. Particularly Mika, who outside a visit to Scotland in her youth, never had experienced such rugged terrain. Everything enthralled her–the red-yellow mountain tundra, snow-melt rivulets, just the crispness of clean air. Chris found satisfaction in watching the interplay between Jaime and Mika. Their open fondness for one another and flirtatious frolic eased his guilt like cold cream to a burn.

Nights proved even more enchanting. As a young child's mouth waters in anticipation as he waits in line for ice cream while other kids all around the parlor tongue theirs, Jaime's veiled lust for Mika could not be contained. Chris and he competed with stories of the starlit sky to capture her attention, but Jaime could not hold a candle to Chris' near lecture of the Southern Cross. As with great shaman through all the many years before, Chris set his aim on the cross. Wisdom of a thousand centuries lie at its feet, he told Mika. Mayan gods share star-drenched baths at its door steps. With the aide of Shaman Dondito and the yagé, it should only be a matter of time before his spirit might return for a moment. Jaime tried to move the conversation to Orion or Gemini or Leo, but Mika already grew weary of their overt attempts at charm and charisma.

"So, Chris, when you say your aim is to soar the lengths of the Southern Cross, how does that work, exactly?" Mika asked, unabashed. "I mean, if your spirit is way out there, what's happening during all this back here? With your being still here? Let alone you're getting there."

"That *is* transcendence," he quickly responded. "It's the oneness of the universe; of everything."

"It's not how far, after all," Jaime added, sensing Mika's displeasure in their competition. "It's how near."

"How near?" Mika scoffed.

"Absolutely," Chris weighed in, returning favor.

"What in God's name are you two talking about?" Mika let out, a hint of betrayal in her tone.

She remained skeptical, at best, after mostly Chris explained his notion of the relativity of the distance of stars. She especially felt more confident in her doubt after noting aloud how enormous the distance between stars nearer to earth are to those not. Undeterred, Chris continued that that is the point. From the Milky Way to which ever direction, the misconception lies in man's insistence that these distances are so great.

What Mika fails to consider, he attempted to convey, minus a cosmic piety he did not realize came across, is that time cannot be a factor in this equation. Not until one becomes able to disregard the trap of time may they begin to comprehend the true proximity of even the most distant stars. At least within our own galaxy, he allowed himself a caveat.

"I don't know. Maybe so?" Mika retreated, beat down by their persistence.

"Only time will tell," Jaime made lightly.

And it worked. They all gently chuckled and lie back to gaze in silence. The vastness soon soothed their thoughts to ease. The next morning, they awoke as if anew, eager to reach their destination and put it all to test. Their desire to be there waxed and waned as the journey reached its fifth day, but that night before their final leg, the anticipation coupled with high altitude, made for a fine evening. They laughed more than debated and took turns expressing gratitude—a practice Chris said would ready their spirits for travel the next twilight.

Jaime said he felt most grateful for his friendships with them and Sharla. He never made close friends with anyone before them, he said. Chris, not wanting to duplicate Jaime, offered having found Shaman Dondito. He suggested they'd understand better in a few days. Mika, momentarily stumped, came up with The Ramones. Chris could not contain his contempt for her choice.

"It's the influence of my life, smart ass," Mika belted. "You shouldn't be so quick to judge, red man."

Chris quickly agreed and apologized. It just caught him by surprise, he pleaded. Mika accepted and said she understood.

"It's hard to express the desperation you feel, sometimes, on the road," Jaime blurted out, catching Chris and Mika off guard. They thought the moment already had passed. "When you've been alone for several days and you haven't talked with anyone you know for several months. It really puts you on edge. Everyone's against you. Everything is against you."

He paused as if a memory of something suddenly became too strong and he had to snuff it out. Moments later he looked at Mika and Chris to gauge the sincerity of their interest. Satisfied, he continued.

"You feel like you'd be capable of anything, if pushed just one more inch or the wrong direction. Especially if it's hot and you haven't been able to shower since whenever. You feel like an animal–a wild animal."

"Once, I set to cross a great stretch of desert during the summer," Chris offered, sensing Jaime's frustration. "Not a desert like you might think, just sand, but a high plains desert, like you find near Pueblo south of the range. They can be just as dry, though. And it had been a very dry summer, that year. So I had run low of water. Poor planning on my part. I noticed the mule behind my horse started to give me that look. A real look, you know. Of life...existence. I knew the horse felt the same. It actually helped me focus. Determined, I found an old cow-feed trough. And luckily, or so I thought, it had some water in the bottom still not evaporated from the last rain–however long that had been.

"I tied the horse up, so to let the mule drink first. As I started to lead him to it, he tried to break free, to race to it. But I held him back, just in time, he pulled so hard. As I held him, I bent my head into the trough and my lips were just to the surface, and just before I went to drink, I stopped. I didn't even know why for a split second, but then I really looked at the water for the first time. It looked like barely warm, unstirred chicken broth. I looked back at the mule. He had quit pulling, waiting on me. I felt honor, more than a warrior in the battlefield. I turned and put my rear beneath the trough and my back against it, but could not tip it over. So I walked the mule back to where I had the horse tied off and tied him too, this time. I used my hands to splash most of the water out of the trough. When we rode away, the mule stopped to smell where the ground had just gotten wet. As he inspected its smell, I looked at him. His left eye rolled up to look at me, only moving his snout a fraction. As he lifted up, he then looked at me briefly. In that look I could see that he knew I loved him. I had saved him from the bad water. Geronimo," Chris smiled with his eyes. "His name was Geronimo. From that day forward something changed in him. He trusted me explicitly from then on. Animals know love. In that regard they are part of us. Vegans may be on to something, I think, sometimes."

Jaime froze, started to speak, but stopped again. Then he couldn't refrain.

"Did you say vegans might be on to something?"

Chris nodded so.

"I..." Jaime shook his head. "If I could only tell you."

"If you could only tell us what?" Mika interjected.

"Oh...hmmf. If I could," Jaime repeated.

"You just said before that we're good friends. If you can't tell good friends...?" Mika challenged.

But the tone of her dare destroyed Jaime's momentum. They waited for him to confess, but nothing came. Mika tried to empathize with Jaime's bad experience of being on the road, but her effort fell flat and they soon nodded off for the night. By the next morning it felt like waking up as kids on Christmas. Magical feelings lie just ahead. They reached the lower village early. Chris introduced Jaime and Mika before presenting more gifts of rice, wine and spices. Chris wanted to save the yagé as a surprise for later.

Shaman Dondito, noticing the abundance of activity, came down from on high to the lower village. He had not paid visit in many months. As such, an extra element of excitement spread about the villagers, and their level of curiosity rose about Chris-the North American Indian whose presence seemed to virtually summon the high priest.

After lunch, song and dance quickly erupted. Chris had not told Mika of the villagers musical proclivities. He watched her closely to see her reaction, but she didn't seem to notice or care how awful they sang. Punk musicians don't have the refinement, he quickly decided.

As the afternoon began giving way to the coming of nightfall, Chris sought Shaman Dondito to inform him of the gift not yet revealed. Demure should never be an adjective used to describe a shaman, so let's just say he didn't over react to the prospect of yagé. Likewise, it must be noted, he did not reject the premise, either. Chris asked Dondito if it might be possible for he, Mika and Jaime to experience together a session, as it were, with him. He expressed no qualms with this, as well.

So as the last remnants of sunlight shone just over the jagged horizon, Shaman Dondito led the three up the mountain to be on high. He moved remarkably well for a man of his age, Chris thought. He whispered as such to Jaime, who instantly acknowledge as much, feeling his own shortness of breath leaving him fatigued. Mika strode along quite smoothly. Jaime thought it might be so because of her telomere drugs.

As they reached on high, Shaman Dondito first led Chris to a pile of wood. Soon they had a perfect fire-large enough to emit heat and capture the stare, yet small enough that they could gather around it tightly, able to grasp hands as Dondito began lightly reciting his ceremonial verses. After a few minutes, Dondito unclenched hands to be able to take hold of the wooden cup filled with yagé. He drank first, then passed it to Mika. A bitterness from the roots caused Mika to cough reflexively. Jaime did the same. Chris consumed his bit without a sound.

Dondito next held a crystal out above the fire, brought it to his forehead, and then passed it to Mika. She simply held it at first, unsure what the Shaman intended her to do. He folded his hands over her one holding the crystal, gently shook it, then handed the button of jade to her and motioned toward Jaime. Mika passed the crystal to Jaime. He held it awkwardly. She replaced it with the jade. Dondito cupped Mika's single hand, again, momentarily, then nodded toward Jaime. Slowly, the crystal and jade completed the circle.

Dondito had them clench hands once more as he began citing more ceremonial verses, his intensity increasing. Jaime felt a sensation fire in his brain, like a neurological sneeze. He felt light in the head and body, cleansed. The sensation of holding hands nearly disappeared. Mika's mind became more akin to a feather, gently being lifted by a breeze somehow coming up from beneath them. A golden light, like filtered through stained glass, began to focus in the center of her perception, though her eyes were completely closed.

Chris's soul left its mooring. As it began to soar, a thousand points of light once again fielded his flight. And again the speed of his ascension increased to the brink of light itself. Just as suddenly, it came to rest. A path outlined in traces of green and red lights came into view. He moved nearer to the path. It seemed as an outline of a staircase leading up. Somehow he felt himself drifting, as if with the lights. Then he settled at the base of the phantom stairs while a procession of souls made their way down, pausing briefly as if to greet Chris, or exchange a quick word, not spoken but still in communication of some sort.

They were the souls of traveled men of the past, some of more recent days, others of long ago–healers and warriors, shaman and teachers, martyrs, poets, mystics and great chiefs. Chris' spirit felt awash in pureness, in truth, filled with light, even joy. After the last one passed, traces of red and green light vanished blurrily. Chris began to move again, but slowly, delicately afloat.

The golden light in Mika's mind became more in focus, now. It appeared as a circle of thick, leaded glass. The light came from beyond, its color a bright yellow, made more golden in nature passing through the glass. It seemed as a sanctuary. She felt enclosed, yet the perception only came from what would be in front of her. She also sensed not being alone, but could not distinguish what other presence might be. Everyone, whomever it was, had come there for the same reason—peace. A peace like she had never experienced; content but easy and beautiful, completely absent of anything else. No one felt to leave.

A single source of light filled Jaime's sense, somewhat dim and distant, yet its mass somehow made if feel near; close enough to touch, almost, it seemed. The perception bewildered him. The deeper he attempted to understand, however, the more it felt both near and far. A sense of warmth then came over him—not a source of heat, rather a sea of security that enveloped his being. The sea was everything. A senata in Bliss major. The light was everything. It's what allowed for the contradiction of it being both something within reach and something infinitely away. It was out there, yet he was somehow right next to it.

Mika's vision of golden light became so powerful, it rendered her unconscious. When she came back to, the streams of gold began to retreat. Seconds later, they were gone, but a sense of the peace remained. Not nearly as strong, yet even that that was still with her felt significant. The journey seemed at its end, so she opened her eyes. Shaman Dondito's eyes were lightly shut, though his chanting continued, softly. She felt light in weight.

Jaime opened his eyes. He noticed Mika. A slight smile formed across her face. Dondito stopped speaking and opened his eyes. He passed something to Mika. Jaime couldn't make out what it was. Then Dondito reached across the fire to hand something to him. The claw of a bear. Jaime used both hands to examine its strength. He admired the symmetry of the claw's curve, and how it tapered from base to point.

Chris now opened his eyes. No one spoke. Shaman Dondito handed something to Chris—also a claw, but smaller than that of a bear. A wolf, perhaps. The effects of the yagé were now in full swing. For many minutes the four of them remained silent around the fire, as if spiritually digesting all they had taken in. Flames from the fire turned to a red-orange glow of coals. At last, Chris stood but still without word. He then simply walked a few yards away and laid on his back.

Jaime wanted to do the same, but he stayed to see what Mika would do. She stood after a brief moment and walked a few yards another direction and also laid down, face up. Jaime now turned his attention to Shaman Dondito. Surely he wouldn't do the same, Jaime thought. And he didn't. He remained seated at the foot of the fire, as if he had always been right there and would be so forever. Jaime could not stop watching him. He liked how the glow from the coals under lit his face. His features reminded him of Sharla, but in a masculine form and aged.

Jaime's knees began to ache from being seated cross-legged for so long. So he moved to stretch out on a side, his head propped up by his hand above an elbow on the ground. An energy swam around his brain, yet it didn't make him anxious, just blissful, quiet and still inside. Chris and Mika must be feeling the same, he thought, as they remained on their backs several yards away. And Dondito, too. The night went on this way for the next hour or more, then the next thing Jaime knew, Shaman Dondito was placing a blanket over him. Morning came next.

Apparently Chris and Mika had moved during the night to also sleep near the fire, Jaime noticed as he opened his eyes, feeling as if a morning fog had settled in his head. Only Dondito wasn't there. He must have gone inside his tent, he guessed. A pain of hunger pinched inside his stomach. He rustled up from the ground and poked the fire to stir Mika and Chris.

Shortly, after thanking Shaman Dondito, the three began back down the mountain. They had apples waiting for them in their food supply. Chris left the remaining batch of yagé with Dondito as a token of their appreciation. Sharing their stories from the night before, it seemed like nothing before they reached the village. They didn't evoke a commotion among the villagers this morning, though. Chores were being performed, so only a glance or two occurred at their return. A few children scampered about four women circled around a bed of coals, which they were using to cook flat bread.

"Wait!" Chris broke the serenity of the scene. "Is that...?"

"What?" Jaime looked the direction Chris pointed. "Is it?"

"Hey, no!" Jaime shouted, moving swiftly toward two boys several yards away. The sword of José de San Martin was being hoisted by one. Jaime quickly raced to the pair and retrieved the bounty. "Where did you get this?" he asked in vain. They did not speak English. Jaime attempted to repeat his question in Spanish, but his tone had frightened the boys and they escaped to their mother's sides.

"Let's get going," Jaime said as he returned with the sword to Chris and Mika.

"Don't worry," Mika said. "They don't know anything about it."

"Still," Jaime lamented. "We've got to be safe."

He slid the sword back between blankets tied to the side of one of the mules.

"Well, we were going back now, anyway," Chris said to Jaime.

A few of the village men, noticing the three packing down the mules to leave, stopped their work and came to exchange good-byes. Jaime thought to question them about the boy having the sword, but decided it might only exacerbate the situation. Everything seemed sincere, otherwise. So they departed. Soon, Jaime raised the question: What to do with the sword?

After lengthy discussion, lasting well into the afternoon, the three agreed that the sword should be hidden away until it might be of use. The next day they chose a spot near a stream Chris said they'd be parallel to for much of the remaining way down. A large tree trunk felled by storm or man or disease rested just into the water's edge with the bulk of its some thirty feet lying at forty-five degrees upon the rocky bank. At its highest point Chris used the small pack shovel they carried to dig a shallow trough. Any farther down the bank would be too close to the river that surely encounters flash floods from time to time and might allow the sword to be washed away.

Here will be safe, Chris said. The tree with its age suggesting it hadn't moved in many years, could serve as their marker if and when the need to retrieve the sword occurs. Jaime agreed but felt hesitant to leave. He suddenly wished he had handled the sword more, had examined it more closely, as if a lover walking out the door for what will most likely be the last time. He wanted one more touch. One more look at its beauty.

"It'll be alright," Mika said, sensing his apprehension.

"Let's hope so," Jaime almost whispered, turning to continue on their way.

They made it to the trading post by late that afternoon, returning the mules and picking up another day's worth of food and water. It was here, waiting for Chris to settle payment inside, as Mika and Jaime sat on a bench that he thought he noticed something different about Mika. He began looking more closely at the profile of her face, but only for a few seconds. He didn't want her to detect his inspection. Chris then came out and Mika stood. Jaime's curiosity would have to resume later.

They hiked another hour before making camp for the night, but the light was already too dim for Jaime to see clearly enough at Mika. The next morning he waited for the right moment, then went next to her and asked anything. Did she sleep well? Had she noticed the moon last night? It was oblong and the dark craters really made it look like a face. Was she looking forward to getting back to Lima? To Beefcake? Although he didn't refer to him as such. And as he continued his ruse of random questions, Jaime continued to examine all about her face as nonchalantly as possible.

"What are you doing?" Mika finally asked, sensing something askew with Jaime's presence.

"What? Me? Nothing," he said, turning away innocently, feeling the answer to his query satisfied.

What Jaime sought within the contours of Mika's face was a sign of age. Not just a simple signal, but that of rapid aging having taken place. Maybe it had been all the sun they'd absorbed in the course of the last week. They were all tanner. But it was something more, he thought. He wanted to wait until back to Lima, though. He wanted to wait to see if Sharla would notice. Having not seen Mika for a while, she'd best detect any discernible difference.

When they returned to Lima that afternoon, the expression on

Sharla's face let Jaime know he'd been right. Mika had aged dramatically. Had she not taken her telomere drugs with her on the trip? Was it the altitude? Shaman Dondito? The yagé? Mika asked for a ride home. Jaime quickly offered for Sharla to do so. He wanted her to have even more time next to Mika.

"So, notice anything unusual?" Jaime asked as Sharla walked back in from taking Mika.

"What, am I blind? What's going on?" Sharla agreed.

"I'm not sure," Jaime said. "Did she say anything?"

"No. Has she seen herself since you guys left? She probably hasn't. I bet she's going in shock as we speak," Sharla said.

Indeed, having shortly gone to a hot shower upon her arrival back home, Mika finished rubbing a towel about her head before wrapping it around her freshly-clean body. As she stood in the mirror for the first time since their journey to Shaman Dondito, the reflection of her image forced a long pause. Her fingers next went in for inspection.

"Eduardo," Mika then hollered.

"Do you see it, too?" she asked as he walked into their bedroom.

"See what?" he replied, sincerely.

"Here! Come here," she cried, moving back into the bathroom and more light.

His silence confirmed her fear.

"Did you forget...?"

"No, that's not it. I took them. Just like always," she answered.

"Then what?" he said.

"I don't know. Oh my God. What's going on?" she cried.

Lines that had not been there only a week before extended out from both eyes. Creases crossed along her forehead. More lines spanned the tops of her cheeks. Her face as a whole seemed to have dropped, only slightly, but it did now seem to sag, particularly below her jaw into her neck. Small lines fanned up from her upper lip and down from her lower one. She let the towel drop to the bathroom floor. Her breasts did not sit as high; the skin across them was not as tout as before.

"Are you seeing this?" she asked Beefcake.

He hesitated to reply. She asked again. He shrugged his shoulders.

"Mas y menos. No se," he then offered before retreating to the safety of the living room.

But she didn't need his observation to know. Something was wrong. Something truly was extremely wrong. She had aged twenty years in two weeks.

Chapter 29

A team comprised of doctors and officials, agents and special officers, even a psychiatrist, flew to Lima. It would have been much cheaper, naturally, for Mika to have flown to them, but they did not want to take any more chances. Perhaps it *had* been the altitude, they cautioned, as she had related to her handler that the break in her not-aging began upon returning from their journey up the Sinola mountains. So as the various men and women poured over Mika's many tests, Sharla revealed to Jaime what she had avoided saying until after his first night back, having wanted one last night with him unencumbered. Chris had even taken a sleeping bag to the museum for the night to give them time alone. She knew once she let this cat out of the bag, it might be sometime before calmness returns, or at least a night anxiety free. Purr.

"We need to leave," Sharla began. "Like, soon. This morning."

"Why? What's going on?" Jaime naturally questioned.

"I don't wanna tell you. Not now. You just have to trust me," she begged. "You do trust me? Don't you?"

"Yes, of course," he said. "But what is it? Why can't you tell me?"

"I just can't," she insisted. "Not yet. I will, okay. But for now, we have to get ready to leave."

Jaime did not know exactly how to react. He wanted to trust her. He did trust her, but this was almost more, somehow. He sat down on the couch. She sat next to him a minute later, running her thin fingers through the back of his hair. He loved it when she did this. Such a simple thing, yet it felt almost magical, somehow. He felt selfish, even, as she continued, for not doing something in return. Ideas of what that could be ran ballyhoo about his brain.

"Where will we go?" he asked, his mind ripe with erotica.

"It doesn't matter," she answered. "We've just got to get out of here."

"But what about my dad?"

"We'll keep working on that. I'm not saying to give up on that. But if we want to be able to continue trying that, we've got to get out of here. Please trust me," she implored, again, not noticing that look in his eye.

"Okay," he replied after a short time, his sexual fever residing mostly.

Thus, they began to load the Land Rover once again. It really wasn't too much—some clothes and what-nots, a portable stereo, a few nicknacks they had collected in Lima. The furniture all had been rented. They packed Chris' few items, as well. Sharla suggested they just pick him up at the museum on the way out.

"And what of the museum?" Jaime wanted to know.

"It'll have to take a leave of absence, for now. It's the least of our worries, really," Sharla pelted. "That's everything, right?"

Jaime asked her to wait in the car while he gave the condo one last look-over. As he walked through, he already felt he was going to miss it all, but it also felt right to be going. Maybe Sharla did know best. The situation with his father might get even stickier if they didn't leave. So this is it for Lima, he thought, closing the condo door. The street meats on a stick, the many varieties of ceviche, care-free beaches, tortora boats, derby hats, Ms. Sanchita. All no more. Chris didn't act surprised when they picked him up and told him of the plan to leave Peru. Maybe he and Sharla were simply home-sick, Jaime thought. Maybe they had hatched this plan to leave, together? He attempted to get more out of Sharla, but she said to wait until they made it for a few hours. What could that matter, Jaime wondered?

Less than a few hours later, though, he didn't need Sharla to confess her reason for wanting them to flee so suddenly. A pair of

LTD cruisers seemed to be tailing them. Jaime put the possibility to test by stopping along the shoulder of highway 22. The cruisers passed, but when Jaime started out again minutes later, the same two were back behind them within five minutes. Where had the hid?

"So they came to the museum, didn't they?" Jaime said, turning to Sharla in the passenger seat.

"From the time it opened, almost, 'til the time it closed," she confirmed.

"What do you think, Chris? Are they just escorting us out of the country, or will the border be sealed?" Jaime pondered, eyeing Chris in the rearview.

"I doubt they'd be going to this trouble just to see us out."

"Ideas?"

"We've got four-wheel drive. They don't," Chris offered.

Jaime turned again to Sharla.

"If we just take it easy, then we can always say we were just going to see the jungle," she posed.

Jaime thought back once again to his exploits in Kettle County. A certain pleasure, one filled of adrenalin and outlaw rebellion, comes with being on the lamb. But sols did not abound, then. He shouldn't have to run this time. He didn't want to drag Sharla and Chris down with him, either. Why don't they object? Of course, home's not exactly around the next block.

"You're really up to it?" Jaime asked Sharla. "And you too?" he looked back at Chris, the LTDs in his peripheral.

"I mean, what can they really charge us with?" Sharla said.

"This is South America, Sharla," Jaime shot back. "Who says they need anything? They just do it."

"Well, if that's true, then we really don't have a choice, do we. I mean, if they're going to do that anyway, then we really do have to get out of here. I think Chris is right," she said. "The jungle is our best bet. We've got to make it to Brazil."

And thus, dear readers, the chase began. For the moment, however, pursuit would be more apropos. Sticking with the plan, Jaime kept the vehicle near the speed limit. Even after taking highway 18 east, he didn't put the pedal to the floor. To the casual observer, none of the hallmarks of a chase could be detected. Tension built just the same.

In Hyánuco they stopped for gas. The two cruisers passed them by again, so Jaime also filled the portable tank equipped as standard on the Land Rover Adventure series. They loaded up with candy bars and bottles of water and a few more junk food snacks. After the split on to 18A toward Tingo Maria, the cruisers returned. There could be no doubt as to their being followed; only to what end?

At Tingo Maria, they caught the 5 north, then hit 18C back east toward Pucallpa. At some point they'd have to cross the Ucayali River. But where? The farther down the east side of the range, the more desolate the terrain appeared. The cruisers kept their distance, but remained behind them.

"There!" Chris shouted.

A side road, hardly visible but there all the same, veered south. Jaime braked hard to make the turn. The road quickly became nothing more than shallow ruts. Jaime dropped the Rover into 4-wheel drive. They were descending the last remnants of the eastern front of the Sinolas. Soon they'd hit the outer edges of the rain forest. Jaime worried if they'd be able to continue at that point. They appeared to have lost the cruisers, though. Jaime stopped and rolled the windows down so they could listen. Nothing. A few minutes later they continued on. The Ucayali stopped them a few miles later.

"Now what?" Jaime sighed, as they all gazed at the slow, flat river for a minute.

"Maybe it's shallow enough, we could cross it...?" Sharla softly suggested.

"Only one way to find out," Chris agreed, stepping out to venture in.

He made it one step knee deep, then it came to his waist. He shook his head and retreated back to the bank.

"I don't want to go back," Jaime pleaded.

The three contemplated what next? After a short while, Sharla spoke again.

"Could we float it across?"

"Maybe," Chris answered. "But even so. What's on the other side? Do you see a trail? You see how thick it's going to be on that side."

Silence ensued until Jaime's frustration boiled over.

"We're not going back! Agreed?"

Chris and Sharla exchanged a quick glance, then nodded so, though only slightly.

"So we've got to float it across. We can do it. There's plenty of lumber here. We build a raft. Then Chris and I will go across until we find a trail, we come back, float the Rover across and we're on our way. It's our only choice."

After the initial stun wore off, they set out to begin gathering fallen sections of trees, trunks and larger branches. Within a few hours, they had enough to start hacking away at the pieces to try and make them as straight as possible and begin puzzling them together to fasten. Chris' small but sturdy tomahawk saved the day, and he had rope aplenty left over from treks up the Sinola. Another three hours later, as they tied off the last pieces of their make-shift uni-vehicle ferry, Sharla let loose a laugh.

"This is just greatness," she said. "The sight of it all. I'm going to write a book when we get back."

"If we get back," Jaime mumbled.

"We have to," Sharla insisted. "Right, Chris?"

But he only looked at her blankly. Then at Jaime. Then he told Jaime to back the Rover to the river's edge so they could tie off on the rear hitch to string a rope behind them when they crossed. They pushed half the raft into the river, then stepped on as the rest went into the slow current, and it carried the raft north as soon as it began to float. Chris and Jaime used long, slender pieces of timber pushing along the river's bottom to guide them across. Fortunately, it only ran six or seven feet deep in the middle. Maintaining balance on the raft proved most difficult.

They reached the other side in little time. The bend of the current caused it to be shallower along this bank, which made it

197

easier to drag the raft out. Finding a trail for the vehicle would require far more luck. They headed north, thinking the current would be pushing them that direction anyway. To their astonishment, in less than half a mile they discovered a way. Perhaps a loggers' trail, the path was well worn, though by the looks of grass and weeds growing in the tire paths, it hadn't been used in some time. Nevertheless, it felt like a small miracle.

Using the rope they had tied off, they pulled themselves back across to Sharla. Once there they decided it was nearing too soon to dark and would be best to camp for the night and make a fresh start of it in the morning. Agreed, they gathered more wood for a fire for the night and Chris revealed a stash of yagé he had set aside for special occasion. Tonight should be it, he said, because a new unknown lay ahead. The yagé brew could clear their consciences for the future.

"You know, it'll be my first time," Sharla reminded Chris.

He flinched inside a little, thinking back on he and Sharla in the jungle. "You'll find it rewarding, I'm sure," he said, careful not to look toward Jaime, afraid he might be eyeing him with suspicion.

Such thoughts of betrayal did not scratch the surface of Jaime's mind this early evening, though. His brain focused instead on Sharla's mention of writing a book about it all. He imagined who would play himself in the movie version. Johnny Depp came to mind first, but it wasn't a good fit, truth be had. Jaime's face was too round. His legs weren't skinny enough. And there's the age difference. Too bad Depp hadn't met Mika's telomere scientist years before, he laughed inside.

Chris passed a Gatorade bottle filled with yagé to Sharla. She coughed as she swallowed the first drink. Chris assured her most people did so and to not worry, it wouldn't hurt her. She didn't look too confident, but took another swig just the same and turned to pass it to Jaime.

"Not tonight," he stopped her instead.

"Well, I don't want to do it alone," she cried.

"Not to worry," Chris let out.

Jaime wished Antonio Banderas could be made to look younger.

He couldn't think of one actor his own age. Chris poured a gulp of yagé down and tried to hand the plastic container back to Sharla, but she raised her hand, no mas. Chris took another swig and put the cap back on. The stars shone in full glory. Jaime wondered if Chris's spirit would make its way to the Southern Cross once more, or might it seek a new source of inspiration?

The day's excitement left them spent. No one spoke. Each seemed content in their own contemplations. Within thirty minutes, in fact, the yagé's affects left Sharla in a deep sleep. She dreamt vividly, though, of life after death. Her spirit took the shape of her old physical self, but in spirit only just the same. The image simply allowed recognition. She traversed along a high mountain ridge that intersected seemingly countless other ridgelines. As she moved along this way, she encountered loved ones from her life–family and friends, and lovers too, though she'd only known a few to this point. Everyone else was doing the same.

Because time was of no consequence, each visit could last as long as desired. Love in its purest form embraced all. Nothing negative remained. A girlfriend from her childhood who had moved away appeared. Sharla knew the girl to still be alive, like herself, and it gave her an overwhelming sense of the dream being more than a dream; more a vision of the future. Her first love then appeared from somewhere. They exchanged words, though Sharla could not discern within the dream what they said, only that it was pleasant and fond. After what felt like a long period, yet timeless also, her father stood before her. They cried, as if for a longing finally being quenched. The vision ended shortly after this, however, as though enough had been revealed and to allow any more would spoil the reality of what will be. It left Sharla enthralled to the possibilities of what's to come and at peace with life, overall–and with a deeper meaning of existence–of eternity.

Already exhausted from the afternoon's agenda, the yagé sank Chris like Miss Delaware's hopes halfway through every Miss America Pageant. Instead of soaring the outer limits of the Milky Way, he too dreamt madly–a rollicking scene of Amazon tribesmen leaping out of trees to ambush the three of them. Little could he know during the vision just how ominous it would be.

They awoke with the sun, hungry and especially thirsty for Sharla and Chris. They wolfed down two candy bars each, wanting to save the rest for rations later, and the same for bottles of water. The prospect of the task at-hand, floating the Land Rover across the Ucayali, left them uneager to get going. Chris broke the spell by suggesting they add additional timber to the four corners of the raft to help with balance and provide more buoyancy.

"This ain't gonna be easy," Chris stated the obvious.

Within an hour they fastened six-foot pieces of timber extending out and across from each corner of the twelve-by-ten foot raft. They spent another two hours fashioning a set of tracks to drive the vehicle onto the raft. They secured two more lines across the river and two more on the near side to anchor the raft up to the bank. Much to their surprise, really, it somehow worked. With the vehicle aboard, Chris and Jaime positioned themselves catty-corner to slowly trudge the raft across. Sharla stood at the rear of the vehicle to not offset the balance. The raft wobbled with the slightest waif of ripple in the current but remained afloat as they made it shakily to the point near the trail they discovered.

In the shallower end of the opposite bank, Chris tied the raft off at each front corner and laid out their Jerry-rigged tracks up the rise of bank. The raft nosed into the water as Jaime began driving it off, but the new extensions dug into the muddy bottom and provided enough resistance for Jaime to drive the vehicle onto the tracks and to the trail. Shouts of jubilation came to a quick halt at Chris' raised hand.

"Do you hear that?" he asked with a serious tone.

Jaime cocked his head to put an ear skyward.

"Is that a helicopter?" Jaime said.

"That's what I thought, too. Come on!"

They quickly bounded into the Rover and started out on the trail, windows down to listen for signs of the helicopter. It sounded close, then faded out, apparently circling near but not directly over them yet. They could only assume it was meant for them. The terrain became denser but remained mostly flat as the trail ensued.

The distinct sounds of the helicopter continued to grow nearer then fade. Each cycle it circled a little closer. When it inevitably flew directly over them, the whirling gnash of air forced down all around them frightened Sharla to the point that she began to cry. Chris yelled above the high-pitched air to try to ensure her that it would be okay. There wasn't anywhere close for them to land. Through the Land Rover's sun roof they could see that ropes were not hanging down, black-ops soldiers were not descending upon them.

Jaime continued to take the Rover down the path, though barely at ten miles per hour. The helicopter simply hovered above them for another five minutes, then flew away, although they could still hear it in the distance for a few more minutes. Would there be a clearing farther ahead–Peruvian G-Men waiting with guns drawn? By the measure of the density of trees and vegetation surrounding them, a clear spot wide enough for a chopper to land seemed highly unlikely. But what could they know.

Chapter 30

The forest only grew more dense the farther along they made it. The helicopter buzzing overhead apparently became disenchanted at the prospect of there being nowhere to land. More likely, they simply gave up their pursuit as the Land Rover and its occupants crossed into Brazil; though where exactly that occurred certainly had not been distinguished by sign or colorful border marker of any kind. Jaime and company were simply happy to believe they had given the overhead followers the slip. Concern for their immediate wellbeing did not fully kick in until darkness swallowed the jungle three hours later.

And with that absence of light a cascade of sounds wildly erupted almost in unison. The rapid, mobile cries of monkeys rang out loudest, but the volume and mass of all else, insects mostly, invoked an underlying cornucopia of creation. Were it not for their natural distress at being literally in the middle of nowhere, in pitch black, no less, the chorus of wildlife might have been something to behold. It felt more like a faux-Indie snuff flick.

They had waited too near dark before stopping to have prepared somewhere to sleep for the night. So after stretching their legs and standing in awe of the scene, they climbed back into the Rover. Conversation evaded them. After a long, sticky, mostly sleepless ten hours, the first rays of morning seeping through eastern canopy tops were a welcome sight. A new set of jungle sounds seemed to accompany the morning, but the end of night at least brought on a feeling of relief for a few minutes.

"How much gas do we have left?" Chris asked, trying to inject a sense of strategy into the mix.

"A little less than a quarter, plus the eight gallons still in the can on the rear," Jaime answered, waiting for Chris to offer more. But he did not. No one spoke for minutes, as if the reality of the situation still hadn't completely arrived.

Soon they continued for another hour following along the same overgrown trail from the day before until it split. The way to the right, to the south, appeared more traveled, but they really wanted to be heading north, if possible. Jaime stopped the Rover at the intersection. After a short discussion, they chose north, the way less traveled; though no allusion to Robert Frost could ease their anxiety. Within less than a mile, they began to regret this decision. They argued briefly whether to turn around or not. Jaime ended the debate with a demanding statement that north is the direction home, and home is where they are headed. The irony of Jaime's mostly nomadic existence prior to his financial windfall and pursuit in South America of the man who helped raise him was not lost on either Chris or Sharla. Yet, they obliged his will without mention. Home did sound good. Particularly so as the density of the forest grew thicker by the minute.

The trail, accordingly, diminished by the second. Within another quarter mile, it narrowed to little more than a wide foot trail. Jaime attempted to keep the Rover moving forward, despite screeches and scraps of vegetation along both sides of the vehicle's body. But soon even this effort became futile. With no room to maneuver, Jaime begrudgingly placed it in reverse. More than an hour later, back at the split, Jaime hesitated once more.

"I just don't see the point in going this way," Jaime whined.

"But it's the only way," Sharla quickly stated. "We've got to find civilization eventually, ya know."

With a heavy sigh, Jaime put the Rover back in drive and down the wider, southward trail they began. For miles this way went on mostly unchanging–a rise in elevation here, a dip there. But then it also began to narrow. Shortly, it faded to little more than maybe an animal trail. The gas gauge read empty. Eight more gallons remained in the spare tank, but what did it matter? Either direction allowed no exit, except back into Peru, where the Ucayali slowly flows. True desperation set in.

"This is serious," Jaime said, half making an attempt at brevity. "Chris?"

"We've hiked for days before," Chris said after a moment. "We certainly can't just sit here expecting a rescue team to show up."

"Just abandon the Rover?" Chris cried, teetering once again on maudlinity.

"Sharla, you up for this?" Chris asked, ignoring Jaime's pity.

"Like you say, there's really no choice," she replied. "Time's wasting just sitting here," see almost pleaded, turning to Jaime.

To their good fortune, Chris' outdoor experience led him to have packed a host of invaluable extra supplies. In addition to his trusty tomahawk, already having proven its worth, he brought along water purification bottles, two backpacks, a compass, a machete for hacking vegetation, boxes of matches in waterproof containers and bags of dried fruit, though he felt confident they'd be able to forage enough food in the jungle. They felt their best shot at finding help would be back north. The remaining gas went into the tank and they returned to the farthest point north they had made it.

As they struck out on foot the trail slowly began veering east of north, Chris noted on the compass. He hoped to keep a more northerly direction, if not somewhat west, toward Colombia and away from the heavier jungle. But he did not bring this to the attention of Jaime or Sharla for the sake of morale. Overhead foliage sheltered them from direct afternoon sun, but the humidity left them drenched in their own sweat. They had enough water for now from what they had purchased at the last stop in Peru. Tomorrow, however, they'd need to find a new source.

They stopped well before dark, soaked like submerged sponges of their own juices. Chris wanted to have enough time for them to construct crude hammocks of vine and rope–anything to keep them elevated above the jungle floor and its host of nocturnal crawlers. Once they accomplished this and built a fire close by to ward off mosquitoes, they were all so exhausted that they found themselves asleep before the sun's final decent for the day.

Awaking early the next morning, Chris did his best to keep their spirits up—not an easy task. He tempted Sharla with notions of how well this would add to the excitement in the book she said she'd be writing about all this. He told Jaime this test would bring good mojo his way, which he could possibly channel toward helping his father gain freedom. They appreciated his effort, but motivation doesn't ease hunger pains and the trail did not appear to be leading them out of the jungle. On the contrary, they knew it to be growing thicker.

The morning wore on slowly. They gained ground only in small increments, slowed by necessity to clear a path by machete much of the way. The threat of large, often venomous insects kept them alert, but the humidity drained their will. They trudged on. Chris said they needed to find a source for water, preferably moving. The task allowed them something to focus on for the time being other than their plight. When they discovered a small rivulet within the hour, it did boost their spirits. Such a simple find, yet so essential.

With their water supply replenished, the afternoon went by faster. A grove of maracuja vines provided a meal of yellow passion fruit. Later they came upon strawberry guava plants, harvesting more for later that evening. They broke for camp early, building new hammocks and another fire for the night. The day's events buoyed their hopes, though Sharla did find concern at Chris' reply to how far until they find people. He didn't know, he answered honestly. It might be days.

The next morning, Chris hoped to gain a more northerly push but a steep rise to the west kept them at a more northeasterly clip. They discovered more passion fruit, as well as figs, to offer some variety. But the way proved just as dense in many spots and by midday Sharla developed a blister on the ball of her right foot, slowing their progress greatly. Before that pre-evening's break to stop to make camp, a sour mood spread from Sharla to Jaime, and then to Chris who felt they neglected to appreciate how much more dire the whole situation would be had he not been so prepared in the first place. They needed some protein in their diet to keep their strength up, Chris said at last to try to break the foul air about them.

"We should kill a snake tomorrow," he offered.

"If we can find one," Jaime commented.

"It shouldn't be too hard," Chris replied. "Or maybe some water holding fish. Or a capybara."

No one said more. The following morning, Sharla questioned if she could continue with her blister, now the size of a small pancake and moist as a jelly fish. Chris agreed a day of rest could help. He and Jaime would go out to try and find a meal of substance.

"Will you be okay while we're out?" Jaime asked her.

"I'll be fine," she said. "What's gonna happen?"

Jaime nodded in agreement. He and Chris set out to hunt for meat. Such a plethora of animals and plants make home in rain forests and part of their beauty lies in each one's ability to survive in such wild environment. Plants compete for light and water. Animals simply try to stay alive, their first and foremost defense being camouflage. Thus, for anyone who's ever watched a nature show on television, the hours of footage edited down to minutes of viewable video belies the fact of just how difficult it can actually be to find a needle in a haystack, or a green-leaf skinned snake within a thousand different shades of green.

Chris and Jaime now knew. Not that they didn't spot a few. But they were too high up or slithered away as they approached. The two concurred, despite Jaime's affinity for monkeys, that they might be resigned to killing one. Yet the furry screechers are no less difficult to encounter.

"Maybe we should go back," Jaime said, growing weaker from the pursuit.

"Back to camp?" Chris asked.

"No. Well, yeah, but I mean back to the Rover and across to Peru. Take our chances getting out through there."

"Maybe? If we can get the Rover back across the river? And if we can get out of Peru? Being locked away without due process doesn't sound too good, either, you know."

"But this. This is just ridiculous," Jaime said, with a laugh half-way between humor and fear. "Our raft is probably still right there. Let's go."

"Yeah, I really don't know how long it might take to find our way onto to something, here, either," Chris admitted.

"That's just it. This could be suicide. Sols abound, remember. I'll hire some good lawyers. Let's go back."

"Let's do it," Chris now easily agreed.

Reinvigorated, our pair abandoned the hunt for protein and proceeded back to Sharla. Shy of Chris' ability to utilize a compass, this process might have taken considerably more time. Retracing one's path in dense rain forest can be more difficult than imagined. After a few miscalculations, however, they did manage to find their way. They could not have guessed what awaited their return, but spears pressed against their necks by nary covered men who smelled of sweat, dirt and oddly tree bark, springing out from lush greenery upon them provided an ominous indication of things to come. They spoke in strange, deep-throated sounds; a language, Chris and Jaime could only assume. The short, thin but muscular men escorted them to where Sharla waited seated on the ground, her hands bound behind her back as six more Amazonians mulled about her.

The men with Chris and Jaime brought them to the others, who quickly used a sort of rope construed of inter-twisting vines to tie their hands behind their backs and nudged them to a seated position to either side of Sharla. One of the men studied Chris' machete, handling it admiringly. More strange sounds of their language then broke out, but only briefly before five of them huddled around Chris, brought him to his feet and began tearing away his shirt. They went to Sharla next, and did the same to her, exposing her perky tits, though they didn't appear overly interested or motivated in a sexual manner. They simply moved to Jaime and did the same.

There our trio now stood, shirtless. The jungle natives all gathered, again, minus two who remained to watch the alien jungle invaders. Those circled spoke in whispers, occasionally stopping to look back at the three, then resume their discussion. This went on for several minutes, until they broke at last and moved back to their captured foe. A slew of more guttural utterances were directed toward the three. They seemed to be growing angry, as if upset by their instructions not being followed.

Finally, one pulled up on a bound arm of Jaime. He wobbled to his feet. Another two did the same to Chris and Sharla. Jaime wanted to cover Sharla's exposed chest. He checked to see if Chris was looking, but just then one of them pushed behind on Chris forcing him to begin walking. Then they prodded Jaime and Sharla and they were now enroot with the rest, Sharla hobbling on her blistered sole. They led them perpendicular to the direction the three had come from and were going. There didn't appear to be a trail, but the men sped on without hesitation. Maybe it was a way, Jaime thought.

They all marched on for what felt like more than an hour, when the jungleites at last stopped. It didn't appear to be a spot the men would use for home. There were no permanent shelters or women. But the ground was well worn. Jaime noticed strands of vine-rope between a pair of trees whose lower branches had been removed on the nearest side of each, and a bed of ashes appeared to be running beneath. Perhaps they hung meat here to dry or smoke?

One of them then pushed Jaime toward one of the trees he had just noted. They pushed more until he faced the tree. A hand clamped down on his right shoulder to turn him back toward them. His back now against the tree, three others quickly surrounded him, using more vine-rope to bind his ankles to the base of the trunk. Jaime questioned aloud what, but it only evoked one of them to roughly place a palm across his lips. Jaime could feel the dirt of his hand upon his mouth. The smell of tree bark filled his olfactory senses.

They removed the binding from his wrists, but then replaced it immediately with his arms now stretched behind the tree, though they didn't fully reach around for the girth of the trunk. Once they finished with Jaime, the same group of men went to Chris and did the same. They finished thusly with Sharla. Jaime could scarcely believe his eyes–the three of them tied to trees in the jungle, like a bad scene from an old Tarzan movie or something.

The jungle men now stood surveying their captured humans. A sense of pride seemed to be on their faces. Naturally, Jaime decided. He looked to Sharla, her face depleted of any emotion. Guilt filled him suddenly. He grew angry again that they had tied her up exposed. He looked to Chris. He seemed stoic, Jaime thought. Like he wouldn't give in to their terror. Then all but two, the same two who had not been included in the huddle from before, walked away. The two left behind shortly dropped to sit on the ground, and then just sat there watching the three of them, without a care, as if this were nothing more than routine.

Curiosity filled Jaime's mind. Where had the others gone? For what? His lips felt sticky–a dry stickiness. It spread throughout his mouth and throat. He could feel the emptiness in his gut, the sting of vine-rope rubbing his wrists raw. He looked again to Sharla. She must be feeling the same. He looked to Chris. Still the same sternness. He's just tougher, Jaime thought. The two watching them barely moved, shifting position now and again, only.

After some hours, as the sun hung low before nightfall, the other men returned. Four women now accompanied them though. They were shirtless, also, Jaime noticed straight on. Their nipples were the largest he had ever witnessed, wide as a saucer with two-inch protrusions like udders. It made him feel better, strangely. Then he felt foolish at the whole notion of caring in the first place. This could be a life and death matter, here. This probably is a life or death matter, here.

The women moved closer to them. They examined Sharla first. Then Jaime. They seemed most enthralled with Chris–perhaps his more reddish skin and darker hair. The core group of men formed a huddle again, as the women now joined with the two left behind to guard the prisoners. One of the women then went to the other group. Then they all broke apart and left, though each in a different direction. Jaime could hear some of them rustling in the jungle nearby.

A woman returned with a handful of what looked like dried

moss. Then a man came back hauling a large leafless branch. Then another also had a branch. They were gathering material for a fire, Jaime decided. This activity went on for some time. Were they going to literally burn them at the stakes, Jaime wondered desperately? The pieces of wood and what-not were being compiled in a stack in front of the three. Maybe they'd distribute it all around them after enough had been gathered?

This collection of wood went on for close to another hour. Just before complete darkness, some of them began arranging the wood into two stacks on either side of the three tied to trees. When they lit the fires by sparks of flint and rock, Jaime could see all of them seated a few yards before the three of them, watching as if viewing creatures from outer space. The jungle men and women continued to study them. Occasionally, one or two would stand to go and stoke the fires. After some time, one of them used a long piece of dried bark as a shovel to remove coals from the bed of the fire and move the still red-hot pieces into the ash pit running between them. He did this until many pieces lay in the ash pit to either side of Jaime.

"They're going to burn us alive," Sharla wailed, speaking out for the first time since the ordeal began.

Her voice invoked a stir among the natives. The one transferring coals stopped. They began speaking to each other, in hushed tones, as if their words might be discerned.

"What are they saying?" Sharla asked Jaime, desperation filling her voice.

"I don't know," Jaime answered softly. "It's like they're deciding something. Chris?"

"What?" he said, half angry. Jaime suspected Chris might finally be growing mad toward him for them being in this position.

Then the conversation among the natives stopped. They all went back to sitting except the one who had been shuffling hot coals, who resumed this activity. Soon he had moved enough coals that Jaime could feel its heat on either ankle. He continued bringing over more, now stacking them two deep. The rest still watched on, seemingly almost incurious, as if they had seen this show numerous times before to the point that now only the grand finale could peak their excitement.

Jaime racked his mind for an idea to stop it all. The vine-rope held surprisingly still tight around his wrists and ankles. He wiggled his hands with earnestness, but it didn't seem to loosen the bind, only deepening the irritation from the coarseness of the rope's texture. He couldn't stop glancing toward Sharla. The grave concern plastered on her face intensified his own anxiety. When he looked to Chris, a resignation of defeat had replaced his earlier stoic countenance. The coals were nearly hot enough that they were starting to burn his skin.

"Why?" Jaime shouted, at last. "Why are you killing us?"

The tone of his voice roused them. Jaime yelled more, sensing it might be their only hope. He repeated why, why, why, as loudly as he could. Finally one of the men moved to Jaime and began shaking him around the shoulders. Jaime stopped screaming. The same man now went to Sharla. He felt of her hair, but oddly so. Then he rubbed on her below her shoulders, slowly. Then beneath a breast. Jaime fumed.

The man groping Sharla noticed Jaime's growing rage. He eyed Jaime, then rapidly dropped both hands to Sharla's shorts and began yanking at them. Sharla now screamed, but he continued pawing at her, as if unaware how to unbutton the shorts. Finally, the force of his effort snapped the top buttons and he pulled the shorts down below her knees. He looked strangely at the purple panties remaining as her last shield of defense.

"Show them your balls!" Chris now rang out to Jaime.

"How? I can't move my hands," Jaime shouted.

Jaime yelled at the man, until he captured his attention. He moved his eyes from the man's to his own midsection, repeatedly. But the jungle man only looked confused, although he did stop his harassment against Sharla. He continued to watch Jaime's mad attempt at diverting his attention away from her. The man now moved to Jaime and seemed to finally deduce the strange suggestion the bound prisoner appeared to be making. He cocked his head in curiosity, then as if the picture at last came into full focus, he let out a primal roar. He went back to the group of his jungle men and retrieved the machete confiscated from Chris. He raised it above his head and let out another wild yell. Jaime's heart beat like a rapid drum roll.

The jungle native hesitated for just a moment, the machete poised to strike. The air tingled. A second of time froze, it felt, before an ungodly enormous flood of electric blue light infused the torture camp in a giant flash, instantly followed by a clap of thunder so loud it split the air with a violence that caused the ground itself to shudder. The instinctive cries from the Amazon representatives could not be heard above the echo of thunder, but they were there just the same. Then a second bolt of lightning crackled through the moist jungle air, not quite as close, but just as crisply, and with it the entire congregation scattered, minus our three whose capacity to flee still remained far less than stellar.

A downpour of cold, clean rain began pouring through the trees. It felt like a gift. Their bodies cooled, but their minds remained mildly in shock. How close to their ends had they been? Minutes? The rain intensified. A smell of smoldering fire filtered up in-between drops of new water. The feeling of relief coupled with the rain's refreshment seemed palpable among the three. Jaime worked his wrists until the vine-rope weakened by the rain finally loosened. He dropped to his knees to unfasten his ankles. Chris was right in-step. They both went to Sharla and freed her.

The rain continued until an hour before dawn. Too dark and lost to move, the three simply sat immersed in the rain through the night. Adrenalin from their narrow escape charged their systems so that being wet and deprived of sleep had little effect. In the morning they would begin finding their way back to the Rover, float it back across the river, then make an attempt to depart Peru through a small border crossing into Colombia.

Ten Most Enduring/Entertaining Enemies

1. Arabs vs. Jews
2. Right vs. Left
3. East vs. West
4. Children vs. Vegetables
5. Good vs. Evil
6. Frazier vs. Ali
7. Westward expansion vs. Buffalo
8. North vs. South
9. Governments vs. Liberty
10. Fossil fuels vs. Earth

Chapter 31

The effects of hunger worsens in stages. In the beginning energy levels drop, the stomach's oldest instinct of survival alarms the central nervous system with pangs of existential aching, eyes blur, and an urge to sleep recurs. We become irritable. These and other factors last for two days or more, before stage two kicks in–mild atrophy within the stomach relieves pain of inanition but the depleted mind also begins to malfunction. Among a brain's more noted circus tricks, hallucinations taking form through voice just beyond one's peripheral or visual tomfoolery–a la, the mirage of water in the desert (palm trees not necessarily included) or an angel descending from the heavens. During their 40-year banishment, more elite Israelites purportedly participated in an ancient form of pinnacle with Gabriel and a few of his winged cohorts.

Back in the jungle, our trio of would-be heroes currently find themselves on the brink of stage two. Unable to relocate their last camp and Chris' supply of survival tools, the three have been forced to a more brutal challenge of existence as they amble for the third day in a direction they hope leads to the vehicle. Since the evening after being abandoned by members of one of earth's last remaining tribes of cannibals, Jaime and company only suspected they were close to being burned alive. They did not realize they were actually being prepared as the main and only course to a charred meat-lovers smorgasbord, dessert–skull marrow al la al dente brain noodles.

"When we get, make it back," Sharla softly tried to speak, her head feeling light as a glass of dry champagne, "I'm going to give to Unicef."

"That'll be nice," Jaime said, walking slowly just ahead. "I'm going to donate to the Red Cross. Chris...what about you?" Jaime asked, their last bastion of light swaying just ahead.

"Hunger weeds out the weak. Earth has too many people as it is."

"What did he say?" Sharla asked Jaime, unable to make out Chris' words from behind.

"He's not in," Jaime answered.

"Not in to what?"

"Charity," Jaime replied.

"Why not?"

"Charles Darwin."

"Do what?" Sharla asked.

"Forget it."

During hunger's second act of stage two, inability to recognize basic thirst sets in. They knew they needed water. Naturally. But starved nerves lose ability to relay as such to the mind. They last drank the previous afternoon, though only sparingly from a small hole of water they happened upon. Chris said they had no choice. If they drank just from the top and only in minute amounts, they might be okay. Jaime and Sharla took the risk.

"Do you smell nail polish remover?" Sharla asked Jaime, seemingly from out of nowhere as they inched on later.

"That's it. Nail polish remover."

"Weird, huh," she said.

A nutritionally bereft body also eventually begins turning stored fat into simple units of energy known as keotene. A by-product of this process is the release of acetone. Hence, our depleted pair are not experiencing hallucination of the nostrils when whiffs of Sally Hansen nail polish remover drift into their airways. Sharla's weakened mind recalled Saturday afternoon trips as a young girl with her mom to the nail salon–Korean tongues flying.

"Does this look familiar?" Chris turned back to ask.

Sharla and Jaime stopped to look around, as if a more careful inspection might yield an overlooked clue. Chris patiently waited.

"Maybe?" Sharla answered after another half-minute.

"Yeah, maybe," Jaime aped.

"I think we might be on the right path," Chris said.

Three hours later, no Land Rover in sight or definitive sign of being any closer to it, Sharla collapsed of exhaustion and dehydration. Weak themselves, Chris and Jaime could do nothing more than wait for her. As the sun later began dropping for the night, Sharla regained a semblance of herself and our desperate trio slowly continued their southward push. Not possessing the strength to construct a campfire, much less suspended sleeping apparatuses, they simply huddled in a small circle for the night. A large, full moon reflecting a sapphire shade of blue soon illuminated the jungle like Beale Street at midnight. They worked their mouths for minutes at a time to force a spit into their hands so as to give handfuls of dirt a paste quality to spread across their exposed bodies and limbs. Insects now were attempting to make a feast of them. Eventually they fell onto each other and slept in broken bits.

Somehow morning brought with it new slivers of hope. They awoke in a nutritionally depleted fog, scratching and weak but determined to force on. Stage three of hunger is complete collapse. Organs begin to fail. Death becomes imminent. Entering the fourth day of their search, Sharla neared stage three by only hours. Jaime and Chris were a day to less behind her. Their pursuit neared to a crawl but Chris kept them moving, drawing will from his mind being convinced he recognized the path they were on and that it leads to the road where they last stopped in the Rover. During the process of starvation a body retains one last wave of adrenalin–one last-ditched source of energy. As the path began to widen for the first time in five days, a slight yet magical spin of spirit lifted through every vein of each of our troubled threesome. The eyes suddenly focus despite a misty haze. When the sparkles of metallic cobalt blue Land Rover reflected through a film of dust and grim entered Sharla's field of vision, she wept. Jaime and Chris

216

embraced. Four 16-ounce bottles of water remaining inside the vehicle, having been more than they could initially carry, never tasted so sweet.

In their emaciated but elated state, they reversed down the way until the logging trail back west toward the Ucayali. Three hours later the slow, often meandering river somehow remained the same. Their hand-crafted timber barge lay in the same spot intact. They decided to just allow the current to carry them north until they could find another spot to unload. Less like post-modern Huck Finn, Tom Sawyer and Becky Thatcher than wretched river urchins, our trio set out adrift on uncharted water. The farther along they went, the milder the river ran. They opted to just continue to float. It felt nice to move without effort.

Just before dark, serendipity played its lucky tune once again, as lights from the small river town of Contamana, Peru peeked above the approaching horizon. Sharla cried again. Shortly, the river twisted like a horseshoe to the west before arcing back east. At the crest of the curve, the boys directed the raft to the shallow western edge where they could run it aground. Jaime eagerly turned the ignition and placed the gear into four-wheel drive. Sharla climbed into the passenger seat and as the Rover splashed onshore, Chris jumped onto the running boards, gripping the luggage rack on top for support.

A gravel road paralleled the river for a quarter mile before another road led away from the river toward town. There they found a small restaurant serving fresh chicken tamales, rice and passion fruit with cassava beer. Sharla cried as she ate. Chris and Jaime fought back tears, as well, emotions ran so strong. Their bellies now easily filled, the weight of their latest ordeal began to sink in more fully. Without a word, they left sols on the table for the meal, stepped back into the Rover and found the nearest hotel Contamana has to offer. A hot shower and firm mattresses never brought such relief. They stayed an extra day and night to aide their recovery.

That following morning, they took the only highway north out of town and continued on to Iquitos and then San Vicente de Los

Lagos at the Colombian border where they crossed without notice or problem. They continued on through the night until they reached San Rafael, Colombia, a remote, small community catering to visitors to a nearby collection of national parks. Had the Peruvian government simply forgotten them? Would they ever know?

For the time being, they did not care. Jaime felt for the plight of his father, but needed to regroup back home for now where he could plan his next move. After another day and night of rest and food and liquids, they set out to make it back stateside. By Central America, they started to at last fully unwind. Stories to recount were practically limitless. Sharla stood convinced she could turn their adventures into a best-seller. Chris thought he might practice the ways of shaman Dondito with those willing near Pueblo. Jaime believed he could find sympathetic ears to his father's cause back in NYC.

"They're having protest parades there all the time," Jaime explained. "Surely, someone, some group knows about the miners in South America. Didn't some of them get trapped for a while, a few years ago?"

"They did. In Chilé," Sharla recalled.

"Well, there you go. So, there'll be something in New York. There's something for everyone there."

"Even shaman?" Chris wondered aloud.

"I don't know? But I'd be willing to bet," Jaime replied.

"Maybe I should do it there," Chris said. "There probably aren't too many shaman in Manhattan. Soothsayers and Tarot card readers. But an actual, legitimate shaman. I wonder?"

As they approached the outskirts of Mexico City, the excitement at being within two days of crossing back into the United States became palpable within the vehicle. The pall of death from its various angles felt far removed at last. As if such threats only occur down there. As if. The party atmosphere in full swing, the remaining miles to Pueblo flew by like shooting stars. Chris wanted to spend time back in his familiar abode, but promised to find them again within six months. Jaime and Sharla both said it felt strange without him as they made their way on to West Virginia. Sharla paid her visit to family, but home didn't feel the same any longer, she claimed. It seemed small, now, she said. Not just in size, but as if the experience of the broader world, the broader universe, left Blacksburg with the feel of a black hole slowly caving in on itself.

"Let's not stay here," she whispered to Jaime on the front porch after dinner at her father's house on the second night. "Let's go to New York. You can try acting, again. I'll write our adventure."

Easily swayed, they left the following morning. Ah, New York—the city of five boroughs, eight dialects, thirty six cultures, forty two languages and the five families. Our brave couple chose the Upper East Side of Manhattan to call home. Though certainly not cheap, it seemed nearest to any form of existence they knew, less circles of high society and blue bloodlines. Not to worry. Jaime kept busy working to have the Natural Anchovy History and Peruvian Culture Museum transported to a space he found available on the Lower East Side. Sharla devoted six hours a day to writing—"Lost in Paradise."

By evening they took in small plays or occasionally fine dining. Jaime could never fully enjoy a meal he knew cost more than a week's worth of groceries. So, they mostly lived day to day in rather simple, routine fashion. After some time, Jaime at last found a company that said it could relocate the museum, its displays, even the aquarium, to New York.

Three months later, stout workers began unloading pieces that comprised Jaime's greatest achievement. Sharla continued plucking away at her work but started growing incrementally frustrated by the overall difficulty of progress. How she now admired the great writers, their depth, their prolificacy. Jaime readily anticipated the North American grand opening of the Natural Anchovy History and Peruvian Culture Museum. With the help of day laborers, in less than a week the newest take on the museum resembled almost to a tea its original appearance. He hired a marketing firm to kick off the North American grand opening and began search for a source to replenish the aquarium with anchovies. Success struck again. An outfit in New Jersey stocked anchovies. The aquarium seemed more dazzling than before. How could anyone not be impressed?

New York plays home to a slew of offbeat attractions–a museum of cast iron ornaments or a city reliquary featuring chips of subway paint, to the Museum of Art and Design's feature on scent or the 3,600-square feet of dirt displayed in the Earth Museum (made all the more rare in an asphalt jungle, apparently). As such, the NAHPC appears completely rational. More than legitimate. Finding a sympathetic ear to the plight of Adrian Holbrook, wearing thin going on the start of year two in incarceration, required far more effort and persistence.

People listen, sincerely with both ears. But of what can be done? Tongues fall flat. A member of the People for the Liberation of Palestine suggested non-violent protest. But where to find the bodies necessary for adequate representation? A tried and tested devotee of Green Peace offered discrete sabotage of key industrial sites relating to mining operations. But such expertise can be difficult to pin down. A representative for the ethical treatment of animals believes an awareness campaign launched on-line should be the first step. Yet how to make anyone aware of how to become aware?

The world is chock full of unjust situations. Where to begin? How to reach an end? Jaime's new found joy in the relative success of the NAHPC quickly succumb to the quagmire of unseen justice, or lack thereof. Another two months passed before the first glimmer of new hope surfaced. And of all people. One particularly damp, chilled November afternoon, as Jaime insouciantly mingled about the museum's patrons, what he thought to be a familiar face captured his attention. He waited for the sleek contours of her silhouette to continue moving around the far edge of the anchovy aquarium's shadow where better light might lend to better recognition.

In more ample light Jaime almost didn't believe his eyes. It looked like Mika Codsworth, only a much older version. Could it be? He quickly reversed his course to circle back around the aquarium so as to be able to walk onto her headways. What about Beefcake? He hadn't noticed him. But as Jaime turned the next edge, it must be her, he thought.

"Mika?"

"Jaime? It is you. How are you?"

"I'm okay. What about you?" he asked in deliberating fashion as his mind could not fully concentrate beyond making out what his eyes delivered.

"I know," she said. "The experiment's over."

"Oh? Yeah?" he smiled. "Ok. Who cares? It's great to see you."

"Right on. I thought this must be you, but then I didn't know for sure. How did you get all this here?"

"Yeah. No. It's me. It's mine. Dollars still talk."

"I guess so. Well, it's great. You've got visitors," she nodded.

"No, it's going good," he nodded again, surveying both directions. "Where's Beef...Eduardo?"

"Yeah, Beefcake. I'm not sure, I guess. Not here, you know....In fact, I'd like you to meet someone else. He's around here somewhere."

She spotted a man eyeing a display in the MRTA section.

"Perfect," Mika said, leading them back to the man.

"Jaime, this is Claude. Claude this is Jaime, the one I said we might find here."

"Ah, yes. Oui. Bon jour," the man offered in a heavy French tongue.

"Hi," Jaime replied, still mostly fixated on Mika's aged face.

"Has there been any development with your father, Jaime?" Mika asked, sweetly.

"No. Still the same," Jaime stated.

"That's too bad. Well, listen, I think there might be another way," she said, alluding perhaps to the un-utilized, still hidden sword of José de San Martin, Jaime wondered? "When will you have time?"

"Tonight, I guess," he offered.

"Perfect. Could we meet for dinner, maybe?"

"Sure."

"Great. How 'bout Motorino's at 9?"

"We'll be there," Jaime said, wondering if he knew of the place? He could look it up.

And so later that evening it came to light the natural connection, as might have been anticipated, stemming from the old adage of the enemy of my enemy is my friend. Claude Perrot explained the long relationship between Peru and France, in reaction to Britain's long history of alliance with Chilé. And though the contemporary state of affairs offers far fewer instances of international intrigue, a confluence of connections still flourishes, both in business and beyond. And being that Monsieur Perrot descends from a lineage of fine French bloodline, mostly from around the Bordeaux region, his capacity to influence must only be described as le magnificent.

With only a phone call, he boldly claimed in a most understated manner, (a more sophisticated brand of confidence Jaime could not recall) he should see to it that the wheels of release be set in motion. Within the month, probably less, Jaime should be reunited with his father once again. It's really not a problem, he added, perhaps for flare. Ooh-la-la.

"There is this manner of the sword, Mika has informed me, though," Claude did then also work in. "I am assuming it will be necessary to return this artifact."

"Of course," Jaime replied, hoping the dread of uncertainty was not flush about his face as it felt just beneath his skin. "Yes. Yes."

Perrot's lower lip jutted out only a fraction, but enough to relay he could detect a reservation in Jaime's inflection of oui, oui.

"How is Chris?" Mika asked.

"Good, we assume," Jaime answered, looking to Sharla. She smiled easily. "We haven't heard from him, since being back, but we expect to any day, now, really."

Sharla smiled again.

"Then it is perfect," Claude spoke up, sensing a lull. "Let us celebrate."

Claude ordered champagne for the table and switched the subject of conversation to the little-known fact of sparkling wine having originated when Roman soldiers forced French slaves to extract grapes from a region of southern France not previously noted for wine cultivation. Such an opposite from Beefcake in so many ways, Jaime thought as Claude continued. The Romantic languages are so fluid, he also decided, as Claude switched back and forth from speaking in English to French. He could just listen to him for hours. Jaime noticed Sharla seemed equally enthralled. He hoped for only similar reasons.

The next afternoon, Claude showed up at the NAHPC, without Mika. He said he spoke with an uncle in France who has connections in Peru and he should hear back from him as soon as the next afternoon. Do not worry, he insisted. He will make this happen. How about the sword, he then added?

"Yes, well.." Jaime mumbled. "As soon as I...I have to talk with Chris, first. He is the one who, well... I will let you know something soon."

"Please, oui. We must," Claude said, calmly. "As I mentioned last night, I am sure it will need to be returned. Without doing so...."

"No. Of course. Without question," Jaime replied. "It will be."

"Fantastic," Claude stated. "Your museum is superb. I really do think so."

Claude looked about admiringly, not focusing on any one thing in particular, but as if to say, it is the whole of this that I am lending such glowing approval. Jaime suddenly realized the pompousness on display. Is it inherited, he wondered? Or had it been taught? He didn't like this man half as much as before this afternoon. Jaime wondered if it had anything to do with his own attraction to Mika?

Five Most Financially Dominant Families Historically

1.   Rothschild
2.   Habsburg
3.   Rockefeller
4.   Warburg
5.   DuPont

Chapter 32

Most stereotypes proceed from at least an inkling of reality. So while some female American drivers of Asian descent may handle the wheel of an automobile better than Mario Andretti, there are indeed others out there whose notion of going with the flow of traffic is about as good as their ability to use an article of speech during the course of uttering the English language. Likewise, not every New Yorker born and raised on the upper eastside of Manhattan can trace their lineage to the British Trading Corporation or the DeBeers Estate, but their money might as well be able to.

Enter one Josephine Anderson, whose familiarity on the New York social scene may only be surpassed by her wanton opinion of any class beneath her–that being all the rest, as it were. Claude Perrot's own filial refinement and proper connections allow him to move about, or at least very near, similar spheres as Mizz Anderson circulates. As such, dear readers, Jaime Gabriel Holbrook finds himself, along with his love, Sharla Jean Evandale, in the midst of le crème de la crème. The particular townhouse overlooking Central Park in which this nighttime soiree transpires belongs to heiress of Scotch tape fortune Cecilia Drummond, her dearest friend being Josephine Anderson. Monsieur Perrot extended an invitation to Jaime and Sharla secretly thinking it might make for devious conversation fodder, which could later be divvied into delightful slices of unctuous humiliation. He did not share this ulterior strategy with Mika.

As for Claude's secret hope that Jaime and Sharla might prove to be a Pandora's Box of sociological snickery, quite the opposite occurred. For it was Jaime who found this band of upper echelon misfits to be the curious matter in his own sociological Petri dish. Having never had the pleasure of cavorting among life's top one-percentile of wealth, Jaime could not have guessed in a lifetime's worth of cavorting how obviously pretense can be worn on one's Versace sleeve. Why, he could only wonder? And then he recalled Chris' belief that money, while certainly affording one a host of material luxuries, in the end actually often robs a soul of life's truly richest treasures–those measured deepest within the heart. And as the old maxim goes, to every rule there always lies an exception, so to tonight's gathering offered a possibility when Jaime encountered the person escorting Josephine Anderson, a man by the name of Edward Kalowski, whose claim to fame and fortune he reported to be made downtown on Wall Street–a derivatives expert, he confessed.

"It's like with Madoff," Kalowski began in response to a comment he and Jaime overheard about that nearly ubiquitous euphemism–shit rolls downhill. "Everything's a Ponzi scheme, if you really think about it. Almost any situation, you name it. An average job, for instance. The guy making twelve bucks an hour. Whoever signs his check is the one getting rich off this guy, right. So how is *that* not a pyramid? We're all taught this way of life from the get go. Our parents, for example. Who holds all the authority, right? Dad smokes two packs a day, but let him catch you sneaking tokes when you're fourteen and he's gonna bust your ass. Or the government. Please! Who dies in their wars? It's not their sons or daughters. Where do they get their money? Do they make it? No! It comes from all of us. Or most of us. You get what I mean. Life insurance. Social Security. Medicare. It just goes on and on."

Jaime nodded in acknowledgment.

"So it kills me when they hang these guys out to dry like they're the only ones. Don't get me wrong, they deserve to be, but I'm just saying, it's the system, too. The whole thing's a pyramid. Any corporation. Any school. Any gang or club or organized crime, or nature even. The lion's share is always going to the top. It's only the crumbs that trickle down to everyone else. What's on the dollar? Huh?"

"Where are *you* in this hierarchy?" Jaime asked, wanting to break his soapbox.

"I'll admit it. I'm nearer the top than the bottom, but that doesn't make it any less true. I've got an insider's perspective, really. I know. I see it first-hand. I do well, but it's peanuts compared to the ones above me."

"Yeah, whatiya gonna do?" Jaime said, employing a jargon he'd picked up since moving to New York. He shook his head and walked away, looking for Sharla, proud to sound like he belonged somewhere, for once. He found Sharla engrossed in something coming from the perfectly round mouth of Claude Perrot.

"What's going on?" Jaime asked as he approached.

"Oh, I was just telling Claude about Chris. I told him how we expected to have already heard from him, so we hoped it would be any day now, that we do," she said.

Jaime nodded in agreement once again. He smiled at Mika. She could really pick 'em. But he shouldn't complain, he thought. Even to himself. This man could be the one who springs Adrian to freedom. Sharla continued sharing more about Chris the Hopi. Claude seemed genuinely interested. Jaime pretended to participate in the conversation, but he could not help but to really take a closer inspection at the rest of the crowd. Everything about them seemed of another world, collectively. Every detail, from the smoothness of their skin to the fullness of their lips, from the angle of their posture to the likeness of their gestures. Just as much as one could group together the cannibals Jaime and Chris and Sharla had survived in the Amazon jungle, these people belonged together. They had always been only around each other. From five-star daycare to parochial school, it had always been like a parliament of owls—anyone not of their kind stands out like long hair at a Republican convention.

Yet as he might have suspected, Sharla didn't seemed fazed.

Maybe she could see it, too. But if she did, she didn't let on. It made him feel all the more isolated, suddenly. Sharla fit in. She didn't, really, but her social graces allowed her to blend in with ease, leaving Jaime as that one oddity.

"Let me see your nails," Mika turned away from Sharla to ask Jaime out of the blue. He extended his right hand to her. She grabbed the three middle fingers. Proof to her claim. "See–thick and strong. Women would die to have a man's nails."

Jaime forced a quick laugh and half smile. Women! Claude Perrot had wandered away from Mika to Josephine Anderson, he noticed. They whispered to each other, like a pair of vultures conspiring to have a carcass all to themselves. If only Chris could be here, he wished. Jaime slowly moseyed their direction. Maybe he could get close enough to catch a word or two. They didn't appear to see him. He circled wide to come in at a better angle.

"One day I'll get there," Jaime now heard Claude saying to Josephine.

"You will, dear. You will," she assured him.

"You'll get where?" Jaime intruded, not caring if it mattered or they cared.

"I'm sorry?" Claude asked.

"You said, 'One day you'll get there.' Where is there?" Jaime explained.

"Ah. Oh, just finances, my good man. You know, big picture stuff."

"But that's just it," Jaime continued his assault. "*There* is *here*. Don't bother with the big picture. Look at the small picture. It's the minutes that count."

"I see your point," Claude offered, honestly.

"Where are you from?" Josephine interjected, fearing her friend being out shined.

"Nowhere important," Jaime replied. "A little bit of everywhere, really."

"I see," Josephine said, now openly studying this unmasked soul, his face, his eyes. "There is here, did you say?"

"Yeah. There is here. Or here is there, you know. It's the

moments that count. Don't worry about the big picture. Just be in the now."

"He's got something, you know," Josephine said to Claude with real surprise in her voice. "It reminds me of this Indian guru my friend was talking about the other day when were at the Guggenheim."

She paused, perhaps for affect. Claude encouraged her to go on–almost as if rehearsed. She followed his cue.

"Well, he told her the same thing. That it's just the moment to moment that counts in life. She said he could like meditate and leave his body and travel the universe."

Jaime's ears twitched.

"Do go on," he threw in for kicks.

"Well, something about the origin of mankind coming from the Orion nebulae. That either aliens long ago mated with, like, Egyptian kings and queens or their DNA made it here on a meteorite and got mixed into the lot even longer ago, you know."

"People speculate the Egyptians had to have help erecting the pyramids," Claude interjected. "And how did the same designs end up across the continents at roughly the same time in history?"

"Well, it's a pretty natural shape, really," Jaime offered unsolicited, turning to find Ed Kowalski ear deep in another conversation nearby.

"Yeah, who knows," Josephine said. "It just reminded me. What you said, about it's the minutes that count."

Everyone nodded in casual agreement.

"Oh, and the king's burial shaft, in the pyramid at Giza, it points to the belt of Orion during the summer solstice, or something. And then the queen's points to Isis, Orion's lover."

"Who did you say you heard this from?" Jaime asked.

"Just a friend of mine," Josephine answered.

"And who did she hear it from?"

"An Indian guy. Like a spiritual guide. He's down off 8th Street or something, on the lower east side. Somewhere in or near Tribeca, maybe."

"It's nice meeting you," Jaime said to Josephine. "Claude, I think

I'll have an answer by tomorrow for you about that sword."

Jaime turned to re-find Sharla. They needed to head to 8th street. Chris could already be in New York. Mika wanted to come the next morning. Before they could escape the party, though, Josephine invited them to an after-hours tapas bar on 56th and 108th East Avenue. Mika and Sharla jumped at the chance to step out with the chic set. Jaime feigned fatigue but wished them a good time.

"Are you sure?" Josephine tried to persuade Jaime. But he wouldn't give in, despite now wondering if Josephine wasn't eyeing him sexually. Had Mika said something to her about his, well, you know. It didn't matter to him. His mind was set on the possibility of Chris being in New York. It's all that counted for the time being.

Sharla and Mika didn't make it back from the late-night romp until the break of day. Jaime grew anxious all morning waiting for them to wake up. Around two they finally put on their faces and released Jaime from his pacing. One might guess that finding someone in Manhattan without a specific address would be at least a challenge, even something as unique as a Hopi Indian Spiritual Guru & Guide. Yet after scouring less than three or four blocks and talking with one bartender, Jaime located the possible location. Lo and behold, bingo! Chris didn't even act surprised when they walked through the single door of his rectangular space. Leave it to Chris to make Manhattan quaint.

"How long have you been here, man?" Jaime asked, his excitement spilling out.

"About two months is all," Chris replied, more sedate than usual.

"Where are you staying?" Sharla asked.

"In Queens. I found a cousin back in Pueblo who has another cousin who paints and came up here to make it."

"Alright. And you've got this going?"

"I knew you would, but how did you find me?" Chris asked.

"Your reputation is already growing, my friend," Jaime said.

"Is that so?"

"Indeed."

Chris contemplated the idea that he might have a reputation.

"We're are you guys?" he then asked.

"On the other end. What they call uptown," Jaime answered.

"Mika, your drugs quit working, I see."

"Yep. I caught up to time in a hurry, too."

Everyone shared a familiar laugh. Then Jaime broached the subject of the sword needing to be recovered from the Siula valley. He explained Mika's tricky French connection and believed Chris might be able to lead one last expedition back into Peru, maybe even seeing Shaman Dondito again. Chris listened attentively enough, but Jaime thought something else preoccupied his full focus. Jaime continued the pitch, but Chris only said at last he'd have to think about it. Then he started in on New York. How being at the epicenter of capitalism and all its wealth had allowed him to realize just how much energy gets spent by people to surround themselves in material comforts. The great vanity, he called it.

Granite countertops, marble floors, designer fashion and wares, sycophant mistresses, young studs, all to impress. All the while their feet are on the ground no differently than anyone else. And it's still just themselves they're left with. And who is that, Chris asked, rhetorically? No matter what we surround ourselves with, he answered his own question, we cannot replace what lies within us. Penetrate as we might, or shield ourselves as thickly as we imagine possible, each is left only with themselves.

"And how many know who that is?" Chris concluded.

No one openly answered, though Sharla's eyes sparkled and Mika stood with a look half in awe and half in comfort of being a part of some inner circle of hidden truth.

"Where are you right now?" Chris asked Sharla specifically.

"What, now?" she questioned.

"Nothing fancy. Just where are you, right at this moment," he explained.

"I'm okay," she replied, meekly.

"No, silly. I mean, where are you physically? Where are we all, right now?

"Your... what is this? Your place, I guess. Your...?"

"That's fine," Chris smiled. "And where is that?"

231

"What?"

"No tricks. You said my place. I'm just saying, where is that?"

"New York?" Sharla whispered.

"Right," he said. "And where is that?"

"Well... the U.S."

"Okay," he went on, "and where is that?"

"Oh, okay," she said. "North America."

"Yes. And where is that?"

"Uh, earth?"

"Right. And where is that?" he repeated again.

"The solar system?"

"Okay. And where is that?"

"The Milky Way galaxy."

"Good. And where is that?"

"The universe," she said shaking her head in amusement.

"Right. And where is that?"

She hesitated.

"I give up."

"And that's just it," he replied. "No one really knows. Where is all this? Where is anything? All we can really know is ourselves. And how many people really even know that?"

All Jaime could see was a vibe between Sharla and Chris. He thought he felt his blood begin to boil, but then realized it actually wasn't. Instead, a sense of pride filled him. Why shouldn't Chris be attracted to Sharla? She is wonderful in so many ways, and it's none other than himself who she shares her life. He glanced at Mika. She began asking Chris where he came up with that. It's an old Indian philosophical riddle, he answered.

"Where do you think we are?" Mika then asked.

"Oh I don't know, either," he said. "I just try to know myself. That's the point really."

"Sure. I get that," Mika emphasized. "But just for shits and grins, where do you think we are?"

Like a politician caught in a question to which he knows the truth will contradict his position, Chris hesitated to answer with a glimmer of discomfort escaping a forced ease.

232

"We're nowhere," he offered at last. "Space, like time, is inconsequential."

Chapter 33

Jaime did not receive an answer to his desire for Chris to go back to Peru to retrieve the sword and put the final push into motion to free Adrian Holbrook. He pressed Chris a few times, but then thought to apply any more pressure might jeopardize any future chance of him going at all. The waiting increasingly brought on more strain. Worse, Mika introduce Josephine to Chris, who then all teamed together to help Sharla overcome her bout of writer's block.

They took to obscure scenes Josephine knew of where avant-garde artists intersperse to be different together. They traveled up Long Island to mark Spring's arrival at beach side villas of established authors. They ate meals prepared by cutting-edge chefs, drank rare wine, captured spoken word performances in burned-out spaces and gazed at distant stars through private observatories; a particular favorite for Chris, no doubt, whose offhand comments of having been there before caught off guard even these more eclectic sorts.

All the while Jaime felt himself fading further into the background. He kept to the museum mostly. By evenings, when Sharla wasn't away, she made things seem normal between them. They made love often and the passion remained. The big balls in the big apple, she sometimes quipped. And her writing did improve, she told him. So he couldn't fairly fault her for trying. But still, he wanted to desperately.

Claude openly questioned how Jaime could idly sit by whilst his father continued to rot in a Peruvian prison. Jaime insisted they were getting closer. It wasn't as simple as he might believe. Time might be a concoction of man's creation, Jaime now scoffed, but it certainly felt to be turning the screws on his wellbeing. And then one afternoon, Chris walked into the NAHPC to report he had decided he *would* travel again to Peru. He had a vision in a dream that convinced him the timing was now right, he said. And Josephine wanted to meet Dondito. They could grab the sword on their way back down.

Three weeks later, Claude announced he would be accompanying Chris and Josephine to Lima. Chris would lead them up the Siula Grande Mountains to visit Shaman Dondito and once they retrieved the sword upon their return to Lima, it could be returned and Claude could then pull the strings to set the wheels in motion to free Adrian Holbrook. What could go wrong? Ahhh, let us count the ways.

For Chris, trouble began clearing customs at Jorge Chávez International Airport. As his turn came about to speak to a customs agent and the routine questions began, something apparently appeared on the official's computer screen and he left his station, asking Chris to hold tight. Where else could he go? A long five minutes later, the official returned with a certain blonde female who Chris had never seen before, but if Jaime could have been there, he would have informed Chris that it might be okay because several months earlier, when Jaime first began his quest to find the man who helped raise him, this same blonde woman had intervened on Jaime's behalf to keep him from the throes of a conspiracy to deliver narcotics rap. This afternoon, however, she did not come bearing reprisals. She did not, in fact, even know of the connection between Chris and Jaime. That is, she did not remember that Jaime had been the one she helped avoid trouble those several months earlier. She did know Chris to be a possible accomplice to Jaime Holbrook, whom the Peruvian government suspected to be behind the disappearance of the sword of José de San Martin in a weak-ass effort to free his suspected communist, labor-union-loving father, Adrian Holbrook.

Yet all was not lost. At least not as far as retrieving the sword and its return possibly playing a part in freeing Adrian Holbrook. For Chris, dear readers, being astute beyond outward appearances and all-around wily creature, planted a map of the sword's location inside a piece of Josephine's luggage, concerned at the off chance he might be detained before the sword could be found. He had, after all, fled Peru with Jaime, as well as radioed several times that the sword was being held as ransom.

Exactly how the Peruvian government came to associate Chris with Jaime, the sword and Adrian Holbrook, only certain American spooks can say, and they're not. So let it just be assumed in this digital age of a nearly omnipotent Big Brother, that the connection was made and Chris' picture did get tagged and marked. No such qualms, on the other hand, precede Ms. Josephine Anderson. And being that Chris also forthrightly informed Josephine to not panic should he not clear customs or otherwise be unable to perform the task—to proceed on with Claude. She would discover the how and the what with minimal effort. The mission must continue.

It only took a few hours after landing before it occurred to Josephine that there must be something to the story Chris had explained back in NYC of the situation in Lima. It took a week, however, before she put things together enough to begin the pilgrimage to find Shaman Dondito. She still planned to retrieve the sword after their rendezvous with the South American mountain high priest. One can always dream. For although Sols do abound concerning Josephine, mountaineering skills are in shorter supply than logic in a snake-handler's sermon. Two days after they obtained rented pack mules to ascend Siula, subsisting on rations of rice, beans and freeze dried fruit became more than Josephine, and Claude's system, for that matter, could endure.

Fortunately, they felt enough effort already had been spent that to return to Lima completely empty-handed would be considered too much a failure even for their fairest-weathered fans to forgive back in the city. Luckily, Chris also anticipated how inept their ability to follow a rudimentary map might be, and so each step from the mountain trading post was spelled out in ultra-basic terms to lead them to the sword's location.

"I'll be damned," Josephine remarked as Claude uncovered the historic sword from beneath the large, dead tree trunk lying at 45 degrees on the bank of the Siula river a half-mile upstream from Pedro's bridge, a rickety number local gauchos use to cross the river when necessary, and convenient marker for Chris' treasure map.

"How'd they come about possessing this, again?" Claude asked.

"Chris said they stole it during an earthquake."

"Remarkable."

Remarkable, indeed.

Perhaps more splendid–Claude's ability to actually leverage the sword for Adrian Holbrook's release. Credit those lingering resentments of British imperialism once again, though. For after hearing only a few sweet syllables of Claude Perrot's French tongue, the Minister of the Interior said he would look into the matter. Claude also dropped the name of his uncle who held a post at the French Embassy in Lima. Less than a week from then, the Lima Hilton concierge forwarded a message to Monsieur Perrot to contact a Mr. Berringer, Deputy Assistant of Penal Detention for Peru, who promptly informed all concerned parties that all one hundred seventeen pounds of Adrian Romero Holbrook would be released the following Lunes.

Josephine, channeling her inner Marine, demanded no soldier of this cause be left behind and purchased Lima's finest legal defense, who easily argued that without solid evidence connecting Chris Tenkiller with the disappearance and subsequent ransoming of the sword of José de San Martin, charges could not be leveled. The following morning, a more oddly assembled foursome one would be hard pressed to fathom.

"Jaime made this happen? No kidding?" Adrian Holbrook could not stop asking.

Although Chris warned against it, concerned that prying ears probably boarded their return flight to New York, Adrian could not contain his emotions and insisted to hear all details of how his son orchestrated his release. So in his quietest whisper Chris told the tale. Adrian fought back tears for as long as he could. When Chris hit the part about the earthquake, the combination of joy and astonishment flooding through Adrian's emotions could not be contained any longer. First class flight attendants produced cloth handkerchiefs.

Next, Adrian explained how his own predicament occurred. He could not convince anyone that his motives did not exceed simply organizing the miners into a union. As if that would be so bad. Adrian had no idea radicals had hijacked the labor movement in South America. He certainly knew nothing of stored sticks of TNT holed away in some MRTA safe house. Chris the Hopi sympathized and turned the subject to how confinement sometimes works wonders on a soul. Adrian nodded in quiet agreement.

"You gain a sense of self, spending so much time locked away," Adrian admitted after a long while. "Your thoughts are all you can really control. It's all anyone can really control. What prison robs a man mostly of is acting on his thoughts."

"Now, at least, you know," Chris whispered.

Adrian nodded quietly once again. He looked across the aisle at Claude, still amazed his son somehow had convinced these strangers to come all this way to Peru to help. He studied Claude's face, recalling how strikingly handsome he looked when he first encountered him at thirty paces. Upon closer inspection, though, he noticed a nose too broad with cheeks outlined in old acne scars and more recent blemishes, which combined to expose a far more mundane appearance.

The farther along the flight continued, the more convinced Adrian Holbrook became that he really would experience freedom again. That he'd taste a chocolate malt, feel the touch of a woman's smooth skin, hear the joy in children laughing. Still, it would take a while for the burden of captivity to fully mollify.

Josephine messaged Jaime and Sharla with the news and flight information so they could be at the airport when they landed. But Jaime grew cautious as they waited to leave for JFK. He sensed a trap, he told Sharla. They shouldn't all be together there at the airport.

"If they're still after you or us, whatever, they're going to get us wherever we are. You're being paranoid," Sharla insisted. "It's fine. Let's be there when he gets off the plane."

But she could not convince him. And so the happy reunion of father and son, and the climax of our story dear readers, occurred several hours later inside their apartment. Trust me when I tell you, though, the moment was sweet and on many levels.

As much as the freedom began to feel real for Adrian, he felt far more deeply that Jaime had gone to such lengths to win his freedom and wanted to remain *his* son. And Jaime reaffirmed any lingering doubt he didn't feel, but suspected must be somewhere within, that this is his father. He would never seek out his mom to discover anyone else. Champagne and tears flowed freely, and scratches upon the surface as to how Adrian and Jaime's mother parted ways. And to mostly Jaime's surprise, the apparent connection between Josephine and Chris. What will the Uptown neighbors say?

Chapter 34

What's in a name? Ed Doveer claimed not much. A rose is still a rose by any other name, he famously penned; although one might question if a daffodil wouldn't be more highly regarded by a less clumsy moniker. Formally registered as the Narcissus, the daffodil, with its feminine form, pedals shaped as the mold of a virgin vulva, tender pistol antennae for front door decoration, looks as delicate as the wings of a butterfly, as graceful as the flight of a bumble bee, as sweet as the nectar of Athena, as soft as a Fall red leaf's downward spiral from its tree—an hermaphroditic creation Georgia O'Keeffe surely found pleasurable to the eye.

Yet daffodil lends the ear to a buck-toothed inbred clad in overalls with no shoes, fingering pigtails on a rickety faded porch–XXX marked on a jug somewhere in the scene. As Sharla neared the last pages of her first effort at being a novelist, she began considering the name by which she should publish. Sharla Evandale just didn't seem like a name that could grace the cover of a book. Not a real book found and sold on the shelves at a real book store. But what?

Josephine suggested Autumn O'Malley. It rings with the sound of literary onomatopoeia, she said. Like words that sing from the pages. Music to a reader's ear. Chris believed she might try a single name. As far as he could remember, an author had never attempted to be as bold as to take only one name. Divas, sure. Pop stars, of course. Actors even, maybe. But a writer? Outside of Voltaire, who else? She'd break ground. Easy to remember, too, he pointed out. Jaime didn't see what difference it made.

"If the book sales, if people like it and read it, then the name, whatever it is, will become household—one that people will associate with being an author," he stated. "Otherwise, what does it matter? No one will remember anyway."

Jaime's father stood perfectly still less than a foot from the thick blue tinted glass of the anchovy aquarium, hearing the discussion of what name Sharla should use as they all gathered at the museum early one afternoon, but not inclined to offer a suggestion. What could he add? It's not his concern, anyway. And the flow of anchovies darting like a fluid body mesmerized him. It eased his anxiety that would not completely allay as he adjusted back to life unconfined. Do the anchovy know they're actually closed within glass? It's such a big space and they have no other point of reference. They probably don't, he thought. They're always only a few seconds ahead or a few seconds behind wherever they're at, practically living in a constant state of now. Perhaps he began to comprehend more fully what Chris the Hopi had spoken of during the plane ride from Peru.

It's the magic of the universe. No matter where or when any one or anything is ever at, it's always just another slice of now. All of life, all of everything only exists within an infinite now. There really is no past or future outside the consciousness of man. In the big picture, it is always now. He turned his attention at last from the schooling anchovies. What a collection, he thought. What a life Jaime stumbled onto. He felt proud as a father, but then quickly questioned if he deserved that feeling. What had he done? Raised him with good character? Hadn't Jaime dropped out of high school to film himself screwing whores. But he eventually did right, Adrian supposed.

Sharla told the group that she'd decide later. She couldn't know in one instant. She hadn't even found a publisher, yet, after all. They should not put the cart before the horse. If only she could have known how prescient that notion will turn out to be. For as many poorly written books are published, it's certainly at the expense of others. Books, from a publisher's standpoint, are not created to be read. They are created to be sold. And if a niche can be found or formed, there will be inevitably printed words to scratch that intellectual itch. Hence, within the confines of most any bookstore, noted or otherwise, there are more than a plethora of nasty little sexual underdog triumphs stories marketed under the guise of romance. There are slews of mostly factual accounts of murderous sociopaths, some even decorated in medals, delivered as mundanely dry as overcooked, leftover scrambled eggs. There are shelves of How To's, from diet to crying. Reams of military conquest. Bounds of words, abridged and not so. Those telling in what order these countless words should be arranged, when to underline or indent from both sides, how not to plagiarize or steal without being detected. Who to vote for and why. And where you will go when you die and who will be there with you, or not!

A much smaller consortium of pages are glued together from the minds of new writers. Not to be confused with new releases, of which an eye-catching display nearest the entrance always will be found. But the majority of works of fiction derive from a handful of authors whose talent or connections were enough to convince an even fewer choice of publishers to take a chance. Small presses are out there, but beyond the world of academia, not many readers venture into these untraditional pages.

And so it went during the course of the next six months that Sharla discovered just how difficult receiving even a rejection letter can be. She made attempt through the usual channels–submission packets of three chapters and one-page summary. Literary agents both small and large were at her disposal. Yet nothing surfaced.

Jaime finished reading it, at last. He offered his strongest support. Josephine, now proudly dating Chris the Hopi, Manhattan Shaman to the Upper East Side, thought she had a solution, at last.

"I do know a playwright, out on Long Island. Maybe he will have an idea," she proposed one evening dining at Balthazar in Soho, where Josephine said artists who have made it frequent, although Jaime didn't see anyone he thought fit the billing, including present company.

But Sharla agreed it couldn't hurt. A few weeks later Josephine drove with Sharla to meet Joe Gagliano (he writes under a pseudonym whose name shall not be divulged for the sake of continuity and Italian pride.) At the bequest of Ms. Anderson, but mostly as result of her secret-from-Sharla sizeable donation, Mr. Gagliano exclaimed to Sharla the wild possibilities he could envision with this work of art.

"Seriously?" Sharla naturally questioned aloud. "Art?"

"Oh, without question, dear." Gagliano delighted. "It's really just a question of which angle will be best. I'm thinking the plight of the working man unfairly imprisoned as the wayward son sets off in search of his missing not-really-his-father will work. But we may tweak it a bit. We'll just have to see."

"Isn't this exciting," Josephine tingled, mildly shaking Sharla's folded knee.

And thus the following Spring witnessed the beginning stages of production for the anticipated October release of "On the Run." Josephine contributed another large stake and served as one of the play's producers. Chris frequently sat in as chief consultant. Jaime attempted to audition for a bit part while in disguise. Or so he hoped. It was Claude Perrot, paying visit one afternoon as guest to Josephine Anderson, who happened to expose the big goof auditioning for the prison guard to be Jaime with hair dyed burnt orange and fake red moustache. Sharla nearly collapsed from embarrassment, until the noted director merely laughed sincerely and said it would not be a good fit here, but he had another play beginning in a few months that had a part Jaime might be perfectly fit to indulge. He'd arrange for a private audition the following afternoon.

My how quickly things can move in a big city. Jaime's multi-month span of melancholy lifted overnight. His personal performance for Shannon Merkel, director Stephen Heinz lead talent scout, went off like a champagne cork just after midnight on the first night of a new year. The part was his. Rehearsals already were under way. Report, she instructed him, the following afternoon at 1:30 to The Playroom Theater where his portrayal of

Jack Wilcox in "Requiem for a Dancer" will commence.

Like a prophecy being fulfilled, Jaime felt more sense of accomplishment than he had ever before. More than after the first sight of Adrian back in the United States. More than from recently printed positive reviews of the NAHPC. Definitely more than from being awarded more money than he might possibly know how to spend. This he owned. This he did. His new raison d'être. Passion flowed within him like boiling magma. Who is this Jack Wilcox character, though?

As he strolled up the street before hailing a taxi for Central Park, his confidence so bountiful it seemed to create a barrier of circumference about his being, strangers here and there appeared to be eyeing him like something to be admired. A fine-feathered bird on display. His chi aglow. The wind across the skin of his face felt supreme. This moment could not last long enough.

Later that evening, Sharla unwittingly poked a hole in his ballooned ego. A top-tier publisher caught wind of "On the Run" being in production and proposed to meet with Sharla to discuss book options. Could he believe it? Her idea from that afternoon desperate on the banks of the Ucayali was coming true. Could he really believe it?

"I knew it when you first said it, sweetheart," Jaime sincerely feigned delight.

"I thought you'd be a little more happy for me," she quickly replied, not fooled by his amateurish attempt at sincerity.

"Don't be silly, darling. I did."

"I don't remember you saying anything," she said.

"Well I don't know if I actually said anything right at that moment, but I thought it. We had a lot going on, you know."

Sharla sighed. What's the point of arguing about it now?

Meanwhile, at the NAHPC, a hair-line fracture undiscovered in the anchovy aquarium succumb to more than a year of outward pressure and stress from one major earthquake, three minor aftershocks, and being transported from there to here. Like an exponential equation, everything seemed minute until it wasn't. Thousands of shattered pieces of glass and 28,000 gallons of salt

Robert Scott

water will attest to this truth, lest any naysayers remain. Not to mention some four thousand flopping, gasping, soon to be stinking bait fish that escaped in less the a minute from the jagged gash shaped like an Africanized daffodil in one side of the aquarium.

Chapter 35

While stumbling out of an afterhour's club near the NAHPC early one morning, a few from the cast of "Mary's Attic" (of all people) discovered a thin sheen of water escaping beneath the museum's doors. By the time anyone official responded, a foul stench of rotting fish covered half a city block. Believing it might be a gaggle of executed prostitutes, however, NYPD homicide detectives were mistakenly first brought to the scene before the reality of the situation became known.

Jaime openly wept when he arrived. Sharla sought to offer support but flinched in repulsion within seconds at the malodorous stench and promptly walked far enough away to avoid the nasal onslaught completely. One official equipped others with surgical breathing masks. Only Jaime refused protection. It would be the last remnants of his prized collection and by God, he didn't care how bad it smelled. He took deep breaths forty five minutes later, as city crewmen bagged the last dead anchovy and the rank air gradually began to dissipate. One officer openly questioned Sharla on Jaime's sanity.

"No... he's fine," she slowly admitted. "He just really loved those fish."

No amount of consoling could squash his immediate despair. The museum dies with the anchovy, he stated, standing alone. There will be no replacements! Mika came the next day, looking beyond even her real age, now, and claimed the display pieces on British imperialism. She said she'd use them as decoration for the lobbies at her shows. Dark lighting and make-up allow her to continue performing, though they hadn't toured coming on a year.

"On the Run" director Heinz said displays detailing history of MRTA could be used as props in the play. Jaime didn't care. As long as nothing remained as it was, left to remind him of the loss of some ten thousand anchovy and their once beautiful artificial home. Such a waste, he lamented, to which Chris reinforced saying how he tried to get city workers to promise to dump the dead bait into the East River—to at least be re-circulated through the cycle of marine life. But they wouldn't go for it. Showed not even a hint of concern, in fact. Chris thought he noticed a chuckle from two of them. Working class, soul-less stiffs!

And thus what should have been a string of ebullient 'now's', slipped into a conflicted fallow state of being—neither glorious or sad, bright or dark, coming or going. Only pallid and stale. Not here, not there. Not even in-between.

During "Requiem for a Dancer" rehearsals, Jaime's mind might slip into focus on projecting the director's desire, but as quickly as the last actors shinnied through the theater's back exit door for the night, despair returned. A state of blah. Turning nocturnal to accommodate theater-life hours could not be helping, either. For although many an animal are predisposed to life nary a glimpse of sun, they are led to behave as such from necessity.

But man naturally rises with the lights of day and falls with its absence. For much of existence, habitually linked to the agrarian cycle of day and night, genetic evolution has reinforced this pattern with each new generation. Certainly only as recently as the advent of electricity have efforts to break from this established ritual occurred. Yes, gas lights and other forms of man-made illuminations allowed activity to proceed through evenings and beyond, but nothing on a scale of any magnitude.

It's part of the mysterious allure of Bram Stoker's Dracula, created at the dawn of the Industrial Revolution. A character who revolts against the sun. Who preys on predictability of human nature to be listless and helpless at night. Who revels in all that is dark. Who is felled by light. Jaime had not developed a taste for blood, but he could not adjust to this reversal of time either. And yet, he stopped in the street one night–if time does not exist, how can it matter, night or day?

A group comprised of bit actors from "Requiem for a Dancer" were hopping the subway to Brooklyn to Ned Jernigan's apartment to party. One of Ned's three roommates scored high-grade medicinal reefer and offered to share. Aside from the yagé experience back in the Siula highlands, Jaime had not partaken in psycho-active substances since he left Los Angeles in a huff. It might have been just what the doctor legally ordered in more open-minded states.

Sure enough his dead-anchovy funk flew the coop not three minutes after inhaling four puffs of the skunky sweet bud. He forgot for a moment that he hadn't seen the sun in three weeks or slipped the big Kahuna inside Sharla for even longer. Everything settled. The world was okay. It sighed with him. He watched the others. Ned seemed filled with joy to be hosting friends. Jeremy, Ned's best friend who landed the co-lead character in the play, waxed philosophical on the merits of nihilism. It didn't make sense to Jaime's mind–there must be a moral line in the sand somewhere–but Jeremy appeared convinced and the faith itself seemed to satisfy his soul.

Ned had three roommates total in the two-bedroom flat. It occurred to Jaime that he should never reveal to these guys his financial fortune. They would never accept him if they knew. Maybe on the surface? But these guys struggle. They each hold part-time work to make ends meet. Reaching their dreams is a fight–a daily battle of how much longer to continue holding on.

"There is no truth in this world," Jeremy concluded after more on the various tenets to Nihilism. "None!"

"Wait. No truth?" Jaime weighed in, now. "But, then, what about that? What you just said?"

"What about it?" Jeremy asked, not offended but somehow

sincerely curious. Or at least his tone made it seem as much.

"Well, you're saying there's no truth in the world–but if that statement in itself is true, then based on what you're saying, doesn't that conflict? How can they both simultaneously be true?"

Our old friend, silence, dearest readers, once again surfaced, in most unexpected fashion, it might be inferred.

"Yeah...okay," Jeremy sputtered half a minute later. "So what you're saying is like that stupid question the high school pseudo-intellectual would always pose to sound smart–if God is omnipotent, then can he create a rock so big he can't destroy it?"

"Yeah, it's called Jerusalem," Ned shouted from the kitchen, not far off in the small apartment. "You're talking about the unstoppable force versus the immovable object paradox. Socrates came up with that one, not your friend in high school, Jerome."

Everyone turned to Ned, hesitated, then lightly laughed, as much at Ned as to his wit.

"But I see what you're saying," Jeremy said to bring the subject back to focus. "It's an interesting point. And he wasn't my friend!" he shouted toward the kitchen.

By the first wisps of dawn, agreement could not be found, but a consensus did form on finding breakfast out. They went to a diner on the block and Jaime wanted to pay for everyone, but decided it might lead to suspicion. When he went the opposite way as they left the restaurant to head back across the East River and uptown to home, that feeling of despair returned. Yet after a few minutes, walking up the steps to catch the R train, he thought it wasn't as severe as from the morning before. A sky of long, thin streaky clouds feathered out from the eastern third of the morning like lavender strands of cotton candy, the sun itself still not visible, but not far off. It looked like a creation, so beautiful. It brought a smile to his face. There's a *truth*, he thought.

Sharla wasn't home when he got there. He couldn't remember the last time she wasn't there since he started arriving home late at night. She probably stayed with Josephine, he decided and went to bed, too tired to worry otherwise. She still wasn't home when he woke up at noon. This new schedule was starting to eat into his sleep, as well. On the way to rehearsal though, he noticed a weird pleasure in the drag in his mind. It gave it a weight, as if it was something. A journey. And showing up, being a part of the shared experience, a cause.

This new sense of purpose propelled him to opening night, which happened in broad daylight because they opened on a Sunday with a matinee. Sharla and her expanding circle that now included Josephine, sometimes with Chris, Claude Perrot, two more trust-funders from Josephine's clique, four actors from "On the Run" and tonight Joe Gagliano and three of his dandy followers, were in the audience somewhere, but Jaime could not discern them through the foot lights' glare.

The performance was exhilarating but it felt too short by curtain call, Jaime thought. The "On the Run" entourage and Jaime went to 123 to celebrate. It was soon into this when the notion of metamorphous surfaced in his mind. Sharla's laugh now came with a slightly back and over tilt of the noggin. Her eyes flowed to Josephine's frequently. It felt so odd to see this, now, here, he thought. The energy at the table, in the restaurant, seemed so alive. But something was different with Sharla; between Sharla and himself. She even looked different, though he'd never be able to put a finger on it tonight.

He noticed across the restaurant a table of two couples. He watched them in glances, not wanting to appear inattentive at his own table. They were not artists he thought. The men wore dinner jackets and slacks, the women dresses, but that mattered less. The men gave it away. They were lawyers, maybe? Or Wall Street guys. The all laughed, suddenly.

Then Sharla laughed again, but her eyes went to his this time. She looked puzzled for a moment. It was him. He hadn't been laughing or smiling when her eyes went to his a second before. He half-laughed quickly but it was too late. She put her eyes back to the group. Jaime watched Claude Perrot. His usual confidence flourished in such environments. Josephine radiated like the center of orbit. She made it appear natural, though Jaime thought she must have had years of practice. Dotting parents. Never a worry for money or love or attention.

She had cast a spell of sorts on Sharla, Jaime now also thought. Chris seemed unfazed by it all, Jaime observed. Yet not because he hadn't been sucked into her gravitational pull. Here he was, after all. But more like the pull of Josephine didn't affect him the same. Like being able to walk on red-hot coals because the soles of one's feet have been conditioned through years of fire. He was Mercury without the sun's exposure baking its surface.

Sharla left with Jaime. It seemed so long since it had just been the two of them. She didn't say anything as they walked along. Or anything in the back of the cab. Or as they walked up the stairs to the lobby of their apartment. Nothing in the elevator, or the hallway.

"That was fun," she finally stated nonchalantly as they walked through the door and she went straight on to the bedroom and into the bathroom where she remained, removing make-up, washing her face, brushing her teeth and whatever else she does. Forty five minutes later she climbed into bed, kissed his cheek and rolled over, contently, as if it had always been this way.

The next night at the theater, it felt more like an opening night. The audience nearly filled the seats and the cast floated abuzz waiting backstage for the first curtain. Camaraderie among actors and production crew left Jaime with a sense of being enveloped in spiritual molasses. Later on, as he left the stage for that night's show, he looked out at it all and it captured his being. It felt like a moment, a picture in his mind he would remember for as long as air filled his lungs; maybe longer. Who knows?

The party afterwards lasted into morning, again. But now that rehearsals were finished, he didn't have to be back to the theater until later that evening. He slept until almost six, waking more recharged than since he could remember. Sharla wasn't home, again. He looked for a note she might have left, but nothing. Maybe it could be interpreted as a sign of security, of trust. Just as easily, though, he thought, it could be seen as a beginning to an end. The question then quickly came to him–do I care?

He had finally achieved his original dream since leaving L.A. Did it taste as sweet as he thought it would? He had nothing when he set out originally. He had more than he could have imagined, now. Yet, strangely, a sense of void somehow filled him. Why? How does yesterday always seem to be wrapped in a sense of nostalgia? Will today have that feel ten years from now?

Chapter 36

For the next three months the play consumed him, though no teeth marks were visible. It surprised him how each night's performance commanded his being so much. Perhaps slight to casual observation, variations to anyone immersed in its production and delivery caused it to feel almost anew each time. Yet as the end of the run approached closer with each night, a sense of dread increased exponentially.

Blocks over, "One the Run" entered full-on smash trajectory. The book also sold well, better than even the publisher anticipated or hoped and was beginning to gain momentum beyond the city. The circle around Sharla and Josephine now sometimes exceeded a dozen. Had they met more frequently and at the same place seated at a round table and intellect played a bigger part, the second coming of Algonquin might have been bandied about, but none of these conditions were met. The spirit of Dorothy Parker need not be restrained.

Jaime removed himself of the malaise soon after it began. He and Sharla were now like passing ships in the night on separate oceans. Chris still remained above the fray, but his own popularity had increased so much, Jaime hadn't seen or heard from him in nearly as long. It seemed incredible that it might have all played out this way. That he might be the one on the outside looking in, despite that that might be of his own choosing. "Requiem for a Dancer" was scheduled to close in three days. A Friday-night farewell, someone called it, though he doubted anyone else had ever used such jargon.

Adrian found work at a body shop in Queens. He let Jaime set him up in an apartment near his work, but insisted that he pay his own way from there. At least for the time being, he explained a little later. Idle time is the devil's handy work, Adrian often remarked.

"Maybe someday when I retire, if you still have any of it left, we can talk about something then," Adrian put it another day rather bluntly. It didn't bother Jaime, though. It made him more proud than ever, in fact, that they were able to finally find him and help to gain his freedom. It also made him realize more so than ever that he needed to have something of substance and meaning in his own life. Maybe theater would be it? He had thought it could be Sharla, or he and Sharla. But a person should never seek wholeness through someone else's, he came to realize recently. He wandered the streets that night, leaving the cast to their own afterhours devices.

He stopped after a while to step inside a small, Irish joint, sandwiched between two taller buildings. He didn't pay attention to the name. Maybe he had wandered all the way to somewhere on the west side? A long wooden bar ran the length of the rectangular room with a shuffle board crammed against the opposite wall and not much space in between. Two older men sat nearly facing one another in the middle. A lone woman occupied a stool at the farthest end. Jaime took the first seat. He asked for a whiskey on the rocks. It had been quite a while since he had a drink. He tried to remember the last time. Besides wine with dinner, that is. Just a drink and nothing more. He couldn't remember.

He liked the feeling of isolation that quickly came to him. A city of eight-plus million and one could still walk into a place and get a feeling of being in Dodge City. Whatever happened to Tashinga and that souped-up Riviera? The notion of it all made him laugh out loud. One of the older guys from the middle peaked around his drink partner to see the man laughing by himself. Jaime didn't care. He laughed again at that.

As the brown liquor absorbed the lining of his stomach, a warm glow quickly rose up into his brain. He downed the rest and quickly ordered another one. The gentle fire inside him intensified and seemed to spread throughout at least the upper half of his body. It amazed him how relaxing the effects of the liquor could be. The bartender motioned his direction to see if he wanted another one, but Jaime nodded his head slightly down and raised his hand barely up to signal his contentment. The bartender went back to the middle of the bar in front of the two older customers. They all seemed familiar with each other; probably sat and stood in the same arrangement many times before, Jaime thought.

Jaime studied the bartender. He was slender and middle-aged and as Jaime observed him further, it seemed, unhappy, but more specifically, disinterested. Was he like Jeremy and Ned and those guys? Was this just a means to some other end? Or was this his end, and that fact left him sullen and long in the face? How lucky *he* had been, Jaime thought to himself. He knew it all along, but at times like this it became more poignant. Jaime stood up to go relieve himself. It must be somewhere toward the back of the place, he assumed, so he went that way.

Before he could make it to the rear of the establishment, though, he slowed to focus his eyes on the woman at this end of the long bar. He couldn't believe his eyes.

"Mika?"

"Jaime! What are you doing here?"

"Same thing as you, I guess," turning back toward the bar. "I can't believe this."

"I know," she laughed. "Have you been here before?"

"Nope. I take it you have."

"It's around the block from this place we used to play back when," she said. "It's a great hole in the wall, you know. I come in here sometimes, just to....How'd you find it?"

"I didn't, really. Just walking around after the show tonight, you know, just going nowhere, really. About the time I thought to stop for a minute, I see this place."

"That's crazy," she said with a wide smile. "Well, sit down."

"Alright. Let me hit the head back here. I'll be right back."

When he returned, they talked about the what-not's of this and that for a few minutes, and then maybe it was the whiskey and his intolerance to its affects, or maybe he finally had the courage at the right moment and her jovial mood made it seem like the right time, but he asked about her age. What had happened, he mustered?

"They don't know," she answered plainly. "I mean, it was experimental all along, you know. So something happened. Something triggered the whatever it was I was taking to stop it from working anymore. They still don't know."

Jaime squinted his eyes and shook his head slightly and pursed his mouth.

"So, that's it?" he asked, finally.

"With me, yeah. I mean, I wasn't the only one, you know. And I really don't know what's happening with anyone else. It's not exactly talked about in The Guardian, you know. And they're not sharing anything with me."

"Wow. Well, you look great, still," he managed.

"Thank you, Jaime," she said and looked straight into his eyes.

He could see now what a strain her relatively sudden transformation from eternal youth to rapid aging must have taken on her. How could it not? She asked about Sharla, then, out of politeness and not wanting it to be all about her. British manners, he supposed.

Jaime answered that Sharla was doing great. Very well, really. And as he included Josephine and the would-be vacuous vicious circle, he knew Mika could sense the displeasure of the whole scene for Jaime. He waited for her reaction.

"You can't blame Sharla, though, really," Mika obliged. "That kind of success can be intoxicating. Especially with Josephine and her people as fuel."

"I just don't think it's for me," he confessed. "It's not that I'm mad at her or anything."

She waited for him to say more. When he didn't, after a moment, she put her left hand on top of his knee.

"You two are so young," she said. The look in her eyes made him think of the initial attraction he had had for her when they first met at the museum in Peru. But he questioned if it were he or his youth she longed for? He touched her hand, taking her fingers between his own. She let their clasp fall between them, held it there briefly, then let go.

"Let's get another drink," she said, as if to mark a threshold. "What are you having?"

"Whiskey," he said, timidly, for some reason.

She motioned the thin bartender their direction. He poured two more whiskeys on ice in highball tumblers and Mika made a toast to innocence. Just as their glasses clanked, four more patrons loudly spilled through the doors. They were young and hesitated momentarily after they entered, realizing their entrance crashed an otherwise serene setting. But they took four stools at the front and their presence soon seemed to add a splash of energy about the place.

The exception among animals is to take but one lover or mate for life. Many, but not all, within the myriad of bird species, for instance, will remain loyal to a single partner. For most other animals, however, sex plays little role in furthering intimacy–procreation rules, with dominant males often commandeering a lion's share of the action. Among no others can it be as good to be 'king'.

Many centuries came and went before monotheistic belief systems led men and women to make life-long commitments at great risk of severe penalty if not fulfilled. Perhaps King Henry VIII's tale of marital dystopia best serves as example (albeit grotesquely self-serving and indulgent) to end that effort, but mere modern-day statistics reveal how rare it is that two people can remain happy throughout the course of an enduring relationship. Not that it doesn't happen, for it most certainly does time and again. Yet more often than not, love simply doesn't last. Hearts grow apart. Motivations alter. Rifts widen. It's the modern condition.

Motivations differed between Mika and Jaime. In addition to a basic attraction she found for him, she still secretly harbored deep curiosity toward Jaime's, well, you know. This temptation had only been stoked of recent upon conversations with and among Sharla.

Jaime just needed attention, primarily. More so than he even realized until being next to Mika for only this short time and the excitement that began to tingle within him at the prospect of being inside and around her. To feel her soft, warm breath close to him.

Another whiskey and the energy between them practically began to glow. Jaime hadn't felt anything this strong in some period. He knew she had to be feeling it too. It couldn't be this strong were it less than mutual. She offered for them to go to her apartment, but he didn't want to wait out the train ride to Brooklyn where Mika stayed, so they made their way to Midtown and Park Avenue and West 50th Street where Jaime sprang for a night at the Waldorf Astoria.

"You can't take it with you," he whispered in her ear as the cab pulled up to the marbled facade.

Neither were disappointed. And while things in this life are rarely, truly equal, as the sounds of blaring car horns began careening up the building walls the next morning, Mika lay soaking in wafts of love wallowing within the fine bedding of their luxury suite, Jaime's body tight next to her own. He lay contently as a cherry atop a dollop of whipped cream on a fudged sundae. The first twangs of guilt held off until just after brunch.

"I know," she said, seeing the look on his face change from go to yellow, then. "Let's not say anything, yet. I'll just see you in a few days, whenever, you know. We're bound to all get together soon enough."

He simply nodded thusly and she stepped inside the open door the bellhop held on the cab. As she pulled away a mix of emotions flooded through him. He wanted it to not already be the next day; for the night and morning to have lasted much longer. He also wanted the stain he brought on he and Sharla to not be there, and yet he felt, strangely, a hint of pride—a sense of power that he could be attractive to more than one woman simultaneously and then act on that fact.

That pride slowly faded the next few days as Sharla suspected nothing. She trusted him. Really trusted him. Or she just didn't care. But that couldn't be it, he thought. No, she had honestly trusted him. It had always been her strongest point–open honesty. Almost, maybe, blindly. And now he had betrayed that. Her.

Despair returned in spades. He felt an itch growing beneath his feet. He began plotting between escape or redemption, when his cell rang one afternoon from Mika.

"Can I see you?" she asked immediately.

"Of course," he answered as much for himself as for the desperation in her voice.

"Meet me at the rink at the park–across the street from the Plaza?" she said.

"Yeah, okay. I'll be there in 30 minutes?"

"Alright. I'll see you then," she confirmed quickly and hung up before he could say or ask anything else.

She wasn't there when he arrived. Or at least he hadn't spotted her right away. He took a position along an overlook so he could see out over the rink and skate rentals. It would be Spring soon and the ice would be closed for the season. He guessed that's why it might be as crowded as it was this afternoon; people wanting to get in one last visit while they still could.

"Hey. Thanks for coming," she said, startling him slightly as he didn't notice her approaching.

"No problem. What's up?"

"Here, let's walk," she said, first. "I wanted to come here because it's out in the open, you know. Lots of people."

"Yeah. What's going on?"

"Well, I'm a little worried, really. Actually, I'm very concerned," she said with an uncertain smile. "Someone has tipped me off."

"To what?" he replied.

"To me," she answered. "It's someone I became friends with back a while ago, and he cares for me, still."

"So what did he say?"

"That I might want to think about getting out of New York, but not just here. To really get out, you know?"

He shook his head otherwise.

"Well, when he says, 'might want to think about', it really means I should do it. It's just the way he puts things, you know. But he means that I need to disappear. As much as possible anyway."

"Why?" he asked.

"I've become a liability, I suppose. He didn't go in to any details. It might have compromised his own position, I suppose, if I knew too many details that they could tie back to him."

They walked east past 5th Avenue along East 59th Street.

"Are you really in danger?" he said.

"I don't know. Maybe?" she answered.

They walked for another minute or two without talking. At 2nd Avenue they turned south and she started again.

"You know, there's so little true freedom left anymore. I mean back in London there's more than ten thousand cameras in the city, now. Every inch of that city is watched around the clock. All the big European cities are like that, now. Here too. And then in Eastern Europe and Central Asia, you've got all the despots and corruption. And China, of course. And NSA out of control. And police out of control. And the kids today, not you I guess, but you know what I mean. So many of them don't even get it."

"I don't know," he said. "Look at all the upheaval around everywhere. It's young people stirring it up, really."

"That's true, too," she offered.

"It's just not the same, anymore, though, I think. That's all. It was the trip up the mountains in Peru. The more I think back on that, the more I've come to believe that it's only possible for people like them to experience real freedom. They don't have any money or possessions, to speak of, I know, but they're free. There's no big brother. No bully police outfits. Or menacing gangs. It's just themselves, their animals, their families, close friends, clean air, you know. Clean water, food. I don't know?"

"It *was* nice there," he whispered. "I know what you mean. We could go back."

She stopped.

"Or someplace like it. They know about there, you know. But something like that."

She looked deeply into his eyes. Her own revealed just how serious this was for her. He wanted only to kiss her, suddenly, but then thought she might misinterpret his intentions. He didn't know himself why, he realized?

"See that place over there?" she said, pointing toward a small garage entrance with a sign jutting out above it: Quantum Automechanics.

He nodded thusly.

"I want to go in there, for a minute. Just to feel safe," she explained, oddly.

"Okay," he said, not knowing why.

"It's a front for a joint operation between M-13 and the C.I.A.," she then explained.

"Yeah?"

"They've got some D-wave computers in the back and other stuff."

"Oh yeah?"

"It's a long story," she shook her head. "But they won't whack me in there and risk exposing their front."

"Okay," he accepted, following her across the street.

Inside the small lobby or waiting area were four chairs, a pair bunched in either side of the right corner. A stand held a coffee maker and some Styrofoam cups and a basket of condiments for coffee. A rack of used magazines stood next to it. Jaime thought it seemed innocent enough, but then how else should it look?

Mika took a seat in one of the chairs. So Jaime followed her lead. A moment later a man came through the door next to an opening and counter where customers might pay for the work. He started out toward them, smiling broadly as if he might ask how he could help, but he quickly recognized Mika and stopped. They exchanged an odd glance before he nonchalantly turned back around and went back through the door. Jaime turned to her.

"Don't worry about it," she responded. "Let's just sit here a minute or so. You want some coffee?"

"I'm okay," he answered. After a few seconds, he asked if she wanted any.

She shook her head no and returned to racking her brain for whatever fix she thought she might find. Suddenly Jaime began to fill with anxiety. They'd take him out, just as easily for guilt by association. He felt to say something to her, to express his anger toward her for having brought him into this matter. But he stopped himself before he did, just in time. What was he thinking? She had done practically the same thing for him when she had Claude intervene on his behalf for Adrian. Maybe it wasn't quite as risky, but still, it was something.

"It'll be alright," he leaned close to her to whisper. "We'll go somewhere."

She smiled so genuinely, so deeply, he knew he'd be leaving NYC for good, maybe within hours.

Chapter 37

They landed in Bolivia. They had kicked around going somewhere in Europe, or Central Asia, even, but decided in the end that it would be too easy for whomever to trace their whereabouts to wherever, there. Central America seemed to offer more desolation. And Mika really wanted to visit Pumapunku.

They flew to the Grand Caymans first where Mika somehow had a connection there to a man who provided them with phony passports–a British ex-pat expert on Photoshop or something. Regardless, Jaime became Miguel Antincio, his mother's Hispanic heritage providing enough cover for the deception to probably work, while Mika became Shelly O'Toole–something about a mix of Irish, Scottish and English making it impossible to dispute, otherwise. And the name just sounds like someone famous. And no one questions the famous, Mr. Photoshop explained during the transfer.

Before we embark on this last leg of our journey, however, loyal readers, let it be noted first that Sharla harbors no ill will toward Jaime, or Mika. She knew for months Jaime wasn't happy, but paid it little mind, too easily busy lapping in her own indulgence of fame and fortune. Only after reviews of her follow-up play, "Stanley's Contradiction," were published did she venture back down from the upper reaches of the stratosphere.

These critiques of "Stanley's Contradiction" were so harsh, you must understand, that news outlets soon went so far as to actually retract initial reviews of "On the Run" and the novel, in that order. Her fall found bottom much sooner than it could have, though, swayed when she reached noon on the new viscous circle; the bones of Ms. Parker, you see, may have moved after all (metaphorically speaking only, of course, since the ashes of Ms. Parker were scattered over various parts of her beloved NYC), some time after a society editor for the New Yorker, or was it the Post? referenced the term Algonquin in an article about the "new play-house set" of Midtown, and in vapid ease Josephine effusively joked how they should each move a seat counter-clockwise every successive encounter.

Three months after the liberal-arts firing squad finished off Autumn O'Malley's literary reputation (Sharla did take this pen name, after all,) her turn around the table at The Plaza (one of six hotels used to meet because they didn't take the habit of actually meeting at the same one, that would be too old fashioned) placed her directly across from a lobby mirror. In that somewhat distant reflection Sharla finally witnessed a real glimpse at the new creature that had emerged from her old self, and one might correctly infer she did not enjoy at all that vision, brief and rather small as it may have been–self occupied, pretentious, bloated ego, just for starters. A moment later, after an involuntary yawp, she excused herself from the circle and promptly left the hotel and went back to what used to be *their* apartment and cried until no tears remained. A week later, she signed off on the lease and returned to Blacksburg where she lovingly squeezed her father's and mother's necks repeatedly. She later found a small house she liked and bought it with money left over from her heydays, took an office job to occupy her time and settled back in to life West Va. style, slow and easy.

Out on the high plains of Bolivia, meanwhile, Mr. Antincio and Ms. O'Toole immersed themselves in all things Pumapunku. For weeks they spent mornings exploring various sections of the site, followed by afternoons of research and early evenings of debate, both among themselves and whichever geologist, anthropologist or scientologist they might encounter over dinner or drinks, or while boating on Titicaca. Jaime found the whole experience to at last provide a new meaning, a better purpose, to his existence. At least for the time being, he hoped.

The notion that mankind's evolutionary development at one time received a boost from high-functioning alien beings, just made too much sense to his understanding. How else to explain so much? Pyramids. Missing link. Red hair, to name but a few. The deeper question soon became how this information had been so carefully covered up for so long. Might Conquistadors of had ulterior motives for invading the Americas? Could word have reached European religious centers of power that answers beyond their scope of restricted dogma existed? Eliminate these charlatans, orders might have been stated. And bring back gold, silver, chocolate and tobacco, just to throw future historians off the scent.

Such a shame, too, Jaime and others shared. With all that is known now about the expanse of the universe, science does not necessarily have to discount the entirety of historical accounts from the old or new testaments. Atoms do not die, they are simply transformed. Is this not the ultimate claim of the resurrection? The shortcomings of man do not necessarily constitute eternal death. Life might continue in one form or another forever.

Also often discussed among Jaime and his new friends, the use of Sumerian cuneiform writing at Pumapunku. How would a Mesopotamian alphabet be in use in highlands of South America more than ten thousand years before Christ? Cuneiform uses a wedge shape as its base font. Most anthropologist believe the shape to be a simple transformation of an early symbol of water: ^

How ironic that two parts hydrogen and one part oxygen might be the foundation of all life, and in this case, written language. Again with that number three. Of course, from this combination of basic elements, all the colors of the universe emerge at the beckon of a ray of light. Aliens must have found water's chemical and physical properties outrageously intriguing—so soft and functional, yet so powerful. Perhaps after a few hundred years of genetic foreplay and experimentation (a host of cranial shapes and forms have been found in grave sites near La Paz, Bolivia; most shapes otherwise regionally located throughout the planet, and DNA test confirm this anomaly) these otherworldly visitors formulated a synthetic water and moved on to replicate life similarly beyond.

The size alone of some of the diorite stones used in construction at Pumapunku (in excess of 100 tons) also means industrial know-how of great expertise had to be available. Did these early men of South America simply achieve levels of industrial capabilities equal to modern man, yet leave no record or proof, otherwise? Or did they receive help from above, as it were, literally?

"Has God ever been lonely?" Mika posed one night sitting outside a non-descript eatery in La Paz with seven others including Jaime, a.k.a. Mr. Antincio.

An hour later after various answers never fully addressed the question, instead focusing on the existence of God, or more, or on the personification thereof, Mika willfully changed the subject.

"Lake Titicaca probably rose during a great flood to as high as Pumapunku at one time, right? If not the actual Pacific Ocean?" A lean of heads around the circle confirmed the possibility and she continued. "I propose, the H-blocks at Puma were built as part of an elaborate system of docking stations for amphibious alien spacecraft."

"Masters of the seas and skies," a scientologist from New Zealand offered.

"Poseidon and Mercury," an anthropologist from Whales added.

"It makes perfect sense," Mika continued. "The first one's who landed probably came in a smaller vessel to explore and sight out the possibility of bigger ships coming in. They constructed a terminal using these massive building blocks to counterbalance the enormous weight of their crafts."

"Why did they leave?" Jaime wondered aloud.

"To get back home," Mika answered on cue.

"Perhaps the flood waters retreated more quickly than they anticipated," the scientologist from New Zealand voiced.

Speaking of home, back in the good old U.S. of A, Chris the Hopi Indian, noted OG Shaman to the Upper, Upper East Side, reached the end of his tolerance for NYC. Not that he didn't find the overall experience a significant learning opportunity or that he didn't immensely enjoy the company of Josephine Anderson and her leisure-set entourage, but while it is possible to take a spiritual warrior out of the desert, you can only take the desert out of the warrior for so long. It was a long stretch of gray, overcast, damp Fall air that really sent him over the edge. The thought of dusty nostrils never tasted so sweetly. Thus, our cash-infused would-be hero returned to Pueblo, spending several weeks eating nothing that didn't have some manner of green chilies in the recipe. Hmmmm.

Back in Bolivia, Jaime contemplated another possible mystery–his initial attraction to Mika. For while she certainly represents an attractive woman, both physically and of the mind, particularly upon their first encounter with her being in her scientifically modified state of eternal youth, but as this attraction did not waiver upon the truth, as it were, becoming reality, and as this most recent bout of time together having increased Jaime's fondness for her in a much deeper fashion than he had ever experienced with Sharla and even thought possible, he began to gain a sense of something eternal between them, of an almost cosmic connection. And so he asked:

"Was I attracted to you, or did my soul just recognize you, like a salmon knows its exact tributary, and pose that recognition as attraction? If time truly doesn't exist, then maybe we go through, well, time, for lack of a better term, in an infinite loop. We reencounter others at the same step in, well, again, time."

"Just because you're referring to time doesn't change the possibility of its philosophical non-existence," Mika responded.

"So, right. Okay. Then that's what I'm saying–that we meet at the same point, time and again, like a point on an X-Y graph."

"Anything's possible," she said.

"I think it is. It truly is."

They both grew comfortably silent, mentally wallowing in all that might be–two souls alight in the dark. In the distance the sound of sirens suddenly drew closer, and louder. Moments later, their mystical spell broken, Mika and Jaime turned their focus to the sirens, now so loud the only question left would be if it would eventually pass. Seconds later, Mika decided they should not wait to find out.

"Let's get out of here," she leaned into him to whisper, not wanting to alert others seated at their table.

Jaime froze momentarily, frightened terribly by the possibility of what might have been the single best moment of his existence instantly being shattered. And for what? By what? Damn the past! Mika could wait no longer. She started off without him. Jaime hesitated one more moment, looking around the table, but finally realized none of these people mattered. Or at least he hoped they didn't. He jumped up from his chair and scurried to catch up to Mika, now at a brisk gait.

They rounded the corner of the building from where they just were. The screeches of sirens came to rest right where they had been. They began to move again, making two blocks. The sound of the sirens were still stopped. They must be questioning those left at their table, Mika said to Jaime.

"Let's keep moving," she demanded.

He obliged, willingly. They turned another corner, made it a few more blocks, turned another corner and spotted an open area leading up a gradual incline covered in natural vegetation–bunch grass and scattered shrubs. They climbed fifty or so yards up and away from the street, then took positions low on their bellies. The sound of the sirens did not start again, but shortly they could hear the sound of engines revving, then accelerating, moving.

"Coming or going?" Mika questioned.

After a second, she answered her own question.

"Coming," she declared.

"They wouldn't use sirens to lay in wait and assassinate you, us," Jaime whispered.

"Or wouldn't they? We'd be thinking what you just said," Mika countered.

The sound of the racing engines grew closer, then stopped nearly at once followed by doors slamming shut.

"This can't be happening," Jaime whispered even lower.

"I'm sorry," Mika mouthed, barely audible.

"Why am I always on the run?" Jaime continued in a whisper.

Mika shook her head, peaked over almost brittle, dry shrub leaves, then rotated and began to scamper away from the lurking authorities. Jaime watched the men as she did. They didn't notice her. He waited another second, then turned to follow.

This should not be, he could not stop thinking to himself, moving crouched as low as he could. Sols abound, for crying out loud. Sols abound! Mika kept moving, low, at oblique angles. She didn't look back. He didn't either. They didn't want to see if they were gaining on them. In another minute, she stopped. They waited on both knees, catching their breath, listening between gulps of air.

"I don't hear them," Jaime said.

Mika turned an ear toward the direction they just were. She shook her head no in agreement. They listened more.

"Do you think they'll be back?" Mika said.

"Probably not. If they don't get us now," he answered.

"No, I mean at Pumapunku. The spaceships."

"Oh, I...," but the non-sequitur caught him off guard. "Maybe? I guess they might? Maybe not, though, if they recreated water somewhere else. Maybe they wouldn't need to?"

"Just out of curiosity, though," Mika said. "Maybe they just want to see how...," but the sound of male voices in the near distance stopped her. They froze another few seconds before the voices grew a little closer, and they were off again on the low run, Jaime leading the way this time, a burgeoning bulge growing, well, you know where.

Top Five Conclusions to Jaime's Next Move

1. They escape the Bolivian authorities and return to Peru to fight for labor rights.

2. Bolivian officials return Jaime with Mika to British agents who then force them into a top-secret sexual pharmaceutical compounding experiment.

3. He goes back to West Va. and sweeps Sharla off her feet and they move to Scottsdale and become sun gods.

4. He finds Chris in Pueblo and buys a tract of desert property and they operate the swankiest spiritual retreat in the Southwest.

5. He returns to NYC and takes Sharla's vacant seat among the new Algonquin round table crew and drinks himself silly before retreating to Algiers following a new generation of beatniks.

"We bought up
Some old memories,
Then failed
To remember from
Peeking in the pipes."

Purchase other Black Rose Writing titles at www.blackrosewriting.com/books
and use promo code PRINT to receive a 20% discount.

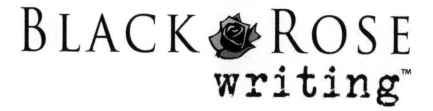

Made in the USA
Lexington, KY
16 November 2016